Praise for Book 1
of the Belleville Family saga

THE HOUSE OF SECRETS: JULIA'S STORY

'This tale is a well developed family saga ... with an interesting cast of characters and some deep secret plot lines that you just know will come back to haunt the main characters later. .... The characters are believable, full of depth and colour; and the writing is fresh.'

Amazon.com 4 stars review

'A well written story that pulls the reader into the era and the family. Looking forward to continuing the saga with book 2.'

Goodreads.com review

'Just wanted to let you know I have just finished reading your 1st novel, *House of Secrets* and can't wait for the follow on story.'

Library Reader via email

'Have just finished *House of Secrets Julia's Story*. Did not know until the last page that it was to be continued. Loved the book - probably the best novel that I have read for some time and now am waiting with great impatience for Book 2 - when can we hope to see it?'

Reader response via email

First published 2017

PMA Books
A division of Peter Masters & Associates
ABN 72 172 119 877
PO Box 5197, Manly Qld 4179
Australia
www.pmabooks.com
Tel 07 3396 4643 • Mobile 0488 224 929
Email enquiries@pmabooks.com

ISBN 978 0 9943276 1 1

Cover design: Neil Deacon, Deacon Design
Email deacondesign@mac.com
Concept: Design Crowd
House photography: Kimbal Baker, Melbourne

TO LOVE, HONOUR & BETRAY

Book 2
in the Belleville family saga

J Mary Masters

About the author

J Mary Masters (Judith) was born in Rockhampton, Queensland, Australia in the 1950s, the youngest of four children. She is married to Peter.

For more than twenty years, Judith has been involved in the magazine publishing industry as a managing editor and publisher.

With plans to retire from full time work in 2017, Judith plans to devote more of her time to her writing career, with emphasis on writing for women readers.

She is a member of the Queensland Writers Centre (QWC) and the Australian Society of Authors (ASA).

You can set up a conversation with the author online

Website	jmarymasters.com
Twitter	@judithmasters
Blog	judithmasters.wordpress.com
Facebook	www.facebook.com/JudithMMasters
Email	jmarymasters1@gmail.com

TO LOVE, HONOUR & BETRAY

Book 2
in the Belleville family saga

J Mary Masters

To the readers of my first novel
The House of Secrets: Julia's Story.

It was your encouragement and praise that kept me
going to write the sequel.

And to my husband Peter
who has encouraged me every step of the way
in my writing life.

AUSTRALIA

BELLEVILLE FAMILY (Prior Park)
Elizabeth Belleville . . . . Mother
Richard Belleville . . . . Son
William Belleville . . . . Son
Alice Belleville (formerly Fitzroy) . . . . William's wife
Paul Belleville . . . . Richard & Catherine's son
Anthony Belleville. . . . . Richard & Catherine's son
Marianne Belleville . . . . William & Alice's daughter

Mrs Duffy . . . . Housekeeper, Prior Park
Charles Brockman. . . . . Manager, Prior Park
Jack Finch . . . . Prior Park worker
Ted Lambert . . . . Prior Park worker
Muriel McGovern . . . . Francis Belleville's mistress
Alistair McGovern . . . . Francis Belleville's natural son

FITZROY FAMILY (Mayfield Downs)
Amelia Fitzroy. . . . . Mother
James Fitzroy. . . . . Son
Julia Fitzroy (formerly Belleville) . . . . James's wife
John Fitzroy . . . . James & Julia's son
Mrs Fry. . . . . Housekeeper

WARNER FAMILY (Armoobilla)
Tom Warner
Jane Warner (formerly Saville). . . . . Former governess

OTHERS
Nathaniel Dodds. . . . . Belleville Family solicitor
Henry Baker . . . . New Belleville Family solicitor

Pippa Jensen. . . . . Julia Belleville's natural daughter
Edith Henderson . . . . Pippa's Great Aunt

ENGLAND

CAVENDISH FAMILY (Haldon Hall)
Lady Marina Cavendish. . . . . Mother, daughter of an Earl
Sir Anthony Cavendish . . . . Father, a Baronet
Catherine Cavendish (now Belleville) . . . . Only daughter

John Bertram . . . . Nephew to Lady Marina

Edward Cavendish . . . . Heir to the Baronetcy

USA

Captain Philippe Duval. . . . . US Army doctor

PROLOGUE

At the end of book 1, *The House of Secrets: Julia's Story,* we left the Belleville family just as Julia Belleville married James Fitzroy in 1947.

Now ten years on, we see the Belleville children all married with their own families, but behind the façade of their wealthy lives, trouble is brewing.

Long held secrets are about to bubble to the surface. All of them will be tested as 1957 becomes a year of crisis for the family and for those they love.

CHAPTER 1: APRIL 1957

It was late afternoon and cool in the shadows of the house. William Belleville strode out the front door in search of his elder brother Richard whom he suspected of avoiding him, although he could see no reason why he should do so, yet the suspicion lingered.

The house at Prior Park had begun to show its age. A team of men was working methodically on its exterior. Unsightly scaffolding covered two sides of the grand house.

'I hope this scaffolding is gone in time for Mother's birthday party,' William said, when he finally caught up with his brother.

'We can't have people arriving and the house looking like this.'

Richard nodded agreement. He thought it was an unnecessary and pointless observation but he didn't say so.

'Have you heard from Catherine? Will she be back in time for Mother's sixtieth birthday party?' William asked pointedly.

Richard did not turn to face his brother but said simply in a low voice that William strained to hear: 'I don't know'.

William hesitated. He had expected a more positive answer. The lack of it left him uncertain as to whether he should press for more details.

It was Richard, in the end, who broke the silence.

'I'm not altogether sure she is coming back for good,' he said, finally lifting his head from examining some cracked stonework.

William made no comment. He did not know what to say. It had not occurred to him that his sister-in-law might not return to Prior Park.

'I had a letter from her yesterday,' Richard said. 'It wasn't a long letter. Rather a short letter really, saying she was struggling to imagine coming back to her life here. She's not happy with it, apparently.'

Richard's voice trailed off.

William wished he hadn't asked the question. The state of Richard's marriage was not entirely comfortable ground between them. Still he pressed on asking the obvious questions or rather almost blurting them out.

'Just like that? She said that? Did you discuss anything before she left in February? And she has Anthony with her? Was she suggesting she remain in England?'

William's mind was beginning to turn over the implications of what he had just heard.

'And what about Paul? Does she say anything about Paul?'

Richard shrugged his shoulders. The arrangements regarding their two sons had not been canvassed.

'I don't know really,' he replied. 'I don't know what solution she sees. I did worry, you know, when I married her that she wouldn't settle here, but then I had to marry her. And I had to come home.'

William nodded but said nothing more. But his brother warmed to his subject.

'She doesn't really go into any detail at all about what's next but if she thinks she is going to bring Anthony up in England, I will have something to say about that, you can depend upon it.'

William was left in no doubt as to Richard's point of view on the matter. He pondered these latest scraps of information for a moment or two.

'You know I did feel there was some tension between you, if you don't mind me saying so,' William volunteered. 'Particularly when you finally declared you didn't want to leave Prior Park. I really think she had hopes of getting you to settle in Sydney.'

Richard at first did not respond to William's forthright analysis of the situation but he did not resent it either, as he might once have done. It was as if he was already resigned to the fact that his marital affairs would become the subject of general discussion.

'What is she going to do with the place she bought in Sydney?'

It was always likely to be the next question to occur to the ever-practical William.

'I assume she'll keep it or maybe she plans to divide her time between England and Sydney,' Richard said, as if she had already planned her future life.

'She may want to visit Sydney while Paul is at school there. Perhaps Anthony will go to the same school eventually, but he's not yet five so that's some time off.'

William, not always the most perceptive of men, for once began to understand the gravity of the situation his brother faced.

'Did you ever seriously try to settle in Sydney?' he asked, out of mere curiosity really, because he felt he already knew the answer.

Almost as soon as he had said it, William regretted it and he said so.

'Sorry, old man, it's none of my business really.'

He put his hand awkwardly on Richard's shoulder. But for once Richard did not resent his brother for his lifetime habit of frankness. He looked enquiringly at his younger brother.

'Could you be happy holed up in a three bedroom flat with traffic roaring past your front door day and night?' he retorted.

William responded as expected.

'No of course not, but I understand it was close to the harbour and a good suburb,' he said, in a feeble attempt to defend his absent sister-in-law.

'Oh yes, it is a good suburb and of course Sydney society matrons were fawning over Catherine because of her aristocratic connections,' he said. 'The few times I was there, I became nothing much more than a reluctant escort.'

He grimaced at the memory.

'I ate their food, drank their wine and admired their views of the harbour bridge and the manicured gardens on which they had expended no personal effort,' he said.

'And hated every minute of it,' he added, unnecessarily, for his feelings on the matter were plain to see

William could see too that Richard was making a determined effort to control himself. He lit a cigarette, the slight tremor in his hands barely noticeable but William could almost feel the tension in his brother. He could hear the rising anger in his brother's voice.

Unsure what more he could say, William was relieved to see Alice and Marianne heading towards them, bringing an abrupt end to their conversation.

At ten years old, Marianne was fast becoming an exact copy of her mother Alice. If there was a lingering disappointment that no more children had arrived, and especially a son, William did not display it at all. In fact he revelled in the tightknit threesome they had become. Another arrival would have been an outsider.

Marianne had been pestering him for a new pony and she never missed an opportunity to badger her father. He enjoyed the game of saying he would not buy her a new pony for years yet, knowing full well that as soon as a suitable animal was found, Marianne would have exactly what she wanted.

'Marianne was helping to set the table for dinner,' Alice said chattily to no one in particular.

Then, linking arms with William, she broached the subject upper most in her mind.

'You know we will have to make a decision on a school for her very soon. Her little local school days are fast running out,' she said.

It had been a source of anxiety for Alice, worrying that William would expect to send Marianne off to a fancy boarding school in Sydney like her cousin Paul, but she had not counted on William's attachment to his only child and his own miserable experience away from home.

'I think your idea of letting her stay with your mother in town during the week is fine. She can go up to the Girls' Grammar School as a day student,' he said without prompting, as if the matter hardly needed discussion at all.

Alice smiled, knowing that it was now settled and the idea she had planted in his mind six months earlier had borne fruit.

'She'll be company for your mother,' William added, as they walked slowly towards the house together, 'now that your father has passed on.'

Alice nodded and smiled her agreement. She gave his arm a small squeeze in thanks.

Her father Jack Fitzroy had confounded the doctors by living much longer than had been expected of a man with a heart condition. He had finally succumbed the previous winter.

Marianne skipped ahead of them, blissfully unaware that she had been the topic of discussion but happily contented with her life, although she missed her cousin Paul who was spending his first year away from Prior Park. She did not think it entirely fair that he had to be sent away to school, but the workings of the minds of adults were a complete mystery to her as yet.

As Alice and William's only child revelled in her secure and happy childhood, another child, not much older than her, was having to face the harsh and totally unexpected realities of life.

Pippa Jensen's life had changed forever, that much she knew. However kindly they said it, however much they tried to soften the blow, she knew that her beloved mother Anne was dead along with her father Harry.

It had all happened in a split second on a lonely country road, they said. Her father had swerved to miss a kangaroo and lost control of the car. The car had rolled many times and eventually hit a tree. They were both dead before help arrived. Her parents had been heading home from a neighbouring property on a back road, the policeman said, when he collected her from the local school.

Now, sitting on a hard high backed chair in the solicitor's office where her father had been the most important client, she tried to act like an adult for the first time in her life but the sobbing would not stop. Tears cascaded out of her blue eyes and down her cheeks, running unchecked. She knew that all that was familiar to her had been snatched away in a single awful moment. She knew she was alone. At thirteen it was a terrifying and mystifying thought.

She tried to understand what the pompous man across the desk was telling her but it was all too confusing. He seemed to repeat himself again and again, slowing his speech as if by speaking slowly he could make her understand what was happening.

She could take no comfort at all from the woman beside her. It was all she could manage to endure, spending the school week with Mrs Hampson, who ran a boarding house for country children attending the local high school. She had told her mother this every weekend. Her mother's reply had been gentle and soothing, reminding her it was just for the school days and the school term. The week would fly by, she had been told countless times. What would there be at home for her now, she wondered? Who would take care of her? The thought crossed her mind fleetingly that she might have to stay with Mrs Hampson for a very long time and she shuddered.

'Your uncle and cousin are organising the funerals for Friday. You will stay with Mrs Hampson and after the funerals are over, we will talk about your future,' the solicitor said, with a note of finality.

With that, he nodded to the stout woman who occupied the other chair and she held out her hand to Pippa, who looked at it briefly but did not grasp it. Instead she ran out of the room and into the street, her tears uncontrollable. She did not know then that worse news was to come. News that would make her future much less certain; news that would rip the very ground from under her feet.

Half a world away, Lady Marina Cavendish stood at the library window watching her four year old grandson playing alongside Joseph, Haldon Hall's elderly gardener, who had provided the boy with a cut down set of tools that were now a constant source of boyish delight. He dug with enthusiasm such that garden soil scattered everywhere but Joseph, patient and unflappable, scraped the soil back into the garden bed, praising the boy all the while for his invaluable help.

Satisfied that her grandson was in good hands, Lady Marina turned away from the window and walked across to the sofa. She sat down with the deliberate air of someone with something important to say. Her daughter Catherine sat in the armchair opposite, flicking through the latest issue of *Tatler* magazine. She looked up when her mother spoke.

'Do you want to tell me what's going on, Catherine, or do I have to play a guessing game?'

It was an opening gambit designed to get her daughter's attention.

This time it succeeded. Catherine discarded the magazine, none of which she had really read, and looked across at her mother.

'Guessing game, Mother? I'm not sure what you mean?' she responded, as if she was more than prepared to play a guessing game with her mother.

'Well, you don't exactly look like a woman desperate to return home to her husband. Or to her child, if it comes to that. Is everything all right between you and Richard?'

Lady Marina, in typical fashion, did not imagine for one moment that this was really none of her business. She sat impassively waiting for her daughter's response.

Catherine stood up and walked the short distance to the window where her mother had been standing just moments before. It was clear she was thinking carefully about her response. What should she tell her mother? Did she know how she really felt? How could she answer her mother's question when she wasn't sure of the answer herself? Or was she sure now?

She turned away from the window but did not move closer to her mother, as if it was safer to speak at a distance.

'If you want the truth, Mother, I'm bored with my life in Australia,' she said finally. 'You know we live mostly at Prior Park with his mother and his brother and his brother's wife. It isn't our home exclusively. I think that's part of the problem. There isn't really much for me to do there. The men, of course, are always occupied with the farm or with business matters.'

She could not bring herself to call Prior Park an estate because it lacked, in her eyes, the prettiness and orderliness of the English countryside. It lacked too the social hierarchy she understood implicitly from her upbringing. Such social hierarchies, if they had ever existed in Australia, had long since disappeared. But to articulate her restlessness in such terms seemed mean and petty.

She started to pace the room restlessly. Her mother said nothing but waited for her to continue.

'Richard is away on business quite a lot,' she said. 'I go with him sometimes but mostly if I travel I stay in Sydney while he goes on to some god-forsaken provincial town. I enjoy being in Sydney but

Richard does not. He's a country boy at heart, it seems. I thought he might enjoy Sydney. To his credit, he did try.'

Her mother nodded, as if to acknowledge that she already understood all that her daughter was telling her.

'You were in rather a rush to marry him, Catherine, as I recall,' Lady Marina said.

'A necessary rush, as you'll recall,' Catherine retorted.

Her mother ignored her response, as if rekindling the memory of Catherine's ill-considered match was a painful episode best forgotten.

'You would have made a good marriage if you had stayed here,' was all her mother could find to say, ignoring completely the reason for her hasty marriage.

'With an illegitimate baby in tow? I don't think so, Mother.'

Neither woman would now say the obvious: that the baby could have been given up for adoption. The eleven year old Paul Belleville had captured both his mother's and his grandmother's heart so completely that to even speak the thought, or think it, was contemptuous, as if it was a betrayal of the child, as if a child could be discarded and forgotten without remorse.

'Is that all that is wrong?' asked Lady Marina, as if she was expecting some unsavoury revelation from her daughter.

'I think it's enough to be going on with,' Catherine said, sure now that she did not want to burden her mother with her deepest concerns.

'So that's why you haven't booked your passage home yet?'

Only my mother, Catherine thought, could impose a special meaning on the word 'home' that mixed contempt with expectation.

'I'm planning to go down to London tomorrow,' Catherine said. 'I plan to do it then. I'll be meeting John Bertram for lunch. He'll be in London for a few days, as it turns out. The air crew has several days rest before they fly the London-Sydney route again.'

Lady Marina remembered John Bertram's prediction clearly that the skies would soon be filling with aircraft flying in from all corners of the globe. She had scoffed at his prediction then and even now, would have been reluctant to admit that he had been right.

'I suppose you will fly back to Australia?' she asked her daughter, although she already knew the answer.

'Yes, of course I will. I can't stand being cooped up on a ship for six weeks when I could get there so much quicker,' she snapped.

Immediately she regretted the small display of petulance.

'It's very safe now, you know. With any luck, I will be on an aircraft with John in the aircrew. That should make you feel reassured. He's very capable, you know.'

'I'm sure he is,' Lady Marina said. 'I'm sure he is. But it seems an unnatural way for people to travel, in my opinion.'

With that, Catherine said no more. She decided it was time to relieve the gardener of the responsibility of entertaining her lively four-year-old son.

It seemed to Catherine that her cousin John Bertram had changed little in the decade or more since he had helped arrange the service at the small lonely church that had opened its doors just long enough for her and Richard to be joined in holy matrimony.

Despite the distances that regularly separated them, they had met quite frequently over the years, his friendship undimmed by the years. It was more than the ties of relationship that made him her confidante; he was Richard's best friend too with the shared experience of air crew in Bomber Command binding them in a friendship nothing could break.

It was unexpectedly chilly for London in mid April, as if the early promise of warm weather had been but a tease to lull Londoners into a false expectation of an early and hot summer.

John Bertram was his usual cheerful self as he perused the menu at Claridge's but he sensed Catherine's low spirits almost immediately and put the menu aside.

'You don't seem your usual bubbly self, if I may be so bold,' he said, studying her serious face and sad eyes.

'Is there something amiss?' he asked, unerringly.

'You could say that,' she said, but she did not elaborate.

After a few moments of silence, he ventured again.

'So let me guess? An argument with your mother? A sick child? A sick husband? None of the above?'

It was John's light-hearted banter that brought a smile to her face.

'None of the above, I assure you,' she said finally, with a half attempt at a smile. 'I'm just feeling a bit down, well a bit more than down really.'

John smiled encouragement at her, careful not to jump too quickly to obvious and possibly inaccurate conclusions.

'I'm not looking forward to going home. I've written to Richard to tell him,' she said.

She pulled a face at the word 'home' as if John really needed the emphasis. He did not.

'Ah, finding life in provincial Australia a little dull are we?'

As usual, he was straight to the point, but his words were so disarmingly honest that Catherine did not mind. She smiled at him, privately relieved that he had arrived at the heart of the matter so quickly and effortlessly, as if he had expected the problem and might even have a solution to offer.

'You understand, don't you? It's about as far from my life in England as you could imagine,' she said, warming to her theme.

'I share almost no interests at all with any of the women I meet. Their worlds are very narrow, it seems to me, and totally dictated by the overbearing demands of their husbands and children.'

As if to apologise for the slight that none of them would hear, she tried to temper the frankness of her outburst.

'Don't misunderstand me,' she said, 'they are thoroughly decent people but there is no intellectual life among them that I can discover. They don't talk about the latest books or plays; they have never been to an art gallery; they may go to the cinema occasionally, that's all. They cook and sew and knit, all the things I hate doing.'

She said no more, knowing that she had made her case poorly. It was left to John to add a note of reality.

'I bet most of those women you speak about don't have any help at home, so I wouldn't imagine they would have too much spare time for their own pursuits,' he said quietly.

'You must know that yours was a very privileged upbringing, Catherine, and by Australian standards, Prior Park sounds like a privileged place too,' he said gently but firmly.

'You're right, John, but that doesn't make it any easier to adapt,' she said, eager to defend herself.

'I used to think much of the social round we had in England was pompous and out of date, and of course, much of it didn't survive the war, but it would be nice to be part of it now – or certain parts of it,' she said, her frankness surprising even herself.

'I'd love to be shopping now for something to wear at Royal Ascot. Mother and father always go, but with father getting older, there may not be many more chances,' she added, wistfully.

'I have to say I wouldn't know about the delights of Royal Ascot, never having moved in those circles myself,' John said, suddenly beginning to see a quite different side to his cousin.

'Oh, it is great fun, I'm told. And the more illustrious side of my father's family have always had an important role at the event,' she said. 'In fact I met a distant cousin the other day – Edward Cavendish. He was very charming and lamented the fact that I would be returning to Australia before the event. I don't think I had met him previously but he could instantly rattle off our distant kinship.'

John Bertram smiled knowingly.

'Perhaps he was one of the suitors your mother had in mind for you?'

He didn't expect Catherine to take the suggestion seriously, but she shrugged her shoulders.

'I don't know. We never really got around to talking about my future. I was only eighteen when the war began and it rather became the focus of our attention,' she said, by way of explanation as to the lack of discussion about her future.

'And then you messed it all up by falling in love with an Australian,' he said, hoping at last to make her laugh, which she did, much to his relief.

'John, you're impossible. Let's order lunch.'

With that, they resumed their close study of the menu. He now knew what was troubling her yet he could offer no solution. She, for the first time, had spoken aloud of her disappointments but could see no solution either.

CHAPTER 2: MAY 1957

There were many days when Julia Fitzroy yearned to be Miss Julia Belleville again. She accepted that her life was now settled but even as her rational mind accepted this fact, still she yearned for something else.

There were very few days when she did not think about the baby she had been forced to give up. She tried to imagine her daughter's life, wondering how she had grown and whose looks she had favoured. Was she fair? Was she like me, Julia wondered? Or did she look like Philippe?

It broke her heart afresh every time to think she would never know. And yet so firmly had she been under her mother's influence at the time, it was only later she began to think she might have resisted her mother and kept her child. She was humiliated to remember she had accepted, almost without question, her mother's decision and then, with very little resistance, her mother's plans for her to marry James Fitzroy. In all these things it seemed she had been allowing others to make decisions for her as if she had no will of her own.

It was only a matter of weeks now until they would celebrate their tenth wedding anniversary. To his father, nine year old John Fitzroy was everything he could want in a son; by his mother, he was loved but it was almost at a distance, as if her heart, broken by the events years before, could never quite love a child again with as much passion.

If he found his mother a little distant, he did not notice. It was the boyish adventures that commanded his attention. It was his desperate need to keep pace with his older cousins, especially Paul, that occupied his mind. His mother, always there in the background, he took for granted as if her presence, permanent and unchanging, did not need to be a matter of concern to him at all, for he expected her to be there whenever he needed her.

Julia had become accustomed to life in the smaller house at Mayfield Downs. She found she did not mind it at all, adopting a less formal routine than her mother had imposed at Prior Park. She was disappointed that her mother almost never visited, preferring instead that Julia visit her on an appointed day each week, usually for lunch.

And so that day of the week had dawned yet again, except on this particular Tuesday, her mother would celebrate her sixtieth birthday. Julia knew the frenzy of preparation at Prior Park for her mother's birthday celebration on the forthcoming Saturday was not sufficient excuse to avoid the obligation.

As she sat down to breakfast opposite James, he raised his head from an intense study of the newspaper.

'Good morning. Are you going to visit your mother today, as usual?' he asked.

Since he rarely asked about her visits to her mother, she wondered why he was interested on this occasion.

'Yes, I am going, even though we will see her on Saturday. It is her actual birthday today, so I can't really avoid it. Was there some reason for your question?' she replied.

He smiled at her.

'No reason, really, I just wondered if everything was all right at Prior Park,' he said, without explanation.

'Why shouldn't everything be all right at Prior Park?' she demanded. 'Is there something I should know?'

'Well,' he said, unsure now whether to share the titbit of gossip, 'I understand from sources, shall we say, that Richard has had a less than friendly letter from his wife. That was what I heard.'

Julia was stunned at this suggestion but outraged too that her husband should be gossiping about her family in such a way.

'Who told you this?' she said sharply. 'I don't believe it for an instant.'

James smiled but did not answer her question directly. Instead he posed his own.

'You may not believe it, but tell me honestly, do you think Catherine has been happy in her life at Prior Park?' he asked. 'Has she joined in the local women's activities or made any strong friendships since she has been here?'

If Julia was surprised that he had given so much consideration to Catherine's situation, she did not say so. Instead she pondered his questions for a few moments before responding.

'Just because she doesn't join in with local organisations and participate in what do you call them, 'women's activities' doesn't mean she's not happy surely?'

He shrugged, not wanting his casual remarks to provoke an argument.

'Well, let's just say I think she was brought up to live a totally different life,' he said diplomatically. 'In marrying Richard, I don't think she thought through the implications of what it really meant.'

But Julia knew, even if he did not, that her brother's hasty marriage had been necessary but she did not want to say so.

'I don't suppose any of us really understand what marriage means,' Julia said quietly, with a quick glance at her husband, whose attention had already drifted back to his newspaper, leaving Julia to ponder how she could raise the question at Prior Park without having to ask Richard directly.

So it was a surprise to Julia when she arrived at Prior Park later in the day to discover that her sister-in-law Catherine had arrived home from England three days earlier, a fact that Julia immediately assumed put paid to the gossip about her elder brother's marriage.

It seemed to her, also, that nothing much had changed in the routine of Prior Park, except that more places were now set at the lunch table over which Elizabeth Belleville continued to reign supreme.

'You should have brought James with you today, Julia,' her mother said, 'then our gathering would have been complete.'

'I would have suggested it,' Julia said, 'had I known that we were to be such a full gathering. I didn't know that Catherine was home, until I arrived here just now.'

She had deliberately meant this to sound like the small rebuke it really was, as if she was being excluded from the intimacies of Prior Park by the fact of living just a couple of miles away. She tried hard not to resent the fact that her niece Marianne now occupied her bedroom. She knew such resentment was unreasonable but still it had felt like her exclusion from Prior Park was now complete.

Her mother, failing to notice the small rebuke, had pointed out that preparations for her birthday party on Saturday were demanding all their attention at present.

It was Richard who, desperate to change the subject, filled the silence that followed the terse exchange between mother and daughter.

'I had a letter yesterday from the manager of the Goulburn Woollen Mill. I've been down there a few times, as everyone knows,' he said.

They waited for him to continue, assuming there was something important he had to tell them.

'He told me some very sad news. One of the big wool suppliers Harry Jensen and his wife were killed in a road accident last month. I went out to their property about ten years ago on my first visit to Goulburn.'

He turned towards his mother.

'You might remember I told you they had an adopted daughter who reminded me so much of Julia. I wonder what is going to happen to the little girl now?'

Long forgotten memories flooded back into Elizabeth Belleville's mind but she was careful not to betray the slightest hint of them on her face. She heard Julia's quick intake of breath but she did not look at her. As this discussion unfolded, she did not once look at her daughter.

'That's very sad,' Elizabeth Belleville said, 'but, if she is an only child as you say, surely she will inherit the property. I hope she has someone to look after her until she is of age.'

Richard shook his head. The rest of the gathering continued with their lunch, only vaguely interested in the conversation.

'Unfortunately, she won't inherit the property. Jensen left the property to a nephew, it seems,' Richard said.

'Well, no doubt the nephew will look after her,' his mother said, wanting to draw the conversation to a rapid close.

'I except so,' said Richard, unaware of the painful memories he had exposed in both his mother and his sister.

'It might be time, though, to sell our interests in the venture, I think,' he said, turning towards William this time. 'I sense that time is running out for wool and woollen mills.'

William looked up from his plate and nodded.

'If you think so, Richard, go ahead.'

Richard was surprised at William's easy agreement but did not stop to wonder what lay behind it.

'We can talk about it later,' he said, turning his attention to his own neglected plate of food.

It was Catherine who asked the questions that had not occurred to William.

'Why do you think time is running out for wool and woollen mills?' she asked, having been almost silent throughout lunch up until this point.

'Well, the world has changed since the war and we are seeing new synthetic fabrics emerge that will be cheaper to produce and easier to care for,' he said. 'It is the march of progress and it is unstoppable.'

He had rarely discussed business with his wife so her interest now seemed out of character, but he did not say as much. That remark, he thought, was best left to a private moment.

'If you sell out those interests, what will you invest in then?' she said, as if it was the next obvious question to ask.

He shrugged his shoulders.

'I don't know,' he said, 'but I'm sure something will come up.'

With that, the conversation turned again to the arrangements for Elizabeth Belleville's sixtieth birthday party, which had been well and truly discussed many times before but which represented safe ground for all of them.

Richard, consumed by his own thoughts, did not initially feel any unease at William's urgent insistence on a private discussion, when he felt the pressure of William's hand on his arm pulling him aside after breakfast the next morning.

Richard slid easily into the armchair opposite his brother in their father's old study. While it had been their domain for more than a decade, there remained, for both of them, the sense that they were invading their father's private space uninvited, yet it was the one place where the privacy of their conversation was assured.

He could see that William's hands were shaking very slightly. It was the first sign of trouble although what trouble would cause William to react in that way he could not imagine.

'What's up?' Richard said bluntly, reaching for a cigarette from the engraved box that sat on the side table near his elbow.

'What's up, you may well ask?' William said pointedly. 'This is what's up.'

He waved a letter from their solicitors in the air as if, by doing so, Richard would be able to discern the contents without him having to spell it out.

'What's old Dodds writing about this time?' Richard asked, almost impatiently, for he had long since given up reading most of the letters, leaving that task to William.

'I'll tell you what he's writing about,' William said, his voice rising such that Richard suggested he calm down, which of course had the entirely opposite effect.

'Nathaniel Dodds has been approached by a young man by the name of Alistair McGovern, who wants to 'claim his birthright', according to Dodds.'

William began to pace the floor. He was agitated by this unexpected turn of events because both he and Richard had considered it would never be forthcoming, even as they had conceded its possibility in the secret deal they had made with Muriel McGovern following the death of their father.

Yet Richard was more sanguine at this sudden and unexpected demand.

'Well, I'm as surprised as you are but we did agree to those terms, as I recall, when we made the settlement.'

William rounded on his brother.

'Of course we agreed,' he said, suddenly irritated by his brother's calm response.

'We did that just to get the woman off our backs and settle her claim so that Mother would never find out. I never thought though that it would come to anything. Who in their right mind wants to turn up at a family's doorstep and announce to the world that 'I'm your father's bastard'!'

Richard could see it mattered a great deal to William that the myth of their parents' happy marriage be preserved.

Their father, they both knew, had, in his lifetime, become the subject of gossip among those who considered him weak and ineffectual; it was important to William that nothing else emerge in their mother's lifetime to further erode his character or his honour, for he knew it would be a source of great shame to his mother. It was something he knew William could not bear to witness.

'Hang on there, William, what's Dodds suggesting or recommending?' he asked, trying to bring the discussion back to the facts of the letter rather than enter into William's flights of fancy that seemed so uncharacteristic of his normally level-headed brother.

William scanned the letter again, as if he did not already know it by rote.

'He says he is writing to warn us, that is all, as he says he had a visit from the young gentleman recently and he 'expressed a desire to see Prior Park'. He writes that misguidedly 'it appears your father must have told the young man about Prior Park'. Dodds also says that he urged him to 'write to us to get permission to visit' but Dodds says here 'I have to say I cannot be sure he will follow my advice'.

'That is the crux of it,' William said finally. 'He could turn up on the doorstep at any time and what do we do then?'

They both sat in silence for a minute or two, considering the solicitor's warning, each wondering what the chances were that Alistair McGovern would have the nerve to walk up to the front door of Prior Park unannounced.

'Do we know anything about him?' Richard asked finally. 'Does

Dodds say anything at all about him?'

William frowned and eventually handed the letter to Richard.

'He doesn't say much more really.'

Richard scanned the letter quickly.

'No, he doesn't except to say he has finished his studies, although he doesn't say what he has studied. I wonder if he gave Dodds his address?'

William interjected at this point.

'It's possible he still lives with his mother in Brisbane. I think I still have the address somewhere,' William said, grateful that his brother seemed to be ready to suggest a course of action.

'You met the mother, didn't you? I think you told me about the meeting at the time we received the demand for a settlement.'

Richard was testing his memory now. The issue had not been discussed between them for more than ten years, as if their unstated pact of silence would ensure it need never be raised again.

'Yes, I met her,' William said, recalling his visit.

'In her defence, I don't know that she knew our father was married when she met him. Perhaps he said he was a widower. She didn't really tell me. All I know is that he spent quite a bit of time with her and the boy when he was away in Brisbane. None of us, especially Mother, knew anything about.'

Richard took a long drag on his cigarette, as if the task of imagining his father in that situation was too painful to contemplate. For both of them, the knowledge of their father's betrayal of not just their mother, but of all of them, had eroded their own happy memories of the childhood they had spent with him, as they came to the realisation that another boy had shared the same innocent experiences with their father that they presumed had been theirs exclusively.

'So what do we do? Wait nervously every day for a knock on the door? Or do we go to Brisbane and confront him?' Richard mused aloud.

Richard's instinct always led him to action. He could not abide inaction. William on the other hand was much more measured yet on this occasion he was easily persuaded.

'I think you're right,' William said finally, as he turned away from the window where his restless pacing had finally ended.

'I think we announce we are going to Brisbane immediately after Mother's birthday,' he said.

'We can say we are going to organise the sale of all our woollen mill interests. I assume you want to sell them all, not just Goulburn?' he said, almost as an afterthought.

'Yes,' Richard said, keen to act and relieved that William had not challenged his decision.

'I do want to sell them all. It's time to move on to a new industry, a new investment.'

'Well, we should prepare to leave on Monday then,' William said. 'Hopefully we can head this other matter off before it becomes an embarrassment.'

'Amen to that,' said Richard, who was keen to escape the confines of the house. 'I think I'll go for a ride. I need some fresh air and sunshine.'

With that, the brothers parted, having agreed on what seemed to them at the time an entirely sensible course of action.

It had been only a matter of weeks earlier that Alistair McGovern had finally confronted his mother Muriel about his father.

In early adulthood, he had come to resemble William more and more, a fact his mother did not remark, having met William only once. His mother had chosen to say very little about his father, hoping that his memory would be sufficient to satisfy her son's curiosity. In that small hope, she was completely wrong and now she understood that.

It was a Sunday afternoon and she was sitting in her favourite chair on the small enclosed verandah of her neat suburban home. All her attention was focused on the small almost invisible stitches she was painstakingly sewing around the hem of a pale green satin ball gown.

She had felt that something had been brewing in Alistair for weeks but she did not prompt him by asking if there was anything the matter. She would not encourage him to ask the one big unasked question that she knew he longed to ask. Whenever he seemed likely to want to discuss the question of his father, she changed the subject. She did not want her son to share the shame of his illegitimacy. It was better, she thought, that he continue to believe that his father had been away at his remote property most of the time as the reason why he had not lived with them.

But she could see, as he framed his questions, that it was a story he was not satisfied to accept now.

He paced the small verandah, hands thrust deep in his pockets, glancing at his mother from time to time until his patience, worn thin by her calm stoic air, finally deserted him.

'For goodness sakes, Mother, can you stop your sewing for just a moment. That's all you seem to do is sew!'

Muriel looked up at her son, her fingers poised ready to insert the needle and thread into the fabric to produce the next tiny stitch.

'Alistair, what on earth has got into you this afternoon,' she said, her voice rising in irritation to match his.

'Mother, I want to talk to you and I need to have your attention. I don't want to talk to the top of your head.'

Reluctantly, she set her sewing aside, careful to make sure the luxurious fabric was not creased. She did not say anything to her son. Instead she sat silently her eyes now fixed on his face.

'I want you to tell me about my father. I want you to tell me the truth. I found this solicitor's letter in a drawer. It talks about a settlement and the end of 'the arrangement, now that your son has reached his majority'. It's dated two years ago.'

He held the letter aloft in his right hand as if he felt the physical evidence, rather than his words, was needed to convince her that he knew some of the facts.

He could see the colour drain from his mother's face yet she remained silent.

'His name wasn't Francis McGovern, was it? His name was Francis Belleville, wasn't it? And I can draw the next conclusion very easily - that Francis Belleville already had a family and you in fact were his mistress. Am I right, Mother?'

There was a contemptuous tone to his voice yet he didn't really mean to hurt his mother. It was the veil of secrecy that he wanted desperately to smash, not her.

'I don't know how you found that letter, Alistair,' she said at last, 'but I could see no purpose in telling you. No purpose at all.'

She paused, trying to frame her words carefully.

'Your father had promised to provide for us in his will but he died before he had the opportunity to do that. That is my belief,' she said. 'So I contacted his solicitor and asked, for your sake, not for mine, for something to make our lives a little easier. Grudgingly they gave me an annual settlement that finished when you turned twenty-one. And that is why you find me sewing so much. It is to make ends meet.'

He looked at her closely. He could see that she was tired. More than that, he could see that she had aged in the past few months. Yet in his preoccupation with his own life he had not seen it.

'Mother, I am not trying to judge you. I just want to know the truth.'

His tone was gentler and she relaxed a little, as if the burden of the secret was being lifted from her shoulders.

'You are right,' she said. 'I was his mistress, as you put it, but when I first met him, I thought he was a widower. He didn't say as much but I just assumed. It was only when I found out I was pregnant that he told me the truth. I expected then that I would never see him again but in fact I think he found solace in our little family. He bought this house for us and supported us. His family never knew about us. He didn't talk about them of course but I picked up a few details from time to time.'

When she had finished, Alistair kneeled down beside her chair.

'I'm sorry, Mother, I didn't want to accuse you of anything. I know how hard it has been for you at times. But you must understand, I remember my father. It's natural for me to want to know something about him.'

She nodded. He noticed a tear running down her cheek unchecked.

'Careful,' he said, gently, 'you don't want to ruin the satin.'

She reached for her handkerchief and mopped at her cheek. In a quiet voice, she told him what she knew of Francis Belleville.

'So you are telling me that I have three half siblings? And that his wife is still alive? And they live on a property Prior Park near Springfield?'

She looked at him, clear eyed now, pleased finally she had found the courage to tell him the truth.

'As far as I know, his wife is still alive and that is where they live,' she said. 'And, I have to tell you, finally, in the settlement with your father's estate, I reserved the right for you to meet them, should you wish.'

Alistair, on his feet again, turned towards her.

'And they agreed to the terms?' he asked, suddenly excited by this unexpected disclosure.

'They did,' she said, 'although reluctantly I believe. William, the only one I have met, handled the settlement. I don't think he told his mother. That is my understanding.'

'So what should I do next?'

He was clearly at a loss as to the next step and looked to his mother for advice.

'Why don't you make an appointment with the solicitor and see what he advises. That is the best thing to do, I believe. That would be a starting point for you,' she said.

'You're right, Mother. That's what I will do, first thing tomorrow. And thank you.'

He kissed her lightly on the cheek and she smiled. Now they did not have to speak about it further and she was glad, very glad. Her grief at the loss of Francis could never be public. It had made the loss doubly difficult to bear. For her, raising her son had given her life purpose but now she could see, as an adult, he must find his own path for she could guide him no further.

CHAPTER 3: MAY 1957

As Julia and James approached Prior Park for her mother's birthday celebrations, Julia was reminded of the time, years before, when it had been her own eighteenth birthday party that had brought the house to life.

As James slowed the car near the front of the house, he glanced across at Julia.

'You do realise we will have been married ten years very soon,' he said. 'It seems such a short time ago that we got married.'

He smiled at her, hoping that she would return his smile but uncertain as to her mood. She did not respond except to nod.

'I was actually thinking of my eighteenth birthday party,' she countered. 'The house looks much as it did on that night.'

He too joined her reminiscences.

'It was the first time I really noticed you,' he said. 'That is, noticed you in the sense that you had grown from a child to a beautiful young woman. You do know from that point I was determined to marry you.'

She turned towards him, smiling this time.

'I'm sorry to disappoint you but I don't think I had any intention of marrying you then,' she said.

In the darkness of the car, he reached across to her, his arm behind her. He had already heard the back door slam as their son John scrambled out of the car and headed straight for the house.

'But you must admit you were attracted to me,' he murmured. 'I could see it in your eyes.'

He kissed her tenderly and she did not resist but pushed him away after a brief moment.

'You'll ruin my makeup and you'll end up with lipstick on your face,' she said, secretly pleased to have a plausible excuse to pull back from his embrace. He accepted her small reprimand with good grace.

'Later, it will wait until later,' he said pointedly.

With that he slid out of the driver's seat and walked around the car to help her out. She took his hand, grateful for the steadying arm as she struggled to balance on the high heels of her evening shoes, realising, not for the first time, that there were few opportunities for her to wear the latest fashions.

Tonight, though, she had made a special effort with a strapless chiffon dress. Yet she would have scoffed at suggestions she was in competition with Catherine, who had the advantage of having acquired the latest London fashions on her most recent trip. She would likely outshine us all, Julia thought, with just a touch of envy.

Upstairs, Catherine was still choosing her frock but with less concern than Julia had imagined, eventually deciding on a dark plum coloured cocktail dress that emphasised her small waist.

She discarded the small matching hat with its wisp of fine net in favour of a diamante clip in her hair and matching earrings. After a quick appraisal in the mirror, she headed downstairs to join the early arrivals, not stopping to add her presence to the receiving line at the front door, where her mother-in-law was first in line to greet the guests, followed by Richard, William and Alice.

If the arriving guests noted her absence from Richard's side, she did not care. Despite the years she had spent at Prior Park, she knew few of them well enough to exchange more than a casual word of greeting. It did not matter to her that they found her aloof and at times unfriendly. She could find no motivation within herself to attempt to change their opinions of her.

And now she found it mattered less and less since her return. She had begun to ask herself frequently which day might be the last she would spend at Prior Park, for her dissatisfaction with her Australian life had only deepened.

It was an hour later that James Fitzroy, exceeding the bounds of kinship, slid his arm around Catherine's waist and kissed her lightly on the cheek. He was slow to release her, his eyes travelling appreciatively over her slim but womanly figure.

Across the crowded room, the warmth of James's greeting did not go unremarked by Richard who had not spoken to his wife all evening. Neither did it go unremarked by Julia who attached no significance to it at all, fully aware of her husband's weakness for a pretty face. She thought no more about it, but it troubled Richard, for no reason he could fathom. But his attention was almost immediately drawn away from the slightly disturbing scene by a firm pressure on his forearm and his brother's low voiced words.

'We have a problem, brother,' William whispered. 'A very big problem. At the front door.'

Richard turned to face his brother, instinctively responding in a whisper.

'What do you mean a very big problem?'

The question hung in the air between them for a few seconds before William answered.

'The problem we were going to solve next week,' he said obliquely.

'Ah, that problem,' said Richard. 'Here? Now? It doesn't make any sense.'

'Sense or not,' William said quietly, 'we have to deal with it now.'

Richard immediately sensed the urgency in William's voice.

'Where is he?' said Richard, looking around the room, alarmed that the unmentionable person might already be mixing among their guests.

'Fortunately, Charles Brockman saw him coming to the front door and, not knowing him, asked what business he was about. He's in the study.'

'Not alone, I hope,' Richard said, certain that the uninvited guest would not be likely to stay put for very long if left alone.

'No, Charles is with him. He managed to attract Mrs Duffy's attention and told her to come and find me.'

Richard nodded, silently relieved at Charles's foresight and quick thinking.

'Well, that's something, at least, although that means that Charles probably knows the whole story by now,' Richard said.

He was already beginning to reassess their chances of keeping the whole sordid episode from their father's life quiet. He was not unduly surprised by William's response.

'It wouldn't surprise me,' William said, 'if Charles already knew about our father's activities. They spent a lot of time in each other's company and there was no one else he would have ever confided in.'

Richard scanned the crowd. He was satisfied no one else had become aware of the gatecrasher.

'Anyway, Charles is loyal. He won't spread gossip,' William said, more to convince himself than Richard.

'I will go and see him,' William said, finally.

'We don't want to both be seen heading to the study together. You come along in a few minutes.'

Richard nodded, happy to let William take the lead, but furious all the same that such an interloper as Alistair McGovern would choose this evening, of all evenings, to present himself at their door unannounced.

Among the throng of guests, it was only Julia who noticed the short, intense conversation between her brothers. She wondered idly what was so important that it must be discussed at her mother's birthday party. In search of answers, she sought out Catherine, who was standing alone at the back of the room, drink in hand, absorbed in her own thoughts.

'You look as though you are a million miles away, Catherine,' Julia said, as she moved to stand beside her and survey the throng of guests.

'Not a million, Julia, not a million miles. Well a few thousand, perhaps. My father will be seventy-four in a week's time. I can't help wishing I was there to help celebrate.'

She took a sip from her glass.

'Are you worried about his health?' Julia asked, as if such a question was expected of her.

'No, not really, he seemed quite well when I was there but then, looking back, I can't help feeling that my mother was trying to warn me before I left that he was not as well as he appeared, but she didn't say anything specific,' Catherine said.

If it wasn't quite the full explanation, it was at least a reasonable attempt by Catherine to explain her lack of enthusiasm for the evening's festivities.

'You must wish that England wasn't quite so far away. I understand that. You must miss your family dreadfully,' Julia said sympathetically.

Without further prompting, Catherine, sensing that Julia's sympathy was genuine, spoke her thoughts out loud for the first time.

'I do. I miss them very much. You know, I didn't really think about what it would mean when I married Richard,' she said. 'I thought it would be a great adventure, and of course, I was pregnant. But I do miss the old life and my home. More than I thought I would, actually.'

Julia was silent, unsure as to whether she wanted to encourage such confidences from her brother's wife.

'I don't mean to criticise our life here,' Catherine said, warming to her theme, 'but I don't find anything very engaging about living here, and the heat of summer is just, well, unrelenting, I suppose is a good word.'

Almost at once she felt that she had gone too far. She put her hand on Julia's arm, hoping she would understand that it was just her very different upbringing that had created a gulf too wide to cross.

After a few moments, Julia looked at her and for the first time saw the sadness in her eyes.

'I understand completely,' Julia said. 'What do you think turned my mother into a bitter and frustrated woman? She made the best of her life here, but didn't expect to live in the country when she married my father. But he loved it here. And it's easier for the men to travel away with their business matters and the like. We're the ones left at home to get on with it the best way we can without that respite.'

It was quite a speech for Julia and she found herself voicing her own half-formed sense of frustration. It was as if a small light had been switched on in her mind.

Looking around the room and noticing that Richard too was absent, she remembered why she had approached Catherine.

'On another matter entirely,' Julia said, suddenly uncomfortable with their shared revelations, 'what do you think Richard and William were discussing so animatedly but in hushed tones a few minutes ago? I don't see either of them now.'

Catherine too looked around the room and could not see them.

'I honestly don't know,' she said. 'They're often locked away discussing business matters but you wouldn't think there would be anything so urgent that it had to be discussed tonight.'

'That was my thought exactly,' Julia said. 'I wonder what's up. They'll be in the study if they want privacy. I might go and see what they're up to.'

With that, Julia started to thread her way through the crowd towards the hallway. If there was some urgent family matter, she wanted to know about it. She no longer felt part of the world of Prior Park, but tonight, in particular, it began to feel, once more, like her home.

Despite her determination to find out what was going on between her brothers, Julia was thwarted by the locked door and the warning hand of Charles Brockman on her arm.

'Charles, are you standing guard over the door? Because that's what it looks like to me. What's going on in there?' she demanded, in a slightly raised voice.

Charles ignored the accusation and responded calmly.

'It's just a matter of business that's suddenly come up,' he said, in a quiet even voice. 'Unfortunately it had to be dealt with tonight. It couldn't wait but they don't want to be disturbed.'

The pressure on her arm increased as he attempted to turn her back towards the dining room where the buffet was being served.

'You should go and see to your mother,' he said, with a discreet insistence. 'She won't show it, of course, but she will feel her widowhood especially this evening.'

It was an unexpected insight from Charles and she was momentarily distracted by it.

'Do you think so?' she asked. 'My father passed on years ago. I think she is beyond mourning him now.'

He smiled and nodded.

'Yes, I agree,' he said. 'To all appearances it would seem that her grieving is over, but it is times like these that you feel the lack of someone close in your life, someone to share the celebration with.'

She had known Charles since she could walk but had never had more than a perfunctory conversation with him. It had never occurred to her, up until this moment, that he had seen them all at very close quarters and there was very little about the Belleville family he did not know.

In a moment of rising panic, she wondered if he knew her deepest secret. She could not ask. How could she ask such a question? There was no way, even by careful subterfuge, to find out how he much he knew. With this thought upper most in her mind, she allowed herself to be led away gently towards to the dining room, all thoughts of her brothers and their secret meeting banished from her mind.

Across the crowded room, she could see her mother, momentarily alone, and looking slightly at a loss. She quickly negotiated the groups of gossiping guests to reach her mother's side.

Charles, for his part, breathed a sigh of relief that he had averted an unfortunate confrontation. He was already in possession of the facts about the young visitor, but he had long known of his existence. He wondered if either Richard or William really knew the depth of his friendship with their father. In the end, he rather hoped not. There were many secrets he had hoped to take to the grave about his late friend and employer.

He did not want to face the family's questions. He did not want to face the choice of betraying the man he had called a friend for forty years or lying to those he also held dear.

Of this, though, he was sure: in the events of the evening, there had been a callous attempt to expose one of those secrets to the family. He rather hoped that the circle of knowledge could be contained to the brothers who now controlled the family. He could see no end to the upset if the knowledge of Alistair McGovern's parentage became widely known. Above all, for Elizabeth Belleville's sake, he felt this must be prevented at all costs.

Within the locked room, the short heated conversation among the three men had lapsed into an unnatural silence.

Alistair McGovern knew himself to be at a considerable disadvantage, now that he had finally found the courage to seek out his father's family. He had only surmised that his existence had been unknown to them until after Francis Belleville's death. Now he had proof. Now he knew for certain he was a dirty little secret, a bastard son that no one wanted to acknowledge openly. A bastard son not entitled to share in the family's wealth. A bastard son who would never be treated as an equal by Richard or William – or even acknowledged by them. He could see they spoke with one voice on this point.

Finally, Richard broke the silence.

'What did you think, coming here tonight when our mother was celebrating her birthday? What did you think you were doing? That we would welcome you with open arms and introduce you to our mother?'

Alistair couldn't help but notice the iciness and threat in Richard's voice yet he found the courage to respond.

'It was coincidence, really,' he said. 'I heard about the birthday celebrations in town and I thought perhaps I could get lost in the crowd. Foolish, I know now, but I wanted to see Prior Park. My father spoke about it to me when I was a child. He painted such a glowing picture. He loved it here. He didn't mention other family. Until I came to know better very recently, I thought he lived alone here.'

At these last words both Richard and William reacted, but differently. William, having taken up his usual position behind the desk, shifted uneasily in his chair but said nothing. Richard, goaded beyond restraint, pushed the younger man back into the chair from which he had just risen.

'How dare you! How dare you presume such a relationship with our father. Why don't you crawl back into the hole you came out of,' he said, his voice rising with each word.

Richard's irritation was palpable, as if every pent up emotion and frustration was about to be released in a moment of raw uncontrolled anger. William saw his brother's right hand clench into a fist but did not rise to intervene. He breathed freely again to see it unclench just as quickly. William hated physical violence of any kind.

Yet he was surprised by the intensity of Richard's anger. Was it the insult to their mother that raised Richard's ire to such a level, he wondered? Or was there something deeper that had prompted his brother's white hot anger? He did not know and dare not ask.

Alistair McGovern was shocked by the rage confronting him and he failed miserably as an advocate in his own defence.

After a few minutes, it was William who took charge of the conversation, for fear that the whole encounter would get out of hand again and end in an unseemly brawl.

'Let's all calm down,' he said quietly, acutely aware that he was looking at a young man who still bore a striking resemblance to himself but he did not mention that fact. He wondered if Richard had noticed. He was not about to point it out.

'What is it that you want from us? Money, I suppose?' William said finally, wanting to turn the conversation to a more business-like footing.

Once again, there was silence.

The room was filled with Richard's heavy breathing as if the anger within him could only be contained for a short time.

Alistair shrugged his shoulders, uncertain now what to say. He paused, considering his answer.

'I don't know really,' he stammered. 'Perhaps money was part of it, but it isn't only about money. I wanted to be part of the family. I belong in the Belleville family. I should have the Belleville name, my father's name. And yes, if there is money, I should share in it.'

Later on, he reflected how he should have stopped there but it was what he said next that set the real tone of the enmity that was to mark their future dealings.

'After all, my father – your father – had some of the happiest times of his life with my mother and I. She adored him. We didn't see him all that much but we had fun when we did. He was relaxed and happy with us, just our little family of three.'

It was beyond any possibility that either Richard or William could sit through this account of a different family life their father had participated in, and even enjoyed, without responding, for he described a family life in which they and their mother and their sister had played no part, as if they were the outsiders.

Richard moved first. In two strides he crossed the room and stood before the young man, who was still seated. He pulled him up by the lapels of his jacket. He came awkwardly to his feet, and would have fallen, had Richard's grip not been so strong.

'If you ever repeat that story,' he said, anger now enveloping him completely, 'if you ever repeat that story, I will kill you. Do you understand me? Do you understand me?'

Richard repeated the threat in a slow deliberate voice.

Alistair was shaking now, aware that his naivety had been exposed and his faint hopes of a proper relationship with his half brothers was at an end. He saw now that he had been stupid to arrive at Prior Park on such an important evening. Far better, he knew now, to have met them both on neutral ground.

But Richard wasn't finished with him yet.

'Now listen to me, and listen good.'

Each word Richard spoke was deliberate. There could be no mistaking his meaning.

'You will be escorted back to your car, you will drive out of here and not stop driving until you are back in your miserable little life and never darken our door again. Do you understand me?'

William sat quite still, not intervening, but watching the young man carefully. Watching his brother too for fear that he would go too far.

'I just wanted to be friends,' Alistair mumbled.

'We cannot be friends,' Richard spat back. 'Don't you understand. My father betrayed my mother and he betrayed us. There is no way we can get beyond that. No way.'

He had already half pushed, half escorted the young man to the door. He opened it, relieved to see Charles Brockman still standing outside.

'Charles, make sure this young man gets on his way straight away.

37

He isn't welcome here.'

It was a curt command. Charles nodded but said nothing, for there was nothing to say.

He ushered Alistair, now ashen faced, down the front steps and into the darkness. He stood feet astride as the young man eased himself into the driver's seat of his borrowed car and headed back down the driveway of Prior Park.

He saw him turn his head taking one last backward glance at the house which glowed bright with light against the darkness beyond.

Charles Brockman did not move until he could no longer see the tail lights of the retreating vehicle. Only then did he head back into the house, getting a cursory nod from Richard as they passed one another in the hallway.

CHAPTER 4: MAY 1957

'What do you think he will do?'

It was the following day late in the morning before Richard and William had the opportunity to discuss the previous night's events privately. It was the question that had occupied William's mind throughout a sleepless night.

'I don't honestly know,' said Richard, who was standing motionless looking out of the window of the study.

'All I know is I had Julia asking me what was going on and when I said it was nothing of interest to her, she seemed very unconvinced,' Richard said, turning to face his brother.

'Just imagine if he starts talking in town. We won't be able to keep it quiet if gossip starts up.'

William said nothing at first, for he could think of nothing useful to say, but, as ever, his approach was the practical one.

'I think we should still go to Brisbane and see the solicitor. I think we should see what he has to say about it all. And I think we should look over the terms of the agreement with Muriel McGovern.'

Richard considered his brother's suggestion for a few moments.

'Well, I think we should go, yes, but I don't think looking at the agreement with Muriel McGovern will help much. I can't imagine she suggested he visit us on the night of our mother's birthday party. From what you tell me of her, that doesn't sound like her at all.'

William nodded. He shared his brother's assessment of the situation.

'I agree. I don't think she put him up to it. I think he did this all by himself. And, by the way, we should both think about how to settle our affairs. Old Nathaniel Dodds suggested it last time I saw him. He said we should both make wills. It didn't seem so urgent then, but perhaps it is now.'

With that, the matter was settled for now between them but each of them wondered privately what havoc Alistair McGovern would wreak on the family. Silently they both cursed him. The fact that he was their half brother meant nothing to them at all.

In the guest lounge of the Criterion Hotel, Violet Cunningham, her hair no longer a deep red in her only concession to her advancing years, listened, at first inattentively, to the ramblings of a young man who seemed intent on getting drunk, despite her best efforts to slow the pace of fresh drinks being set before him.

For her, Sunday was usually a quiet day with the public bars shut and only the few hotel guests to wait on. For once she wished for more customers to give her an excuse to escape from the troubled young man's increasingly garbled story.

He grabbed her by the wrist as she attempted to walk past his table. She could see that he was determined to find an audience for his misery.

'Hey there, Mister,' she said, quickly pulling her arm back from his weak grip. 'Don't do that again or I'll call the manager.'

He did not know that Violet had never 'called the manager' in her entire working life, such was her confidence in her ability to handle any situation with the hotel patrons, so he apologised profusely.

'I'm sorry,' Alistair said, his words only slightly slurred. 'It's just that I've been rejected by my father's family and I have no one to help me or listen to me.'

'Well, I'm sorry for you,' Violet said. 'I am sorry to hear that you have problems, but we all have problems and we just have to make the best of it.'

But this sudden interest in his story only acted as an encouragement rather than as the discouragement Violet had intended.

'You probably know the family; they're local,' he said, looking up at Violet, trying to gauge her interest. 'I bet the sons come in here to drink when they're in town.'

Such an invitation to gossip had never failed to engage Violet's attention in the past and it did not do so this time.

'And what family would that be that you're talking about?' she said in reply, certain that the revelations would turn out to be of no particular interest but she decided to play along anyway.

'The high and mighty Belleville family of Prior Park. That's who the family is. They are the ones who don't want to know me.'

There was a hint of vicious pleasure on Alistair McGovern's face as he observed the sudden spark of interest in Violet's normally impassive countenance. She could not resist asking the next question, despite a vague feeling of annoyance that this nondescript young man possessed inside knowledge of the most influential family in the area that she did not.

'So what have you got to do with the Bellevilles of Prior Park?' she asked, still unconvinced that he would really have any news that would surprise her.

He did not bother with a long explanation.

'As it turns out, I'm the father's bastard son, in the true sense of the word if you'll excuse the language, and they don't like it. I tell you they don't like it one little bit. Not one little bit.'

He repeated the words again but Violet was used to the repetition of drunks as if their words held particular fascination for their audiences. So she waited until he was silent before asking the obvious question.

'So you're saying that you are Francis Belleville's natural son, if I'm to understand you correctly?'

He nodded, the headed moving up and down in an exaggerated fashion.

'That's right,' he said. 'Francis Belleville seduced my mother and I am the result. All the while he had a wife and three children at home. And I thought he just went away to work on his cattle property for six months and then came home to us. I thought his name was Mc-Govern. I thought he and my mother were married. They acted married. We were a family. But it was all a lie.'

Again he emphasised the words, as if he could still not quite believe that the little family he remembered was a sham.

'And now they don't want to know. They don't want to hear about their father's other life. They threw me out,' he said, bitterness and bile rising in his voice.

'They threw me out of my father's house like some mangy dog. Told me not to ever come back. They made sure that I left too. The estate manager stood in the driveway and watched me drive away to make sure. He had a grip like a vice on my arm. He was very strong. An old man, but very strong. I'm sure I have bruises I can show you to prove it.'

Violet held up a restraining hand.

'There's no need for that,' she said, alarmed that he might at any moment strip of his shirt to prove his point.

For her part, she could visualise the scene readily for it was played out repeatedly on any particularly rowdy night in any bar in the town. It was the idea that he had actually been to Prior Park, walked up to the front door and asked to see who? Mrs Belleville? one of the sons? that most intrigued Violet.

'Do you mean you've been to see them at Prior Park? Who did you see?' she said, no longer holding herself back from the story but now keen for any detail, however insignificant, because she knew for certain she would be the only person to know about it, or at least, the only person outside the small group of people already involved. She knew with absolute certainty that none of the Belleville family would ever mention it.

'I saw the two brothers – William and Richard. I was intercepted, so to speak. It was just last evening, on the night of Mrs Belleville's sixtieth birthday party. I went, thinking I could just blend in with the crowd to see what the place was like. I'd heard people in this very lounge talking about it and I asked them where it was. The house is very grand you know. They must be rich.'

For a few minutes, Violet was silent trying to imagine the scene at Prior Park which she had never visited but had heard much about.

'Had you ever met them before?' asked Violet, incredulous that this unremarkable young man could devise such a daring plan all by himself.

42

'No, I'd never met them. My mother dealt through their solicitors when my father died. There was some small grudging settlement then to help us – I was only ten at the time – but there was never any direct contact with the family, except once.'

He paused, sipping at his beer which had sat unnoticed on the table before him for some time.

Violet had been turning over the story in her mind.

'So, do you think anybody ever told Mrs Belleville about you?' she asked. 'As I understand it from local gossip, William and Richard inherited everything although Mrs Belleville continues to live at Prior Park.'

He nodded.

'Yes, William and Richard got everything and they do all the business work. My mother had met William. She told me that, but only the once she said. All other contact was via the solicitor. I only found out about all of this very recently,' he said finally.

Violet could see that the young man was totally spent at the effort of telling her the story, which she did not doubt for one minute. Having seen William Belleville on several occasions, it was the likeness between them that she now noticed for the first time that persuaded her the story was true.

'So what are you going to do now?' she asked, for it seemed a perfectly straightforward and reasonable question.

'You may well ask what I'm going to do now,' Alistair said, a strange look coming over his face.

'You may well ask that question. I don't yet know,' he said, emphasising the word 'yet', 'but they will be sorry one day. They will be very, very sorry.'

With that, he rose from the table and pushed his chair back.

'I need some fresh air,' he said, already half way to the door.

'I think that's a very good idea, Mister,' Violet said out loud to his retreating back.

His words had unsettled her. There was a malevolence in the tone that worried her. With any luck, he would be gone from the hotel by the time she arrived for her shift tomorrow because she was sure now that she did not want to encounter him again.

43

She cleared the empty glasses from the table and headed towards the bar. What he had told her was, she now realised, a secret the Belleville family would do almost anything to keep, especially from Mrs Belleville. She wondered idly how this information could be used to her benefit but she could not immediately see a course of action. For the time being, it would remain her secret, she decided, even though it was the most delicious piece of gossip she had heard in years.

Elizabeth Belleville would have remained entirely unaware of the unwelcome visitor to her birthday party had it not been for her daughter Julia, who decided to ask her brother William what had kept him and her brother in deep conversation in the study for so long during the party.

William was too late to issue a warning to his sister, whose direct question to him was overheard by her mother who was at that very moment coming down the stairs to supervise the clean up, an unnecessary task as it turned out, for the house had already been returned to its usual neat and tidy state.

'Hello, Julia, I didn't expect to see you today and what's this you are asking your brother about? I didn't see any unexpected guests last night,' she said, as she neared the bottom of the stairs.

'Good morning, Mother,' Julia said in response. 'I hope you enjoyed your party.'

It was said without much enthusiasm, merely as a matter of form.

'Yes, I enjoyed it,' Elizabeth said, 'but at sixty, one finds these events a little tiring. So what have you been asking your brother about? A gatecrasher at my party, by the sound of it.'

William, desperate to head off any probing questions, took the easy option.

'Ah, it was just a fellow we met in Brisbane and put a business proposal to. He didn't realise it was such a bad time to call, so we said we'd see him next time we're down in the city,' he said.

It was the extent of William's capacity to embroider an explanation so he was quick to add.

'Alice and Marianne are waiting for me. We are going to pick up her mother and take her back to town,' he said hurriedly.

With that, he was gone, desperate to deny Julia the chance to ask further questions, for he was sure that he would tie himself in a knot of lies from which he would not be able to extricate himself.

Julia, dissatisfied but lacking the opportunity to ask either of her brothers about the incident, went in search of Charles Brockman who, she was sure, would be able to provide some answers.

Elizabeth Belleville, herself hardly satisfied with her son's responses, nevertheless shrugged off the incident as unimportant.

Charles Brockman too was doing his best to avoid Julia on the day following Elizabeth Belleville's birthday party. It was no more than instinct that drove him to avoid her, for he sensed that she would want to know much more about the events of the evening than he was willing to divulge.

The appearance of Alistair McGovern at Prior Park had come as no surprise to him. It was only the timing of the young man's visit that had caught Charles off guard. It seemed a ludicrous idea that anyone should arrive at Prior Park uninvited on the night of a big celebration. Whoever had put that idea into the young man's head he could not imagine.

Charles had kept many secrets over the years – about his friend Francis Belleville, now dead more than 10 years – and about other members of the family. Some of the secrets he had discussed with Mrs Duffy, the Prior Park housekeeper, who had become his friend and confidante over the years, but there were other secrets that he had shared with no one and the existence of Alistair McGovern had been one of them.

He could remember very clearly the conversation with Francis as if it was yesterday. He did not know if Francis, in telling him, had been seeking advice or had felt it a burden too great to shoulder alone. He did not know and did not ask.

Instead he offered his opinion for what it was worth that Francis should at least provide for the mother and the baby. He had never suggested that Francis should become part of their lives, which it now appeared he had done, for William had given him a succinct précis of the events that had occurred.

But how, possessing so much knowledge, was he to keep it from Julia, if she started to ask probing questions?

Better to avoid her, he thought, and hope that it would soon be forgotten, so it was that he found himself riding in the most remote corner of Prior Park's vast acres, only to encounter, once again, a surreptitious meeting that reminded him so much of his discovery of Julia's secret assignations with an American Army officer years before. He still did not know the full story surrounding her love affair. If asked, he would have said very little, claiming no knowledge at all, but privately he felt he had pieced together the whole sordid story, despite never having discussed it with any member of the family, Francis included.

As he had done before, he reined in his horse and sought cover behind some bushes that grew conveniently in a clump close to the path well worn by the constant movement of cattle. He patted the side of the mare's neck to calm her, for he had been riding at a solid pace for some time.

Just ahead, he could easily make out the familiar figure of Richard, dismounted from this horse, helping Jane Warner remount.

His first thought was that Jane Warner had ridden a long way to be where she was. In fact she had ridden what he thought was an unreasonably long way for a morning's ride. Armoobilla, where she lived with husband Tom and young Tom, the growing boy on whom the father lavished his attention, did not share a boundary with Prior Park although anyone familiar with the country, as Charles was, would ride a shortcut through Mayfield Downs but in doing so, would risk being seen by James Fitzroy or his men. The more he thought about it, the less he was convinced that the meeting was accidental.

Desperate not to be seen, Charles eased his horse quietly out of the bushes and headed back the way he had come, but not before he had seen Jane bend down, balancing herself carefully in the saddle, to kiss Richard, not as a friend might kiss another friend, but as a lover.

Charles wished with his whole being that he had ridden another track, that he had never witnessed this betrayal. Once seen, he could not forget it. He shook his head sadly for he knew then that Richard's marriage was in serious trouble.

He was too close to them all. It mattered too much to him. For the first time, he wondered if he mattered to them at all.

He shrugged his shoulders glad there was no one else to see this futile gesture. He dug his heels into the mare's flanks and encouraged her into a gallop, desperate for the concentration that hard riding would demand for he could find no pleasure in the knowledge he now possessed.

Pippa Jensen was looking at her bedroom with its deep pink and white wallpaper and luxurious carpet for the very last time. The shelf where she had kept her dolls and teddy bears was already bare, the imprint of the toys outlined in the dust that remained.

'I will not cry,' she thought to herself, 'I will not cry.' But it was a promise to herself she was struggling to keep.

As the tears welled up, she remembered how her mother had often sat on the bed and together they had talked and laughed and shared a bond that was now broken. Her life, as she had known it, was over. Her beloved mother gone, lost to her in a single careless moment. Her father gone too, but she did not mourn him with the same sense of grief. As yet, she did not know why but she knew, instinctively, that it was her mother who had loved her unconditionally, who had loved and cherished her and who was now lying dead under a pile of brown earth. With her had gone the home she cherished and the life that she had known. It was all gone, lost forever.

As she turned to go, she found herself face to face with her cousin Andrew. It was a face in which she could find no sympathy or understanding. He had forced her out of her home. Now he had little to say to her. He would not even make the pretence of a hollow gesture or a kind word, such was his determination to claim the inheritance his uncle had so generously bestowed on him.

Earlier, he had met the solicitor and signed the necessary documents that had given him the right to take over the properties, for they could not be left unattended. Pippa's future mattered less to him now, for he had been assured there was no legal obligation for him to let her continue to live on at the Essex Downs homestead. He would be the rightful owner. Harry Jensen had left his adopted daughter almost no stake in his considerable wealth, apart from a modest annual income that would end on her marriage.

It mattered little to her now, for there seemed to be almost no one who cared for her welfare. It was only her mother who had cared and she had left her what little private money she possessed. The home she had once known and loved meant nothing without her mother. Now she was leaving it for the last time, to live with her mother's aunt, she had been told. Where she lived no longer mattered to her for no one could replace her mother, who had been the centre of her world and that world no longer existed.

As she turned to walk down the few front steps leading from the verandah for the very last time, Andrew stopped her with a light touch on her arm. She looked up and saw his hand extended towards her. In his right hand, he was clutching a crumpled envelope.

'Here, you should have this. I found it in your father's safe, but it is addressed to you,' he said brusquely.

Across the outer envelope, Harry Jensen had written the words 'For Pippa'. It had not occurred to Andrew Jensen, now that he was in sole charge of his uncle's affairs, to read the letter or to hand it to the solicitors. Instead, like his uncle before him, his first inclination had been to discard the envelope in the wastepaper basket but he paused, smoothed out the envelope, and left it on his desk. He did not know what the envelope contained but decided, without further inspection, that it was likely to be some trivial matter, so he set it aside to give to her later.

At the bottom of the stairs, a car was waiting to take her to the train in Goulburn for the journey to Sydney, where she had been told she would be met by her Aunt Edith, who was expecting her. As far as she could remember, she had met Aunt Edith twice and then only briefly. She carried with her only one bag. The rest of her belongings would follow, they said, by transport.

'What is it?' she said, hardly able to disguise her dislike of her cousin, who was already talking of the changes he would make to the home she had once loved.

'I don't know. Didn't read it. But it must concern you as it has your name on it. Get your Aunt Edith to read it for you,' he said. His words stung her as if to say she was too young and too stupid to read a grown up letter.

'I can read it myself, thank you,' she retorted, and grabbed the letter from him, almost ripping the envelope in half.

'Have it your way,' he said, already uninterested in the contents of the letter and totally unconcerned for her welfare.

He watched her climb in beside the driver, who was one of his more reliable station hands. Within minutes all that remained to remind him of her presence was the empty bedroom and the cloud of thinning dust settling back into the landscape.

He turned and walked back into the house, satisfied that one problem was now behind him. What an absolute stroke of luck, he mused, that his Uncle Harry had no sons. Now all this was his and much sooner than he had ever dared hope. Life had certainly dealt kindly with him, he decided. He spared not one thought for his adopted cousin Pippa such was his preoccupation with his own good fortune.

Chapter 5: May 1957

It had taken Richard and William a day's hard driving to reach Brisbane by sundown the previous day yet neither man showed the after effects as they entered their solicitor's office early the following morning.

Each had expressed their concern privately that Nathaniel Dodds might be getting too old but, out of loyalty, they did not for a moment consider moving their affairs to a new firm.

'Gentlemen,' he said, nodding to each in turn, 'before we start our meeting I have some news for you. I am retiring at the end of June. I'm getting too old now to manage everything. I have sold my practice to a new man and I am happy to introduce you, if that is what you choose, or you may look around elsewhere.'

'Well, Mr Dodds, I can't say I'm surprised by your decision,' William said politely, 'but it will be difficult to work with someone new. You have such knowledge of our affairs that simply can't be gained by reading a set of accounts.'

The solicitor smiled faintly, revealing a rarely seen set of yellowing teeth.

'Other clients have said the same, Mr Belleville,' he said in a voice that was completely devoid of emotion. 'Other clients have said the same, but there comes a time when we all must give up our work. There is a good man taking over from me. I'm sure he will serve you well.'

He sat back in his chair, waiting for one of them to reveal the specific reason for the meeting.

It was William, once again who responded, describing the ugly scene on the night of his mother's birthday party.

After hearing William out, Nathaniel Dodds sat in silence for a few minutes, as if weighing up carefully the advice he would give to the two brothers.

'It is a difficult situation,' he said finally.

'I believe your father probably intended to make provision for him in his will but like a lot of people, he thought he had plenty of time to do it. As it turned out, he did not. He died before he could even instruct me on the changes he wanted to make. But I do not believe that any changes he would have made would have included directing that this young man, who is the source of the trouble, become part of the family. Not at all.'

He paused slightly, as if made breathless by the effort of speaking about such an unsavoury topic.

'I do not believe he ever intended your mother to find out about his extramarital activities, if I may call them that,' he said, choosing his words carefully.

'I think he would have proposed a settlement which required the recipient, shall we call him, to agree not to contact the family. How he proposed this might have been done and kept away from your mother's knowledge, I don't know. We have in fact only been able to keep the earlier settlement quiet because you dealt with everything, Mr Belleville, while your brother was overseas,' he said, nodding in William's direction.

'Although, of course, now that I think about it, your mother didn't really feature in the disposal of the estate except to have a lifetime right to reside at Prior Park, because she has her own money. And nor of course did your sister because she will inherit her mother's money, so we were fortunate in that regard.'

William nodded in agreement.

'Fortunate indeed, Mr Dodds, and fortunate too that our estate manager Charles Brockman was able to head off the unwanted guest before he was seen,' William said.

'I think, and this would be my advice,' Nathaniel Dodds said, 'I should write to the young man, asking for a meeting but I would also need a proposal. In my experience, an offer of money would be the only inducement that is likely to secure his silence. Do you both agree?'

He looked first at William and then at Richard. Both men nodded, but this time, it was Richard who spoke.

'You're right. We have to offer him money. If it is too little he will feel slighted; if it is too much, he will feel he is important in our eyes and then he may not keep with any agreement he signs, which is probably unenforceable anyway.'

Nathaniel Dodds agreed.

'His signing of any document won't have much force in law if he comes bothering you again, but it does demonstrate you are serious about not wanting contact with him.'

He waited then for them both to agree to the course of action. He wanted to be sure that the two brothers concurred with his advice.

'Let's do it,' William said. 'We have other matters to discuss. Richard feels we should liquidate our woollen mill interests, and, as you have been suggesting for some time, we should both make wills.'

Nathaniel Dodds almost always took his instructions without comment but on this occasion he raised an eyebrow at the decision to sell their interests in the woollen mills.

'You're both set on this then, selling your woollen mill shares?' he asked, looking from one to the other.

'We are,' Richard said. 'I think over the next decade we will see a lessening in demand for woollen fabrics as cheaper synthetic fabrics take over. I want to be in a business of the future, not of the past.'

'Very well, if that's your decision, I will put your shares up for sale at market price,' Nathaniel Dodds said.

'Because of the size of the holdings, I may have to sell them in several parcels, but it shouldn't be a problem. There are many who still have faith in that type of business, even if you do not,' he said, making as strong a point as he dared, for it was clear he did not agree with the decision.

Both Richard and William waited while he wrote a detailed note for they knew from experience that he was careful to document every meeting and every point agreed.

'Now, to your wills,' he said, finally, satisfied that he was clear on their instructions for the other matters.

It was Richard's turn to spring a surprise.

'I think, apart from provisions for our wives and William's daughter Marianne, Prior Park and the other business investments should be left to my two sons equally once William and I pass on,' Richard said.

It took some minutes for Richard's suggestion to register fully with William, for he had not considered any possibility beyond leaving his share to his daughter, having first made provision for his wife Alice. To hear now that his brother wished to exclude Marianne, most probably because she was a girl, left him speechless at first but he quickly regained his voice, and it was an angry voice, raised in defence of the rights of his only child.

He turned towards his brother, his anger barely controlled.

'How dare you suggest Marianne be excluded from the inheritance because she is a girl! Just because you have two sons doesn't give them any more rights than Marianne to inherit Prior Park.'

William was on his feet now, physically confronting his much stronger and taller brother.

'How can you just sit there and insult my family like that,' he said, his voice loud and angry.

Richard's plan had taken him completely by surprise and he was angry that his brother could even consider such an unfair and unjust arrangement.

'Mr Belleville, sit down please and let's discuss this logically,' Nathaniel Dodds said, in an even careful voice. For one brief moment, he thought the brothers would come to blows.

'Let's first hear your brother's reasons behind his suggestion.'

His tone was soothing; his gestures matching his words.

Richard, so convinced was he by the practicality of his suggestion, had hardly assembled convincing arguments to support his stance.

'Well, William,' he said, 'Marianne is likely to go off and marry who knows, could be anybody. Her husband would then have a big say over what happens and I don't want my two boys to have to deal with that, quite frankly.'

William almost sneered at the suggestion.

'And your two boys, mightn't they go off and marry who knows and be similarly influenced by them. I think it would be grossly unfair to Marianne not to share in the inheritance and I won't agree to it.'

It was a flat refusal from William. He was incensed at the insult his brother had so casually uttered. It was clear Richard, so engrossed in his own family problems, had not noticed how much William doted on Marianne.

'I wasn't planning to leave her out altogether,' Richard said, in a conciliatory tone. 'I thought we could set up a trust fund for the wives that she would inherit once they are gone.'

'No, I won't have it,' William said flatly, his anger still evident. 'Once provision is made for our wives, Prior Park and all the family assets should be left with my half going to Marianne; your half being divided between Paul and Anthony.'

'So in effect, Marianne, under your suggestion, gets more than each of my two boys?' Richard shot back, uneasy at this latest suggestion, which seemed to disadvantage his two sons.

'Well, to me it is simple,' William said, and he proceeded to set it out for his brother in unnecessary detail.

'You and I are equal partners; I leave my share to Marianne; you leave yours between Paul and Anthony.'

The solicitor, although long used to family disagreements where wills were concerned, harboured hope the pair would resolve the issue without further intervention from him, but seeing the intransigence of the two brothers, he finally offered a suggestion. It was clear he was on William's side in this disagreement.

'Let me draft the wills as you suggest, William, and then you should both discuss the provisions with your wives and, may I also suggest, with your mother. Let's see what her point of view is,' the solicitor said, in an effort to bring the meeting to a close.

They both grudgingly agreed.

'OK, we'll do that,' Richard said finally. 'I'm planning to stay on a few more days so perhaps I could call in and take the draft documents back with me. You can get your clerk to call me at the hotel when they are ready to be picked up.'

The old solicitor nodded, pleased that an unseemly row had been averted, at least for now.

Together, Richard and William headed back towards their hotel. It was some minutes before the sullen silence between them was broken. It was William who spoke first. He could not let the issue of their wills go unremarked.

'I don't think you really thought through that will business,' he said. He did not want the argument between them to escalate further.

Richard shrugged, as if it was now of little importance. He did not want to continue their argument in public.

'Let's not discuss it now. Let's look at it when we have the papers from Dodds,' he said.

William nodded, satisfied that Richard would at least consider his point of view.

'By the way, does Catherine know you're planning to be away longer?' William asked, for the news had come as a complete surprise to him.

'No, I didn't tell her before I left,' Richard said, without offering further explanation.

'Well she'll want to know why you're not with me when I return,' William said, imagining the cross examination he was likely to endure from both his mother and Catherine at Richard's absence.

'Just tell them I want to look into some investment opportunities, now that we are selling the woollen mill shares,' Richard said, unconvincingly.

'And are you?' William asked, for it was the first he had heard of it.

But his brother did not reply. They walked on in silence towards their hotel.

Pippa Jensen did not immediately read the letter her cousin Andrew had reluctantly given her at the very last moment on the day of her departure from Essex Downs. Instead, she had placed it carefully in her bag, deciding there and then that it was something to be read and understood away from prying eyes.

In fact, it was several days before she could bring herself to read the letter.

Alone in her bedroom, she carefully drew the letter out of the envelope and unfolded it. She moved towards the window where the light was better so she could read it.

Dear Pippa, the letter began.

You will be reading this letter as a young woman. I hope your father has prepared you for it for he knows what it contains.

I think this news will come as a shock to you, that you are an adopted child. Mr and Mrs Jensen are not your natural parents. They adopted you after you were given up for adoption by your mother. I am your natural father.

I will not reveal the full name of your natural mother, but her first name is Julia. She is most likely married now and has other children. It's likely her husband does not know she had a baby out of wedlock.

I was posted to a Queensland city during the war when I met your real mother. We had been seeing each other for some time and then I was sent overseas to another job. I did not have much notice of my departure. It was only after I was gone that your mother discovered she was expecting a baby. As I wasn't around to marry her, her family made her give the baby up for adoption. That baby was you.

I found out about it only after the war was over. Your mother Julia wrote to me care of my own mother. The letter was among my mother's belongings when she died. My letters to Julia had obviously been intercepted by her family and she never heard from me again.

I was a doctor with the US Army during the war. Now I am a surgeon in New York. I have given you my address below.

When you read this letter, depending on your circumstances, I would love to hear from you. But you must consider the feelings of your adoptive parents too because I am sure they love you as if you had been their natural child.

Your loving father

Philippe Duval

She sat for a long time on the edge of her bed, trying to understand what the letter meant. She read the words again and again. There was no comfort in them for she had learned that the mother she adored was not her real mother and the man she had thought was her real father was not her real father at all.

Now she knew that her real father was in fact an American. And her real mother? She could only guess.

Deep in her heart, she now understood, for the first time, why her father had been cold towards her. She was not his child. He had never wanted her. It was only her mother who had wanted her, who had chosen her and who had cherished her, as much as if she had been a child of her own body.

In the privacy of her room, she wept until the pillow beneath her head was damp to the touch and her eyes red and sore.

A terrible emptiness gripped her. She had been given away like an unwanted puppy.

Each day, she spent what seemed like hours looking out of her bedroom window onto the leafy street beyond, yearning for the vast landscape of Essex Downs, but all she saw were the neat suburban houses, one after the other, stretching along the street and all she heard was the noise of the traffic as it drove by.

Already, she was used to the routine of the household with the small tea table set daily for two, the blue checked cloth fresh every day and the white china carefully arranged, as if someone important was coming to visit.

Edith Henderson, widowed and with no children of her own, had been chosen by Pippa's mother for a duty she never expected her to have to fulfil but now, with the responsibility suddenly thrust upon her, she was determined to do what she could for the now orphaned child, whom she barely knew.

She was a patient woman with the same kind and caring nature that Pippa had so loved in her mother, so each day, she offered the young girl just the slightest encouragement to talk, even as she repeated the same reassuring words.

'Now, are you sure you have everything you need, Pippa, because if you don't you must let me know and I will get whatever you want.'

Pippa remained very still, her stony face hardly revealing any emotion at all. She responded politely but without enthusiasm.

'Thank you, Aunt Edith, I'm fine.'

There was silence for a few moments as they both finished their meals.

'You know you will be going to school next week. It's just around the corner. The principal at Meriden, who is a friend of mine, has agreed to let you join the school, even though you weren't enrolled there, given the circumstances.'

Aunt Edith waited for the effect of this announcement but Pippa merely nodded but said nothing.

'It's a very good school with some very nice girls there. I know you'll find it very different from what you are used to, but I'm sure it won't take long before you make some friends,' the older woman said, trying to keep any hint of desperation from her voice, for she did not know how to put the girl at ease.

There was something heartrendingly painful about the small wary eyes and the self contained emotionless face that looked back at her from across the table.

She had not said it before but now she felt she must.

'I didn't say it before, not properly,' she said, 'but the loss of your mother, and your father, was just so shocking I could hardly believe it. I hoped it was a nightmare from which I would wake and find it all a big mistake.

'Unfortunately it wasn't,' she said quietly.

Pippa looked at her mother's aunt with a little flicker of interest, understanding for the first time that the loss of her beloved mother had been felt by others as well, not just by herself, for she had thought herself alone in mourning her mother. Now she could see, for her aunt was close to tears, that her mother's death had left others bereft as well.

'I don't really want to talk about it,' Pippa said finally. 'All I want to do is cry but crying doesn't achieve anything at all, because when I stop crying, my mother is still dead, nothing has changed.'

She wanted to say, but everything has changed; it was all a lie, but she did not.

Aunt Edith stretched her hand across the small table and touched Pippa on the arm. It was the faintest of touches, but it was strangely comforting to the girl, who did not pull back from it.

'We must be strong for each other,' Aunt Edith said. 'That's what your mother would want, for us to comfort each other, because your mother was as close to me as if she had been my own child. I loved her as much as if she had been.'

Tears slid down the older woman's cheeks. She brushed them aside impatiently, but more in impatience with herself, for she did not want to show this weakness, and yet the tears could not be stopped so easily.

Pippa drew in a deep breath, fighting back her own tears. She got up from the table and began to clear the plates. She suddenly felt uncomfortable, uncertain in this new place and uncertain in the discovery that there was someone who could grieve as deeply as herself.

It was only the memory of her mother that kept her going. Without her mother, life seemed impossibly bleak and uncertain. And, now, in the midst of her pain and her heartbreak, she kept reminding herself that her mother was not really her mother. It was knowledge that struck at the core of her being.

Over and over again, she wondered why she had never been told and she could find no answer. But in the depths of her despair there lay a glimmer of hope, an address in New York. Would she dare? Could she dare write to the man who proclaimed to be her father?

Later that night in the privacy of her bedroom, she sat down to write a letter. She did not know where to begin.

In her still childish handwriting, she started to write on the blank page. She began 'Dear Father .....'.

By the merest chance, Jane Warner avoided seeing William Belleville on the morning he checked out of the hotel. Seeing him at the reception desk, she walked quickly but unnoticed into the dining room where breakfast was still being served. She sat down at a vacant table that had just enough of a view of the entrance to the dining room in case he entered but was far enough removed from the entrance so that he would not see her.

The waitress brought her tea but she declined the offer of breakfast.

Her hands shook just a little but she doubted anyone would notice.

She had practised the answers to the obvious questions any acquaintance would ask but she was pleased to avoid William in particular. He was too close to Richard and while Richard had described his brother as 'unimaginative' she did not want to put this to the test. It might never have occurred to him to link Richard's delayed departure with her presence but she could not take the risk, so she stayed at the table long after her tea had gone cold to be sure of avoiding him.

Only after she was sure the she would not see him did she venture out into the foyer to approach the reception desk herself and ask for her room key. She was about to turn away from the desk when the hotel receptionist called her back to receive a message. She recognised Richard's handwriting at once. She quickly tucked the envelope into her handbag, preferring to read it in the privacy of her room.

She smiled and thanked the young woman at the desk whose attention had already moved on to the next guest. She hoped no one had noticed the slight flush in her cheeks. It had taken only a couple of very small white lies to arrange her trip south alone. Her reasons had not aroused even the slightest suspicion in her complacent and wholly contented husband for whom their mundane and predictable life together was entirely satisfactory.

Back at Prior Park in the absence of Richard and William, the routine of life continued for Alice and Marianne and for Elizabeth Belleville, who had yielded more and more of the running of the household to Alice, leaving Elizabeth free to follow her own interests.

She missed her sons when they were absent but most of all she missed the eleven year old Paul Belleville who had quickly established himself as her favourite grandchild, having the natural advantage of being the first born. Still she was happy to have the two younger grandchildren in the house, but she found the boundless energy of the youngest, Anthony, tiring and at times irritating, although she tried hard to hide it for fear of upsetting Catherine, who had hoped for a daughter with her second child.

On this particular morning Elizabeth Belleville had written a long overdue letter to her cousin Jean Dalrymple. As she descended the stairs to place the letter on the hall table for posting, she paused at the sound of Catherine's voice on the telephone. It was not the fact of Catherine speaking on the telephone that caused her to stop; it was the soft almost inaudible level of her conversation.

To Elizabeth, it seemed entirely out of character for Catherine's cultured voice could normally be heard throughout the house whenever she spoke, particularly on the telephone. The lowered tone and the almost whispered responses concerned Elizabeth Belleville yet she did not want Catherine to know she had been overheard, so she turned quietly and retraced her steps back to her sitting room upstairs.

She sat down at her desk, this time with no particular purpose in mind other than to wait until she was sure Catherine had finished her telephone call. There was something that troubled her about Catherine's recent behaviour but she did not understand or know what the cause was, but she knew instinctively that she did not see in Richard and Catherine the quiet contentment that existed between William and Alice.

In recent times, she had commented to Alice that Catherine was using every excuse to spend more time in Sydney, away from Prior Park, but Alice had only countered by saying that Catherine wanted to make sure Paul was happy at school.

What troubled Elizabeth Belleville, and this she did not say to Alice, was that Richard seemed to worry less and less about his wife's absences.

This, she decided, was the problem at the heart of it all yet she knew she could be no more than a powerless bystander in witnessing what she now thought of as the disintegration of her elder son's marriage. For Elizabeth Belleville, this was an alarming and unhappy prospect. For the first time, she felt powerless to intervene.

CHAPTER 6: MAY-JUNE 1957

Richard paced backwards and forwards along a short stretch of the concrete pathway that led through the Botanic Gardens towards the river, not out of impatience, but out of expectation.

He glanced at his watch. She wasn't late. It was just that he was early to their assigned meeting place, so he lit a cigarette and watched the smoke dissipate into the chilly early evening air.

Meeting late to avoid scrutiny had been her idea. He understood why she thought it was necessary yet he did not think there was much risk they would see anyone they knew. He had declined to take up the membership of the club his father had frequented just a few hundred yards away so he had not built a circle of acquaintances in the city who might have recognised him.

It was then he caught sight of her, walking towards him through the trees, careful to avoid the public pathway.

Richard ground out his cigarette in the dirt and walked to meet her. In the shadows, they embraced, his lips on hers, words hardly needed between them.

They broke apart but still he held her, as if letting her go was a risk he did not want to take.

'I'm so pleased you came, Jane,' he said. 'I wasn't sure you would, in the end.'

She put her fingers to his lips to silence him.

'I had said I would come, but you didn't believe me.'

He stopped her then.

'You said you would wait for me, remember, all those years ago so forgive me for being a bit cautious.'

She smiled. He relaxed his embrace.

'I don't want to talk about that now,' she said.

She turned away from him, her face momentarily hidden from him.

'It's a deal,' he said quietly. 'No re-opening of old wounds. We'll just enjoy the moment. We'll just enjoy the few days we have together.'

They walked hand in hand for a short way. To passers-by they looked like any other happy couple. It was only in their nervous glances left and right that they both betrayed their fear of being recognised.

It was some days later that James Fitzroy delivered the news of Richard's delayed return to Julia. He enjoyed the small victory the superior knowledge of the goings on at Prior Park gave him over his wife on this rare occasion. In the normal course of events, it was Julia who relayed all the news of Prior Park to him so she was taken aback to hear that only one of her brothers had returned from the trip south.

'Apparently, he wanted to stay on to look at some business opportunities,' James said, offhandedly, for he was no longer interested in the topic.

'And he didn't tell Catherine beforehand?' Julia asked, her voice betraying the hint of anxiety she had meant to hide.

'Not as far as I am aware,' James said dismissively.

'He seems very unsettled at the moment,' Julia said, unsure though whether James was still listening to her.

'There was something on the night of mother's party that upset him and William and I don't know what it was,' Julia said, in no expectation of a response from her husband.

James looked up, suddenly interested again in the direction of their conversation.

'There was indeed something that upset them,' said James, teasingly. 'There was indeed.'

It was his tone that made Julia turn to look directly at him. Instinctively she knew then that he was in possession of some information about the incident that he had not shared with her.

'You sound as if you know more about this than I do,' she said. 'With Richard and William away, I had been trying to see Charles Brockman but if I didn't know better, I would think that he has been avoiding me. I expected to see him on my ride yesterday but I am almost certain he spotted me and rode off in the other direction, before I could reach him.'

James set aside the newspaper he was pretending to read. He got up to refill his whisky glass from the decanter on the sideboard.

'So why do you think Charles Brockman wouldn't want to see you?' he asked, in a tone of unconvincing innocence.

'He doesn't want me to ask awkward questions, I suppose,' she replied. 'He doesn't want me to ask who it was that came to Prior Park on Saturday night, because I know he knows.'

Julia had ignored the obviousness of his question.

'So why would he be so evasive, do you think? You obviously think he has a reason to be evasive?' he shot back.

It was not so much James's questions as the tone of his voice that alerted Julia to the realisation he knew much more than he was telling her. He enjoyed the rare moment of triumph, of knowing something she did not.

'You know who it was, don't you? You know who came to Prior Park and wasn't admitted. Tell me, who was it?' she demanded, annoyed now that he had remained silent and not shared the information with her.

He took a slow deliberate swig from his glass before responding. He sat looking at her appraisingly.

'Do you really want to know? Are you sure you want to know?' he said, finally. 'I would have preferred to wait and speak to Richard or William before telling you because I'd actually prefer one of them to tell you.'

She could see he was being serious, regretting perhaps that he had teased her and reluctant now to share with her what he had discovered.

'Why must everything always wait for Richard or William? Why can't I know? I have as much right to know something that affects

64

my family as they do,' she said pointedly.

James was silent, considering whether or not he should tell her. He knew he had made a tactical error in goading her, yet that was exactly what he had done. It was exactly what he could not resist doing. He knew he should have mentioned it quietly to William and Richard and suggested she be told before the story spread, but it was too late for that now. The responsibility now fell to him and he did not relish it, because after all, it was only gossip he had heard, and he did not know how reliable it would prove to be.

He was serious now, unsmiling. He moved to her side, as if physical proximity would render the scandalous news he was about to impart more bearable.

'I can tell you what I heard in town yesterday,' he said, his voice softer now, 'but it would really be much better coming from your brothers. William is back. Why don't you go and see him tomorrow?'

She shook her head.

'If you know something, and I don't, I want you to tell me now.'

There was a hint of rising anger in her voice that she tried unsuccessfully to stifle.

'Very well, if you must know, there was a young man who, I understand, came to the house on Saturday night during your mother's party and was eventually turned away by your brothers,' he said. 'I heard gossip yesterday at the Criterion Hotel that the young man they turned away claimed to be your half-brother. He claimed that your father was his father.'

Julia gasped out loud, an unmistakable expression of her disbelief. He could see at once she was sorry now that she had pushed him into telling her what little he knew.

'Who told you this story? You can't be serious,' she said, turning to look directly at her husband, whose expression told her immediately that he was deadly serious.

'I'm sorry. I don't know any more details than that. That's why I didn't want to tell you. Really, you should ask William,' he said before adding a note of caution.

'But remember, if you didn't know, it's likely your mother didn't know either, so don't go asking her or asking William in front of her.'

She was silent for a few moments, as if absorbing the new information, trying to form it in her mind and reconcile the memory of the family she had grown up in with the new knowledge that her beloved father might have fathered another child. A thousand unanswerable questions crowded in her mind but she knew immediately that James could answer none of them.

Eventually, she spoke but even to her own ears, the words sounded unconvincing.

'It's probably just some crackpot who met my father at some stage and decided to make an outrageous claim because he thought there would be money in it. What do you think?' she asked, almost pleading for him to agree with her.

He shrugged, not knowing and yet knowing; knowing that the young man he had glimpsed leaving the hotel was the spitting image of William; knowing too that the man he knew Francis Belleville to be could have been capable of such deception. Above all, he knew the probable outcome would be to destroy Julia's belief in the father she had loved unconditionally. This much he knew for certain, even as the full details were yet to be known.

'I don't know, to be honest,' he lied convincingly. 'I don't know anything else. It's best that you ask William tomorrow, but remember, do it quietly in a private place where you won't be overheard. I imagine Richard and William will be doing their best to contain this story, especially for the sake of your mother, so don't create a scene with him.'

She nodded briefly, as if the advice was unnecessary.

'I'll go and see William first thing in the morning,' she said, anxious now to bring the conversation to a close.

'If I go early, I should be able to see him before Mother is up and about, otherwise it would be difficult to get him alone.'

James's silence she took for agreement with her plan.

He was sorry now there was no way to spare Julia from what he imagined would be a sordid unhappy story for she knew too much now not to want to know the truth. For the first time, he understood just how painful the truth was likely to be and there was nothing he could do to make it easier for her.

The following morning was cold, in fact colder than the weather had been in years but Julia knew the crispy white frost covering the ground would soon disappear as the sun gained strength. It was rare for frost to linger beyond the first couple of hours after dawn so she was not deterred from the mission that had kept her awake most of the night.

She was by now a very competent driver so she could have chosen the ease of driving over to Prior Park but instead she saddled her horse, a bay mare she had christened Jezebel. She had chosen the horse herself against James's advice. He had declared the horse too nervous in temperament for a lady rider. Twice she had been thrown from the horse, a fact that she never revealed to James who had failed to notice the bruise on her upper arm from the most recent clash between horse and rider.

The cold morning had left Jezebel more fractious than usual but Julia, having decided to ride, ignored the quivering nervousness of the horse.

Having settled herself in the saddle, she reached forward and patted the side of Jezebel's neck to calm her. The horse seemed to respond to the quiet whispered words from her mistress and broke into an even paced trot as they left the horse yard near the house.

Once on the main road, Julia urged the horse into a more energetic pace towards the turnoff to Prior Park, which was only a short distance. As she neared the Prior Park turn, she pulled on the reins to slow Jezebel to walking pace. It was just at this point that three kangaroos in full flight bounded across the roadway immediately in front of the horse and rider.

The horse, startled by the suddenness of the movement, reared. Julia, caught completely by surprise, struggled to hold her grip on the reins and keep her seat in the saddle. The horse reared again before Julia was able to regain her balance and this time her grip on the reins gave way.

Moments before her head hit the hard gravel road she managed to free her left foot from the stirrup. Her horse, free of the burden of its rider, bolted down the road.

Left behind, Julia lay still on the deserted roadway, her fair hair falling loose over her face and blood trickling slowly down the back of her head.

James had only been vaguely aware that his wife had left the house very early. He had assumed they would breakfast together as usual so he was surprised when the housekeeper told him she had already left.

'Are you sure she's gone, Mrs Fry?' he asked again. 'The car is still here. Surely she didn't ride, did she?'

'She did, Mr Fitzroy,' the housekeeper confirmed. 'She didn't take the car. She had a cup of tea and went out to saddle Jezebel. She said the horse needed some exercise.'

'Thank you, Mrs Fry. I don't like that horse you know. I think it's unreliable,' he said.

'Well, if I may say so, it's very hard to tell your wife that. She doesn't seem to want to listen to much advice, although I'm sure she's a very good rider.'

This was as far as Mrs Fry had ever gone in criticising Julia. She had accepted Julia as mistress of the house but, despite the years, the pair had never warmed to one another. It was to James Fitzroy's mother that Mrs Fry owed her loyalty.

James smiled ruefully.

'Ah, you know my wife too well, Mrs Fry. She won't listen to me either, for that matter. She is very headstrong. Very spoiled, I think, by her family.'

It was the most he had ever said about Julia to the faithful house-keeper, although he knew instinctively how Mrs Fry felt about Julia. As much as she tried to hide her feelings, it was the occasional word or look that betrayed what she really thought.

'So why was she so anxious to see her family this morning at Prior Park?' the housekeeper asked. 'I doubt her mother would be up and around for another hour or two at least, I would think. Their house-keeper Mrs Duffy tells me that she has breakfast in her room most mornings and doesn't appear much before ten, so if she wanted to see her mother about something, she would have been better off going much later.'

James smiled, knowing full well that the one person she wanted to avoid on the visit was her mother. He answered vaguely.

'I don't really know,' he said. 'Perhaps she just had the urge to get an early start.'

Mrs Fry said nothing more but it was easy to see she was unconvinced by his explanation. She began to clear the breakfast table.

Charles Brockman was hardly paying attention to the road so familiar was it to him so he almost missed the crumpled figure lying near the Prior Park turnoff.

He was quick to bring the big old Bedford to a halt, loose stones scattering from behind its dusty wheels. The vehicle had barely stopped before he was out of the truck cabin and down on the roadway striding quickly towards the still figure.

He knew in an instant it was Julia. There was no mistaking the blonde hair and the slim figure. He could see she was dressed for riding but there was no sign of her horse.

'Damn,' he said under his breath. 'That bloody horse. I knew it was no good.'

He knelt beside her, feeling first for her pulse, and then gently turned her on her side. For once he did not know what to do. By himself, he could do little except lift her in his arms and lay her body across the bench seat of the truck. He was desperate for any sign of life from her, however small. He was sure she was still breathing.

He coaxed the truck to life again and eased it around the turn, driving as fast as he could towards the house. As he neared the house, he pressed the horn repeatedly, the noise of it deafening him momentarily.

First out of the door to see what all the noise was about was William, followed by Alice and then Catherine and the rest of the household, except for Julia's mother. Charles jumped down out of the truck cabin and motioned urgently to William.

'I need help here. It's Julia,' he yelled.

He yanked open the passenger door and together they lifted the limp figure off the seat, before William took the full weight of his sister's body in his arms.

'What the hell happened?' William shouted at him.

'I found her on the roadway just near the turn in,' Charles replied in a sharp rapid burst of words that told the story in as few words as possible.

'She's obviously been thrown off that bloody horse of hers.'

It was William's turn to yell, to make himself heard above the general commotion that now enveloped him.

'Get the car out for me, Charles. It's no good taking her into the house. She needs to go to hospital,' William said, as he stood helplessly in the midst of the agitated onlookers.

Charles, pleased to have something useful to do, strode towards the garage which now housed three cars. The Buick, which had been a favourite of William's, was rarely driven now so he opted instead for the new Holden, its two-tone blue paintwork still in pristine state.

William looked at the others clustered around him.

'I'll take her to hospital now,' he said, without waiting for agreement.

Turning towards his wife, he gave her the most difficult task.

'Can you go and tell James, Alice, and then he can bring whatever you think she'll need,' he told his wife who did not relish the task of delivering bad news to her brother.

'I don't think there is any time to waste,' William added, as he turned towards the car that Charles had brought round to the front of the house.

Alice nodded, clear now on what she must do.

'I'll go now,' she said, heading back in to the house long enough to get her handbag and her coat, for the morning was still chilly.

Shocked at the sight of her sister-in-law, Catherine, without being asked, volunteered to tell Elizabeth Belleville what had occurred.

Together, William and Charles laid Julia carefully across the back seat of the car. William quickly settled himself behind the wheel and let the clutch out rather sharply, shouting one final order to Charles Brockman as he did so.

'When you find that bloody horse, Charles, make sure you have a rifle with you to shoot it.'

With that he was gone in a whirl of dust, memories of an earlier time when he had been run off the road by the American Army truck came back to him. Julia had been injured then and his mind ran quickly to the unforeseen consequences of that incident.

This, he worried, was far more serious.

He pushed the car as hard as he would dare on the dirt road, unconcerned now about the new paintwork. His only concern was for his sister, who was showing few signs of life. He cursed the distance he had to travel to hospital but he knew it was her only chance.

James Fitzroy was surprised to see a car driven by his sister come speeding up the Mayfield Downs driveway. He walked down the few front steps from the verandah to greet her as she brought the car to a shuddering halt.

'What's up, sis?' he asked casually. 'Had a row with William?'

Her first words were breathless and garbled, such that he had great difficulty in understanding what she was saying.

'It's awful. It's Julia,' she blurted out.

She paused for a moment, to calm herself and to force the words to come out sensibly.

'What about Julia? What's wrong?'

Now he was fully alert, aware that the reason for his sister's early morning visit was serious. A little calmer now, Alice stressed each word so she would not have to repeat it.

'Julia came off her horse, just near the turn off to Prior Park. Charles Brockman found her lying on the road.'

He interrupted her then, desperate to know but fearing the worst. He had to ask.

'She isn't dead, is she? Tell me she's not dead.'

He was almost yelling now, unable to keep the rising anxiety he felt in check.

'No, she's not dead. We're sure she's unconscious. William has headed into the hospital with her. He told me to come and tell you the news.'

With that he turned taking the verandah steps in one athletic leap. Before Alice could say anything he returned, car keys in hand.

'I'll go after them. He'll take her to the General Hospital. I might even catch them if I put my foot down.'

Alice did not try to stop him for she had known that he would go straight away.

'I'll get some things for her, a nightgown and such, if that's all right,' Alice said, but she doubted he heard her for he was already in the car, revving the engine hard.

Alice turned towards the house, seeing Mrs Fry for the first time.

'What is it, Mrs Belleville, what's the matter?'

Alice had always thought it odd that the housekeeper had retreated from the use of her first name, now that she was married. She would have much preferred to still be called Alice but she did not remark it.

'Julia has come off her horse, just near the Prior Park turn off. Charles Brockman found her. It was lucky he was coming along with a load of hay he picked up early this morning, otherwise who knows how long she might have been there.'

Mrs Fry wiped her wet hands on her apron absent-mindedly.

'I said to your brother even this morning that horse was no good, now look what's happened,' she said, shaking her head at the whole sad story.

'Is Mrs Fitzroy going to be all right? She's not badly hurt, I hope?'

Tears gathered in Alice's eyes and threatened to spill down her cheeks. The shock of seeing Julia lying apparently lifeless in William's arms was almost too much for her. Seeing this, the housekeeper put her arm around her and drew her into the house.

'We think she's unconscious,' Alice said, through her sobs. 'It looked to me as if she'd had a nasty blow on the back of the head. But I'll have to get some things for her and take them in to the hospital.'

Now the housekeeper began to exert the same motherly pressure on Alice that she had done through the years Alice was growing up.

'I think you should have a cup of tea first, my dear,' she said tenderly, for Alice had been a great favourite with her.

'Then we can get some things together for Mrs Fitzroy. Another ten minutes won't make any difference.'

Alice succumbed to the gentle pressure and found herself sitting at the kitchen table, the surroundings comfortable and familiar. Despite Julia's complete redecoration of the homestead, the kitchen had been largely untouched, except for a coat of paint and some new appliances.

The hot tea was too warm on her lips and she put the cup down to let it cool.

Mrs Fry sat opposite, shaking her head.

'I don't know what she was doing riding off like that so early this morning, but I know she was heading for Prior Park. Your brother said he didn't know why she was going so early but I heard the tail end of their conversation last night and she said she wanted to see William first thing this morning about something,' she said.

Alice looked up, quite obviously totally at a loss with the direction of the conversation.

'I have no idea what she wanted to see your husband about, but whatever it was, she was very on edge this morning, that I do know,' Mrs Fry added.

Alice, calmer now, shrugged her shoulders.

'I have absolutely no idea what Julia might have wanted to see William about,' Alice said finally. 'I will ask him though when I see him at the hospital.'

She got up then, her cup of tea only partly drunk.

'We must get some things together for Julia. William will need me,' she said, knowing that Mrs Fry would understand completely.

Together they headed towards the master bedroom to pack a hospital bag for Julia, both desperately hoping that she would have need of the nightgowns and toiletries they were choosing from among her belongings.

Chapter 7: June 1957

'Tell me about what you did during the war?'

'Tell me why you dumped me and married someone else while I was away at the war?'

Richard lay sprawled across Jane's bed. He wanted to know the answer to his question first. He did not want to talk about the war. He did not want to drag up all the terrible memories which had begun to haunt his nightly sleep.

She sat up and looked across at him, drawing the sheet around her body.

'If you must know the truth, I thought I was pregnant,' she said quietly.

'To me?' he asked, wanting to be sure of what she was saying.

'Yes, to you,' she said.

'And were you?' he asked.

He had never considered the possibility that her young son might be his. He was sure he had been born too long after his departure for Canada.

'No,' she said. 'I wasn't as it turned out but when Tom Warner took an interest in me shortly after you left, I decided to accept his offer. I couldn't run the risk of being pregnant with no one to help me.'

'Not a great love match then?' he asked.

'No, not a great love match,' she said, 'but we've managed to get along together.'

At this statement, he reached across and pulled her towards him. She nestled in his arms.

'If you were happy with your husband, Mrs Warner, I wouldn't be in your bed.'

He said it teasingly but there was a grain of truth in his words. But she was determined not to let him get away with such an outrageous statement.

'And if you were happy with your wife, Mr Belleville, you wouldn't be in my bed.'

He began to kiss her and his hands began to explore her body but she pushed him away gently.

'I think it's time we got up, don't you? The housemaid will be knocking on the door any moment and then it will be a mad scramble.'

He laughed.

'Yes, we mustn't be caught together,' he said, although he had made no move to return to his own room. 'We don't want to be fodder for the newspapers in some lurid divorce proceedings.'

She was serious for a moment. Was divorce a possibility? Is that what he was proposing?

'And what happens now?' she said.

Amidst the heady passion of rekindling their relationship the future had not even been considered.

If he heard her question, he did not acknowledge it. Just then the housemaid knocked on the door and Richard disappeared hurriedly through the connecting door to his own room.

Back at Prior Park, an uneasy silence engulfed the house as those who remained went about their daily tasks but the atmosphere of the house was far from normal.

Catherine, having volunteered to deliver the bad news to Elizabeth Belleville about her daughter, could do nothing more than offer constant reassurance there was every sign that Julia would be fine.

In the intimate surroundings of Elizabeth Belleville's private sitting room, a place that Catherine rarely visited, the atmosphere was especially tense.

'Are you sure you've told me everything, Catherine,' Elizabeth asked querulously for she was not at her best in the morning.

'You really think Julia will be fine?' she asked, a question that she had now repeated at least six times by Catherine's count.

'I'm sure she will be fine, Mother,' she said.

The word 'mother' sat uncomfortably in Catherine's response. The word trailed off uncertainly, for she rarely used it at Prior Park, preferring to reserve the name for her own mother of whom she spoke very little to her Australian family.

In truth she was rarely asked about her family, except for a perfunctory enquiry every now and then from Elizabeth Belleville or Alice. She rarely answered in any detail because she knew that they, in turn, would struggle to feign interest beyond their first banal but well mannered enquiry.

Elizabeth Belleville drained the last of the tea from her silver teapot into her fine bone china cup. She sipped at it and then put the cup down. Uncertain as to whether she should remain, Catherine stood up and turned towards the door.

'Don't go, Catherine, don't go just yet,' Elizabeth said.

She was much calmer now, aware that all they could do was wait for news from the hospital. Catherine turned and resumed her seat. For the first time, she took note of the furniture in the room. It was old-fashioned but comfortable, with several well-padded chairs and the beautifully made, highly-polished writing desk, not large like a man's, but small and elegant, designed for a woman who would not be cluttering it with ledgers and accounts but invitations and handwritten letters from relatives and friends.

'Was there something you wanted? Something I can help you with?' Catherine asked the questions cautiously.

'When is Richard due back?'

Elizabeth Belleville asked the question directly, without preamble, as if she was wanting to judge not just Catherine's response but the way she responded.

'Tomorrow, I believe,' she said briefly, without further explanation.

With her short answer, Catherine had hoped to put an end to any further questions. She did not want to lie outright but neither did she want to draw her mother-in-law into their increasingly unhappy situation.

Elizabeth Belleville could not fail to notice the reticence in her daughter-in-law's response but she was not deterred. She had thought about this moment for some time and was determined to ask the questions no one else would have dared.

'Are you happy here with your life, Catherine? Are you happy with Richard?'

Catherine avoided meeting Elizabeth Belleville's steady gaze; instead she got up and walked to the window, hoping the view below would offer some distraction, anything at all, to release her from this conversation.

She paused. In the silence she could hear her own breathing, the increased rhythm of it betraying her rising anxiety at the question. Elizabeth Belleville did not attempt to fill the void. She waited patiently for Catherine to answer.

'To be honest, I don't think this is a conversation you and I should be having,' Catherine said, finally, as she turned away from the window.

For once, she was surprised by Elizabeth Belleville's response.

'I agree with you,' Elizabeth Belleville said. 'It's not a conversation you and I should be having, but I fear that it is a conversation you and Richard should be having and you're not. Am I right?'

Once again there was a long silence.

'You are right,' she said reluctantly. 'We haven't talked at all. If you must know I wrote to Richard when I was in England and about to come back, saying I couldn't imagine settling back in Australia permanently, but since I've been back, we haven't spoken about my letter at all. He simply doesn't seem to want to discuss it.'

She had avoided saying she did not want to settle back at Prior Park. She drew back from uttering such an insult to her mother-in-law.

Elizabeth Belleville merely nodded, for she had heard the response she had expected. It had been clear to her for some time that both Richard and Catherine were restless and unsettled but she could only guess at the cause. Now she knew for certain.

'You must talk to him when he gets back, Catherine,' she said. 'You must try to work this out between you. You have two boys to consider, not just yourselves.'

'I am aware of this,' Catherine said. 'I am fully aware of my responsibilities, but is he?'

She was immediately sorry she had posed such a question out loud. If she was looking for someone to share her concerns with, that person would certainly not be Elizabeth Belleville, who looked up in alarm.

'What are you suggesting? That my son doesn't love his two sons? That he isn't aware of his responsibilities as a husband and father?'

Catherine stood up and picked up the tea tray to return it to the kitchen. She was desperate now to end the conversation which had already gone too far.

'Of course not. I'm sorry I spoke. I didn't mean to say that,' she said.

'I promise Richard and I will sort things out. I don't want you to worry about anything at all. And don't worry about Julia, I'm sure she will be fine.'

As if suddenly remembering the reason for Catherine's visit to her sitting room, Elizabeth Belleville thanked her daughter-in-law.

'You will let me know if there is any news from William or James? I'm sure William will telephone when there is anything to report,' she said.

'I will come and tell you straight away,' Catherine promised, as she closed the door behind her, relieved to have put an end to the probing questions.

In the end, she had resorted to platitudes which she hoped would settle the issue with her mother-in-law. But the nagging uncertainties and doubts remained. She knew she could ignore them no longer.

One question, and one question only, continued to occupy her mind: what exactly was it that had kept Richard away from Prior Park for days after his brother had returned? Was it really business or was there something else? The doubts had begun to nag at her and now they could not be settled without confronting him on his return, but on the flimsy evidence of her own instinct and some idle gossip, she drew back from the accusation that she knew would tear them apart.

Preoccupied with her own thoughts as she placed the tray on the kitchen table, she attached no significance at all to seeing Tom Warner, a riderless horse in tow, hail Charles Brockman who was supervising the unloading of the hay that had been the reason for his early morning trip.

She stood for a moment at the kitchen window, watching, as Tom Warner tied the reins of the riderless horse to the rail. She recognised the horse immediately.

On impulse she walked quickly out through the back door and crossed the yard. Having heard William's impulsive order to Charles Brockman to shoot Julia's beautiful but ill-tempered horse, she was determined to intervene to save the mare from such a fate.

As she approached the men, they both greeted her deferentially.

She immediately went to Jezebel, speaking softly and stroking her sweating neck, all the while her expert hands checking for any cuts or abrasions the animal had suffered, but she found none. Slowly, she undid the saddle and handed it and the saddle cloth to Charles in one steady movement. He was astounded at how quiet the mare had become under Catherine's careful and gentle handling.

'She's being very well behaved for you, Mrs Belleville,' he said, with clear admiration for her ability.

'Well, Charles, I had a very flighty filly to ride when I was young and just learning to ride, but my father said I should understand the animal, and in the end we formed a very good understanding. I never had any trouble with her,' she said, although explanation of her obvious expertise was hardly necessary to those watching her calm the temperamental horse.

She turned towards Tom Warner, surprised now to see his young son with him.

'Where did you find her, Tom?' she asked, more out of curiosity than any real need to know.

'Young Tom and I were riding the road boundary fence. We've had some stock get out lately and we were looking for the spot where the fence must be down. We found the mare cropping the grass on the edge of the road a couple of miles from our house,' he replied.

'How did you know who it belonged to?' Catherine asked, without realising there would have been very few properties in the district able to afford the luxury of keeping such a well-bred animal for the simple pleasure of riding.

He smiled at her but replied politely.

'Well, I wasn't sure, but I guessed it would either be Mrs Fitzroy's or your mount, Mrs Belleville, so I thought if I brought it along here to Charles, he would know.'

Catherine smiled back at him.

'Of course, I wasn't thinking. Most of the horses around here are hard ridden stock horses, not horses ridden for the simple pleasure of the exercise.'

She glanced at young Tom Warner, now a sturdy twelve year old. He sat in the saddle as if he had been born to it. His father had dismounted but he had not.

'You should be in school, young man,' Catherine said teasingly.

It was his father who replied for him.

'I let him off school today. His mother's away in Brisbane for a few days, needed to see a specialist doctor, so I said he could have a couple of days away from the lessons to help me with the work.'

Catherine smiled and nodded but this time the smile was forced. Was it just a coincidence that Richard was in Brisbane too or was there some truth in the gossip she had heard recently?

She walked Jezebel towards to the stables. Jimmy, the youngest of the four station hands, looked after the horses so she handed over the reins to him, with instructions to give the mare a good rub down, good bedding, and plenty of feed and water.

She walked back towards the house slowly, not knowing what to make of the news she had just heard about Jane Warner. It seemed ludicrous. It seemed too much of a coincidence to matter at all yet somewhere in the back of her mind, a small seed of doubt had begun to take hold. Exactly how she would tackle it with Richard she did not know.

It was the shrill sound of the telephone that brought her back to the present and she hurried into the house to answer it.

By the time James had reached the hospital, Julia was already beginning to come around. He found William sitting beside her bed, glancing anxiously from doctor to patient and back again, clearly concerned for his sister but furious with her too.

The nurse had bathed the bad cut on the back of her head and was in the midst of creating a turban of white bandages when James strode into the room.

'How is my wife? How is Julia?' he demanded, noticing William in the chair beside the bed.

William stood up and went around the bed to greet James. He put his hand on his arm, in a small gesture of comfort.

'She'll be fine,' William said, the relief in his voice obvious to everyone in the room.

'The doctor says she has had a nasty bang on the head and she mustn't become excited or agitated,' William added.

James approached the bed, looking for the signs that William had assured him were there. Julia opened her eyes briefly and smiled at him. She murmured something but he could not catch the words.

It was then that the doctor put a restraining hand on his arm.

'Your wife will be fine, Mr Fitzroy,' he said, 'but you must let her rest. She's had a very nasty bang on the head.'

James heard the words but it was the calm authority in the doctor's voice that reassured him.

'We will keep her under observation for several days, Mr Fitzroy,' Dr Aidan Murphy said. 'In that time, I don't want a stream of visitors to your wife. I want her to have peace and quiet to recover.'

James nodded. He was now slightly less grim-faced than he had been on arrival.

'I'll see to that, doctor,' he said, with emphasis. 'I'll see that my wife is not besieged by well wishers.'

Dr Murphy nodded.

'She has been very lucky, you know,' he said. 'If that blow on the head had been in a slightly different position, I don't think we could have expected such a good outcome.'

James nodded, aware of just how bad the accident could have been, for he had imagined such an outcome on his rushed trip to the hospital.

'I think it will be some time before your wife rides again, Mr

Fitzroy,' the doctor said. 'And only then, might I suggest, on a more docile animal. Judging by the old bruise on her upper arm, this is not the first time she has come off.'

James looked at him directly.

'I had no idea, to be honest. My wife goes out riding several times a week. She has a new mare, not of the best temperament I'll agree, but I didn't know she had come off the horse previously. She didn't tell me,' he said, a hint of defensiveness creeping into his voice, as if he was being accused of being responsible for his wife's riding accident.

'Well, I suggest you don't let her ride for a while and certainly don't let her ride that horse again. I'm sure you can find her a more reliable mount,' the doctor said.

With that, he was gone, responding to an urgent summons to treat another patient.

James began to thank William profusely for what he had done but to William it seemed almost inappropriate to be thanked for saving his own sister.

'She certainly won't be riding that horse again,' James said, lowering his voice so that only William would hear.

'No, she won't indeed,' William said, although he did not think it was quite the time to tell James he had ordered the horse to be destroyed. Time enough for that revelation when they both left the hospital.

It was Catherine who received the news of Julia's recovery from William, who was now starting to worry that his own wife should have already arrived at the hospital, although he did not say as much to his sister-in-law.

Elizabeth Belleville, alerted by the ringing telephone, walked slowly down the stairs, all the while listening intently to Catherine's side of the conversation.

Catherine replaced the receiver and turned towards her mother-in-law, grateful that it was good news, not bad, she was delivering.

'That was William on the telephone. It seems that Julia is going to be fine,' she said.

'The doctor is going to keep her in hospital for a few days, under observation, and after that he wants her to have a quiet few days at home. No more riding for a while and no more riding Jezebel, apparently.'

There was no mistaking the relief they both felt at the news.

'Thank goodness for that,' Elizabeth Belleville said. 'I was preparing myself for the worst news. I do wish she would give up riding.'

Pre-empting Elizabeth Belleville next request, Catherine was quick to relay the doctor's orders.

'According to William, the doctor doesn't want a lot of visitors coming in to see her just yet. He wants her to have complete rest.'

'Of course he doesn't want a lot of noisy visitors crowding around her,' Elizabeth Belleville said.

'But I can assure you, that restriction does not apply to her own mother. In the absence of my sons and Alice, I'd be pleased if you would take me in to see her. I shall not be satisfied until I see my daughter with my own eyes.'

She paused then.

'I wonder if we should go first to her house and get the housekeeper to pack a bag for her?'

'There's no need for that,' Catherine said. 'Just as William was ringing off, Alice arrived with a bag for her, so everything has been taken care of.'

Elizabeth Belleville nodded but said nothing more. It was clear the relief she felt at the news of her daughter's recovery.

So for the time being Catherine could do nothing to allay the small seed of suspicion that now surrounded Richard's absence from Prior Park. She realised that, had a well-meaning friend not alerted her to the possibility of his interest being engaged elsewhere, the news that Jane Warner was also absent from her home would have been of absolutely no consequence at all.

Chapter 8: June 1957

In the past few years, Philippe Duval had convinced himself he had hardly thought at all about the daughter he had left behind in Australia. Time had dimmed the memory of his visit to the orphanage in Goulburn but not the memory of the small golden-haired girl he had glimpsed for a brief moment on the railway station platform as his train pulled away.

A part of him had always hoped that little girl was his daughter, for she looked happy and secure alongside her mother. It was little enough to cling on to, little enough to sustain a memory of love, a memory of loss and a memory of what might have been.

It was not only the loss of a child but the loss of the woman he had loved that every now and again came unbidden into his mind. Thinking about her with another family, with another man, in another life had been at times too much for him, but he had endured it. He had eventually moved on with his life, at least that is what he had tried to convince himself he had done. Julia Belleville had been his secret, never shared, never mentioned, never discussed. It had been a part of his life that he alone would ever know. He had vowed never to share it with anyone.

Everyday life had been easy enough for him to live, superficially happy with his busy hospital routine and his determination to be the best in his field of neurological surgery. He accepted the plaudits of his peers with modesty tinged with satisfaction. Among it all, he was thankful there had been little time for personal reflection, little time to dwell on what might have been, and even less time to consider the real reasons for the failure of his short, ill-advised marriage.

Now he was alone again, returning once again to live in his small Manhattan apartment, freed of the obligations of a marriage he had quickly discovered he hadn't wanted. Happy to be free.

It was late afternoon, and he was tired but satisfied from a day of surgery. The light was fading fast so he could not see clearly. His mail, an odd assortment of large and small envelopes, lay on the coffee table unopened. He had not bothered to open his mail in days. Mostly the smaller envelopes would contain bills. Among them, he knew there would be the final letter from his lawyer regarding his divorce from Jennifer, which was now just a formality. A marriage reduced to the exchange of letters and the unsavory business of money. He did not find any pleasure in the process, only sadness, for he felt that he alone was to blame for the failure. In his heart he had known he lacked the commitment to make the marriage work yet he had gone ahead anyway, out of a sense of duty underpinned by a sense of expectation.

Looking back, he had always known it would fail for he was the one who had held himself apart, who had not committed to the union with his entire being. Yet he had denied it when she challenged him, even though he knew it to be true and even as he spoke the words of denial, the words rang false in his ears. It was a simple fact: Jennifer was not Julia, but he could not say that. He could not tell her of the beautiful young Australian girl whom he had loved and lost. He could not say out loud that no one would take her place in his heart, even though he expected never to see her again.

As he flipped through the envelopes idly tossing each one aside, he paused as he noticed one envelope addressed in childish handwriting. He reached over to turn on the lamp so he could read more clearly and it was then he noticed the international postmark. Did it say 'Sydney, Australia'? He could not make it out because the postmark was blurred, the smudged ink illegible.

His hands began to tremble, almost before his mind had begun to consider the possibilities of what the letter might contain.

He eased open the flap of the envelope, careful not to destroy the return address on the back. The address was meaningless to him.

Was there a suburb of Strathfield in Sydney? He did not know. But the state was New South Wales, that much was clear.

With great care, he smoothed out the crumpled pages. In the glow from the lamp he could see the words he had never expected to see.

Dear Father. The words seemed to jump off the page at him. He could hardly get beyond them. He read and reread them, as if frightened to continue.

He stood up too restless now to sit quietly and read the letter. For the briefest of moments, he thought it was a hoax but he read on, struggling at first to make sense of the thirteen-year-old's incoherent thoughts.

Dear Father, she had written, I am writing to you because I do not know what else to do. My mother is dead but now I find out that she was not my mother after all and that I was adopted. My cousin Andrew – well, is he really my cousin now because he does not write to me – gave me a letter the day I left home. He said my father had addressed to it me, but then he is not my father really as it turns out.

Now that both my mother and father, or the people I thought were my parents, are both dead, I cannot continue to live in my home. In fact it isn't my home anymore, because it now belongs to Andrew. I thought I would live there forever.

I loved my mother dearly. But now I am living with her aunt, which is all right, but I am living in the city and I don't know what is to become of me. What will happen when my aunt dies, for she is quite elderly. She must be sixty at least.

Your letter to my father says I was to have your letter to me when I turned 18 but with father dead too, no one bothered to check. Andrew just gave me the letter. It says that you are my father and that you were in love with my mother, but I don't know who she is except that her name is Julia. You said the war separated you and they made her give me up because she wasn't married. Why didn't you come back and marry her? Then everything would have been all right. But now I don't know what to do.

Nobody tells me anything. I am going to school and trying to behave but I don't care for the girls and they think I am a country bumpkin.

Which is not true, but because I don't have a mother or father, they think it is all very odd. How I envy the girls when their mothers and fathers come to the school. Aunt Edith does her best but it's not like having a mother.

So, I decided to write to you, because you left the letter for me so you must feel something for me.

I hope you get this letter. I hope you reply to me. I cry for my mother Anne every day but it comforts me in a strange way to know that my real mother is probably still alive and that you are still alive. At least I hope so.

Can you help me? For I have no one else to turn to.

Your daughter

Pippa Jensen

PS I have not told Aunt Edith about this letter nor about the letter you left for me. I managed to keep it away from her. She knows I think that I was adopted but she did not tell me so if she does I will have to act very surprised, but I don't suppose she will tell me just yet. I am only 13 by the way. Perhaps you do not know that.

PPS I have a gold locket chain that has always been with me. My mother Anne said it was special but she did not say why.

Philippe stopped pacing the floor. He stood for a long time by the window although there was nothing to see now but the lights of the city. In the few minutes it had taken him to read the letter, he knew immediately his entire life had changed forever.

It seemed such an inconsequential thing this letter – two sheets of paper torn from an exercise pad, the childish handwriting on the small envelope – it might easily have never reached him. It might have dropped from a mail bag at any point on its journey of thousands of miles or it might have been delivered to the wrong address or discarded by an unhappy postal clerk. But it had not and he silently thanked God for it.

He tried to imagine his daughter now, on the cusp of adulthood. Would she resemble Julia? Or would she resemble him? Those thoughts occupied his mind briefly. Uppermost in his mind was how he would respond. He could write to her but with her aunt not knowing, would she even pass the letter to Pippa? Perhaps Pippa had decided to tell her what she had done but somehow he doubted it. He had been totally unprepared to hear from his daughter. He had never expected it. Now that it had happened, he did not know what to do.

He did not know what expectations his letter of more than a decade ago had raised in the girl. Could he now take responsibility for her? Could he pretend he had never heard from her and ignore the letter? It was a fleeting thought dismissed almost as quickly as it had occurred, for he knew he could not ignore her. She had reached out to him for help. It was then his thoughts turned to Julia.

The desolation of knowing what might have been overwhelmed him. He could have borne the idea of his only child being brought up by others in a happy, contented family. What he could not bear was the sadness of knowing that family no longer existed and his daughter had been cast adrift. He could see then, very clearly, that her future depended on him and him alone.

He sat for a long time, trying to decide what he must do. He must help his daughter, that much was clear, but how?

For the second time in his life, he began mentally to prepare for the long trip to Australia in search of his daughter, only this time with more assurance that he could find her. But what then?

To that question, he could find no immediate answers except that he was prepared to do everything in his power to make amends to the child who had been abandoned. His and Julia's child. The child who should have borne his name, the child who should have enjoyed his protection from the moment she was born.

Back in Australia, Julia, who had been the focus of her family's concern, was now ready to leave hospital and return home four days after her riding accident.

As she left the hospital, she was supported by a not very concerned nine year old John, who had never seen his mother ill and did not suppose she was really ill now. He had been given strict instructions by his father James to help his mother to the car, but such an instruction exceeded the understanding of a healthy active boy who was never known to stand still for more than a minute, so he was already yards ahead of his mother as they approached the car.

It was James who held the door for her as she slid into the passenger's seat.

'Oh, I have such a headache,' she said, her hand feeling for the bandage that was still wrapped around her head.

'I'm not surprised, coming off the horse like that. You could have been killed,' he said, his words sounding harsher than he intended.

'I was just unlucky, James,' she retorted. 'I've never had any problems before.'

He gave a derisory chuckle.

'That's not what the doctor said when he examined you,' James said.

'Oh, what did he say?' she asked, as if she did not already know the answer.

'He said it was clear you had come off the horse previously, judging from old bruises on your upper arm.'

He wasn't going to back down this time and let her have her own way.

'So I can't hide it then?' she said, with half a smile. 'I'm not the horsewoman I always thought I was.'

'No, apparently not, and that mare was just a bit too temperamental. We'll find you a quiet old nag too old to get above a canter and too experienced to get over-excited by a mob of kangaroos. That should keep you out of mischief in the future,' he said.

He smiled. He was relieved more than he could say that she had survived the experience with nothing more than a headache.

'You put your family through quite a trauma though, I have to say. I don't think your mother was amused.'

Julia pulled a face.

'It is difficult to amuse my mother,' she said, 'as you well know.'

James let the clutch out carefully as he eased the car away from the front of the hospital. He was normally an impatient aggressive driver but on this occasion he was considerate of his wife, not wanting to cause unnecessary bumps.

'Don't be surprised if your mother comes over to visit tomorrow.

She will be keen to tell you exactly what you should do about riding in the future, and I imagine it will be not to ride at all,' James said.

It was John who took up the conversation from the back seat where he had been listening half-heartedly to his parents.

'I don't know if Grandma will be over tomorrow. When I saw Marianne this afternoon after school, she said the house was in uproar,' he said, without any understanding of the import of his words.

'Apparently there was a noisy argument between Uncle Richard and Aunt Catherine when he returned home and she is threatening to leave. I imagine Grandma will have something to say about that.'

Julia turned in her seat, as far as she could, so she could see her son properly. She had almost forgotten the reason for her unplanned visit to Prior Park on the morning of her riding accident, but John's recounting of Marianne's gossip was something totally new and unexpected and clearly not related to what had happened on the night of her mother's birthday party.

She did not notice the ghost of a smile cross her husband's face.

'What are you talking about, John? You and Marianne shouldn't gossip like that about other people.'

Faced with this accusation, John retorted loudly.

'They aren't other people. They're family. Marianne knows everything that goes on. She's quiet like her mother so people don't notice her but she hears everything.'

Julia couldn't help smiling at this spirited defence of his cousin, who at fifteen months older was a natural ally for the younger boy, especially with Richard's older son Paul away at school.

Julia was tempted to press him for more information but she did not. If there was trouble in her elder brother's marriage, which she had suspected for some time, it was best to hear it from a more reliable source than the wild imaginings of a nine year old who would struggle to understand the implications of what he had been told.

Silence settled among the three of them as they headed home. Of the three of them, it was James who could have provided more information but he chose not to say anything at all, knowing that what he already knew was much more than Julia could have imagined, but only because he had made it his business to find out for sure something he had already suspected.

Elizabeth Belleville's sitting room was too small a space for Richard Belleville to pace successfully although he did try. He was not enjoying the largely one sided conversation he was being forced to endure with his mother, who did not see any reason why she should not interfere in her son's life.

'So, this is a fine mess, I must say,' she said, hardly expecting his agreement but feeling compelled to say it all the same.

'Your wife has accused you of being unfaithful to her but you say nothing in your own defence. Tell me that this is all just a figment of her imagination. Who is it that Catherine's accusing you of seeing? Some barmaid I suppose or someone you've met on your business travels.'

The fact that it had not occurred to Elizabeth Belleville to look to the past for an answer to her question was a brief moment of relief for Richard, who had responded to his wife's unexpectedly explicit accusations with a shrug of the shoulders and a very evasive answer that had only fuelled the argument he did not want to have with her.

He had known for some time that she was unhappy, yet he had chosen to ignore the issue and go his own way, not with a deliberate desire to hurt her but in the unspoken belief that their marriage was probably doomed anyway and it was only a matter of time. He did not want to admit that he did not know what to do or how to reclaim the passion he had once felt for her.

Above all, he wanted to keep Jane Warner's name out of the discussions. Finally, he turned to face his mother, who sat waiting patiently for his response.

'Mother, I think this is something Catherine and I will have to sort out. I'm not going to answer your questions. In fact it is none of your business.'

He added the last words as an afterthought, almost as a direct challenge to her need to control everything that happened in the household.

It was the first time Elizabeth Belleville could remember that one of her children had refused to answer her questions. She was stony faced, struggling to hide her rising anger.

'You think this is none of my business? How can you say that,' she said, her voice louder and more forceful than she intended.

'Of course it's my business. It affects my grandchildren,' she said, citing them as her primary reason for interfering.

'Someone has to stand up for them and get their parents to see commonsense,' she said too loudly for comfort, as if it should have all been quite apparent to him that she was much more than an interested bystander.

'Do you think Catherine and I aren't very well aware of our responsibilities to our children?' Richard said, his tone remarkably even given the circumstances.

'Well, it doesn't seem like it to me,' Elizabeth Belleville retorted.

'Mother, let's leave it, shall we, before we say anything we will both regret. I came to see you only as a courtesy. Catherine and I will let you know what we decide to do.'

With that, Richard brought the tense discussion to a close. Elizabeth Belleville, far from happy with the direction of the conversation, sat in her armchair for some time afterwards. She simply did not understand what was wrong.

Here her imagination failed her utterly. She did not see that Catherine wanted more in her life than Prior Park and Richard could offer and Richard, knowing that, had turned elsewhere for reassurance.

To Elizabeth Belleville, a marriage, successful or otherwise, was to be endured. She had long suspected her own husband of dalliances but had never confronted him. Why couldn't Catherine do the same, she pondered? Richard was good looking and charming, like his father. Perhaps it was the curse of the father visited on the son, a roving eye capable of charming any woman he desired. She tried and failed to imagine her other son William in the same predicament.

Having drawn a too obvious conclusion, she silently resolved to advise Catherine to turn a blind eye to her husband's activities. That was the only sensible course of action and that's how Catherine should approach it, Elizabeth Belleville decided.

She became quiet in her mind, satisfied that she had alighted upon a sensible solution that would restore order to the household. It had not occurred to her that Catherine would ignore her advice.

Despite young John's assertion that his grandmother would be too overtaken by events at Prior Park to visit her daughter, it was mid-afternoon on the day of Julia's return home that she noticed the car driven by Alice pull into the Mayfield Downs driveway.

Julia was lying on the verandah on a daybed that had been hastily arranged with pillows to make her more comfortable. Her head still ached so she welcomed the inactivity for once.

She did not notice her mother until Alice brought the car to a stop very close to the front steps, as a courtesy to the older woman.

For the first time, Julia observed how her mother had aged. There was a hint of a stoop in her normally upright bearing. Some strands of grey hair had escaped from her usually very neat hairdo.

Julia greeted both visitors with a cheery 'hello', determined to convince them that she was none the worse for her horse riding misadventure, as she liked to call it. She knew she simply must endure the lecture that was coming from her mother.

'Well, you gave us all a terrible fright, my girl,' Elizabeth Belleville said to her daughter, as if she was a thirteen year old again.

Alice was more understanding, although she had endured the shock of seeing Julia's apparently lifeless body in William's arms.

'I'm so relieved that you're back home again and not badly hurt,' she said. 'It was just terrible seeing you like that.'

Alice reached out and squeezed Julia's hand in a spontaneous gesture of relief and pleasure at seeing her sister-in-law looking so much better. She had been about to give a graphic account of just how badly Julia had appeared immediately after being found on the road, but drew back at the last moment, realising that Elizabeth Belleville hadn't actually seen her daughter at the very moment when they had all feared she was dead.

Julia in turn was grateful that Alice avoided the indiscretion of being too frank in front of her mother. She had already endured quite enough comments on the topic of her riding accident. She was in no mood to listen to more.

At that moment, as if by some unseen command, Mrs Fry, who had seen the visiting car approach well before Julia had noticed it, appeared with the tea tray which was a welcome diversion for the patient, who did not want to talk about her accident at all.

What she did want to talk about was the gossip she had heard via her young son but she did not know how to approach it. As it turned out, it was her mother who, suspecting that gossip might have travelled to Mayfield Downs, decided to broach the subject.

'I hope young John hasn't been telling stories about his Uncle Richard and Aunt Catherine,' Elizabeth Belleville began.

'I know he and young Marianne are very close and it's possible that Marianne might have overheard a private conversation between them,' she said.

It had been an inspired guess on Elizabeth Belleville's part that the two children might have been the primary channel for gossip between the two houses. She had not considered that there were other less direct ways for gossip to pass. Alice though was quick to jump to the defence of her daughter.

'Marianne wouldn't go spreading gossip and telling tales,' she said, except that by defending her daughter she had confirmed without realising it that there was gossip to spread.

Julia smiled, knowing that her young son's account of the uproar at Prior Park was probably very close to being accurate. She decided there and then that a direct question was the best way to get to the bottom of the matter.

'So what was this argument about between Richard and Catherine, because that's what I heard it was?' Julia asked, looking from one to the other, but without directly implicating the two children.

Alice shifted uncomfortably in her chair. She would have been happy to discuss what she knew with Julia, but not in front of her formidable mother-in-law. Alice and William had discussed it all in the privacy of their own room, for it was a matter of grave concern to William.

It was left to Elizabeth Belleville to answer her daughter's question. Her answer was dismissive, as if the whole episode had been exaggerated.

'I understand there has been some uneasiness between Catherine and Richard. She hasn't settled since she returned from England a month or so ago. I think she probably feels she's missing out on things with her own family,' she said.

'I think Richard has been a bit unsettled because of it too. He prefers life at Prior Park and likes the business trips that take him away but maybe he doesn't want the same sort of life that Catherine enjoys. They will have to work it out. That's what I've told them. That is what I expect them to do.'

Julia thought her mother's view of events was probably only part of the story but she asked the obvious question nevertheless.

'And are they going to work it out because I heard there was talk of her leaving?'

'Well, I won't hear talk of that,' Elizabeth Belleville said, as if the decision was hers and hers alone and it was a decision she could ultimately influence.

Julia smiled. She noticed a quiet smile play across Alice's face too and the pair exchanged a knowing glance.

There was much more to this story, Julia decided, much much more but it would have to wait for another day.

CHAPTER 9: JUNE 1957

It was just a few days later that James Fitzroy met William Belleville quite by chance. James was quick to take advantage of the unexpected opportunity.

He had walked only a few yards from the garage where his car was being serviced when he saw William heading in his direction.

He raised a hand in greeting to attract William's attention. As they came together, the two men shook hands warmly. James could see at once that William was preoccupied but William's first words were entirely predictable.

'How's my sister getting on?' William asked, already aware that she was well on the way to recovery but that a polite enquiry would be expected of him.

'She's much better, thanks, William,' James said. 'She is really up and about now, thank goodness. She's recovered much quicker than I or anyone else expected.'

'I'm very relieved to hear it,' William replied. 'When Charles brought her back to the house, I immediately thought the worst.'

James nodded, fully understanding just how traumatic the whole scene had been for those who had witnessed it.

'By the way, I know the horse is at Prior Park,' James said, 'what have you done with it?'

William looked slightly bemused for a moment, having entirely forgotten about the horse.

'Well, yes, I'd forgotten about that,' he admitted. 'I was going to dispose of it, if you get my meaning. That was my immediate plan when I found out what had happened to Julia but when Tom Warner brought it back, Catherine seemed to take a fancy to it. She seemed to be able to calm it down, so it's just in our stables at the moment.

'We're taking good care of it,' he added, although he expected James to be quite uninterested in the welfare of a horse that had caused so much trouble.

James gave a half laugh.

'It can stay there, as far as I'm concerned,' James said. 'We don't want it back. I didn't want her to buy it in the first place.'

William nodded and shrugged his shoulders.

'I know just how stubborn Julia can be,' he conceded. 'We'll see what happens. Perhaps it will be a stock horse. I think Catherine has other things on her mind just now.'

The fate of the horse was of very little consequence to either man, now that Julia was well on the road to recovery and she had accepted she couldn't ride it again.

'By the way, your mother and Alice came to see Julia a couple of days ago,' James said. 'I understand there was talk of an argument between Richard and Catherine but Julia said your mother didn't think it was of any great importance. Is there anything in it?'

William feigned surprise at the question.

'Anything in what?' he asked.

There was no subtlety in James's very direct answer.

'Well, I heard that Catherine was threatening to leave and accusing him of seeing someone else,' James said bluntly

Standing in a public street gossiping about his brother was not something that sat easily with William and he rounded on James, as if James had been the source of the problem and not merely a curious bystander to it all.

'I don't really think I want to discuss my brother's marital affairs here in the street,' he said, in a quiet but determined voice. He almost hissed out the words.

James had expected William to be straight with him so he was momentarily taken aback by William's reaction.

'Hey there, don't forget your family is my family too,' he said bluntly. 'I am not an outsider trying to find out the gossip.'

'Fair enough,' William said. 'I didn't mean to imply anything. I just don't like talking about my brother behind his back, so to speak.'

James moved then, hoping that William would follow his lead.

'Let's walk down to the Criterion and have a drink together somewhere quiet so you can tell me what's going on.'

William was half inclined to reject the invitation but he did not want to have an argument with James that would attract attention so he fell into step alongside James and they walked in silence towards the hotel.

It was only after their glasses were half empty that William relaxed and seemed prepared to give James at least an abridged version of events at Prior Park.

When he had finished, James sat silently assessing the information he had just been told, which was exactly what he had expected to hear, although he did not say as much to William.

'So you are telling me that Catherine accused Richard of seeing another woman and she's threatened to leave and go back to England?' James said.

William nodded bleakly, for he was unhappy at the prospect of his brother's marriage not being the success his own marriage was.

'That's the story in a nutshell,' he said, nodding his head.

'Do you think there is any truth in the accusation?' James asked, testing now to find out how much William really did know.

'I don't know to be honest,' William said. 'When he stayed on in Brisbane recently after I came back home, I thought it was for genuine reasons, because we will soon have some cash on hand to make new investments. Perhaps it was for something else entirely but I don't know, to be honest.'

James pondered his response for a few moments. He knew he was not being entirely honest with William but he persisted with his questioning.

'So, how would Catherine know anything about it, if Richard was seeing someone else while he was away from home?'

To anyone but William, the extent of James's questions might have seemed unnecessary but the thought did not occur to William.

'I don't know,' he said. 'I think a friend might have phoned her to say that she had seen Richard with someone else or had heard something. That's all I can think of. Alice said she did get a call recently that she didn't speak about and was very cagey about.'

The discussion was beginning to make William feel more and more uncomfortable. He wished that James would stop asking questions. He began to feel that little by little he was betraying his brother's trust.

And James, sensing that William had at last confided all he knew, remained silent on the topic of the identity of the other woman. He did not see any reason at all to share her name with William but he was certain of it, all the same. William it seemed was blissfully unaware of the gossip that swirled around the town regarding the goings on at Prior Park.

It was James who then turned the conversation to the other matter that had ultimately been the cause of Julia's horse-riding accident.

He finished his glass of beer and motioned to the barmaid for another. He looked back towards William, who had declined the offer of another drink.

'Do you know why Julia was going over to Prior Park so early on the morning she came off her horse?' James asked.

William eyed him cautiously as if he was suddenly wary of anything he might be asked.

'No, I had no idea she was even headed our way,' he said. 'I thought she was just out for an early morning ride, although now that you mention it, it was very early for her to be out. It was a very frosty chilly morning. It would have been much better for her to ride later once the frost had gone.'

It seemed that such was the level of concern over her accident, no one at Prior Park had stopped to ask the obvious question: why was Julia out riding so early on a slippery frosty morning?

'She was coming over to tackle you and Richard about the young visitor you unceremoniously ejected from your mother's birthday party,' James said, noting with a half smile the look of horror that appeared briefly on William's face.

'I don't know what you're talking about,' William said, trying desperately to sound convincing in his flat rejection of James's assertion.

James leaned forward in his chair.

'Of course you know what I'm talking about, William,' he said pointedly, noticing how William avoided his gaze.

'I was there, remember, at the party and I saw Charles Brockman manhandle someone out the front door and stay there on the driveway until that uninvited person had driven away.'

William said nothing because he could think of nothing to say, his silence adding weight to James's recollection of events.

'I later heard from someone else - shall I call that person a reliable source – that a young man was getting very heated in the dining room of this very hotel, claiming that he was your half brother,' James said.

This latest revelation shocked William for he clearly had no idea there had been any discussion of the matter away from Prior Park.

'This young man claimed that you and Richard had thrown him out of Prior Park and told him never to return, or words to that effect,' he said. 'He claimed that you were denying him his birthright, whatever that means.'

James paused to see how this latest disclosure was being received. William had turned pale. He was sweating although the weather was mild. He could not easily conceal the disgust he felt at what James was telling him. Finally, he nodded as if resigned to the need to take James into his confidence.

'I didn't know about that,' William said finally. 'I had no idea that he was mouthing off like that. No idea at all.'

He took a deep deliberate breath and spoke, it seemed, with some difficulty.

'You're right, James,' he said. 'That's who he says he is, but Richard and I are determined not to recognise him or to have our mother find out. It would be just too awful to contemplate my mother hearing news like that.'

William suddenly looked up at James, the truth dawning on him that James had, in fact, kept their secret from his own wife.

'Did you tell Julia? I take it she was coming over to us to ask about it?' William said.

James relaxed in his chair, confident now that William was being frank with him.

'Yes, I did tell Julia what little I knew, because she badgered me to,' he said. 'But I really only had gossip to go on. I thought this news was better coming from one of her brothers but I did caution her not to say anything in front of your mother, hence her early morning visit, hoping to avoid her mother.'

James took a long swig on his beer.

'Knowing what it's about, I understand why you would want to keep it quiet, but you should tell Julia the full story,' he said. 'She deserves to be told.'

William nodded.

'Well, you handled it as well you could in the circumstances I guess,' William said. 'And you're right. She does need to be told. We are trying to buy his silence. Our solicitors are working on it, but they haven't been able to do a deal with him yet.'

'Well, I hope they manage to buy him off for all our sakes,' James said. 'I don't think we want your father's bastard making a public spectacle of himself and embarrassing everyone.'

William winced at his choice of words which seemed unnecessarily vulgar.

'Well, as it happens, I agree with you,' William said. 'It's not very pleasant and we certainly don't want my mother finding out. It would be a terrible shock to her.'

'I take it there's no chance he's a fraud?' James asked. The thought had only just occurred to him.

William shook his head.

'No, I've met the mother,' William said, which was something James had not expected to hear. He was silent as William continued on, clearly remembering an encounter from years back.

'In fact, it wasn't long after my father died,' he said. 'Richard was overseas still. It seems the woman had been my father's mistress for quite some time and none of us knew about it. He bought her a house in Brisbane. That's why he went down there so often. We had no idea at all.'

He could not bring himself to look at James. He felt the shame of the sordid story, as if he had somehow been responsible for the deception.

Now it was James who was deeply shocked at this latest revelation. He had been totally unaware of the depth of the deception that Francis Belleville had perpetrated on his family.

'You must feel pretty bad about it but it was your father's fault, not yours,' he said. 'You mustn't feel the shame of it because the blame, and the shame, belongs elsewhere, entirely with your father.'

'I know that,' William said. 'If only I could be sure this young fellow would settle for some money and leave us alone, all would be well, but I'm not sure of that at all, and that's what worries me.'

William stood up abruptly. He glanced at his wristwatch.

'I must go and collect my car and get Alice from the hairdresser's. She'll be ready for me now, I think.'

James laid a friendly hand on his arm.

'Thanks for telling me the whole story,' he said. 'I understand it's a painful topic but I still think either you or Richard should discuss it frankly with Julia. And you can be sure I won't be gossiping about it.'

'And if you think I can help, let me know. It concerns my family too, you know,' James said finally.

William nodded his thanks, knowing that it would probably fall to him to tell his sister about the whole sordid business.

William felt it was almost too much for him to deal with. He decided he would at least share the story of Alistair McGovern with Alice. She would be shocked but he knew instinctively she would support him and their actions.

It was only afterwards as he was walking back towards to the garage that it occurred to him that Julia herself was the guardian of a similar deeply-held secret that would have dire consequences if it was ever revealed.

It was, in fact, the secret he still carried regarding his sister that was the greatest burden, for it was knowledge he would never be able to share with anyone, even Alice.

As he walked back along the street, he prayed there would never

102

again be a time when the issue of Julia's discarded child was discussed at Prior Park, as the issue of his father's illegitimate son was being discussed now.

It was the sins of his father returning to haunt them long after his father's death which made him feel unsettled, as if the past could never be guaranteed to remain just that: the past.

For a few moments, James watched William as he headed up the street away from the hotel. He was about to head in the opposite direction, along the roadway that ran along the riverbank towards his mother's house, when he was stopped by a light touch on his arm.

Violet Cunningham had not been serving in the lounge but she had recognised the two men who were deep in conversation. She did not want to miss the opportunity of finding out anything more to add to the delicious gossip she already possessed about the high and mighty Belleville family.

'Ah, Violet,' James said, 'I didn't see you when we came in.'

'How are you, Mr Fitzroy?' she said, in a tone she reserved for familiar well-heeled customers. She did not wait for his response.

'I couldn't help noticing you were having a very serious conversation with Mr Belleville? Nothing amiss, I hope,' she said, almost overstepping the bounds of propriety in her eagerness to know what had been discussed between the two men.

James smiled, knowing full well what Violet would be very keen to find out but unwilling now to add to her store of gossip, despite her having been the one to share the gossip about Alistair McGovern with him.

'No, I was just catching up with my brother-in-law,' he said.

But Violet was not to be so easily dissuaded from her original mission.

'Of course, I know how you are related,' she retorted. Violet's accurate knowledge of the inter-relationships of all the important families of the town and district would have satisfied even the most meticulous genealogist.

'So no more news of the young man I told you about?' she asked straight out, without preamble.

'No, no more news,' he said, 'and I hope you haven't been spreading gossip as we don't want his wild claims generally known.'

James hoped his words would act as a check on Violet's natural tendency to gossip with a handful of favoured hotel patrons and her intimate circle of female friends.

'No, I haven't said a word,' she said, lying convincingly. 'And before you ask, I haven't seen that young man back here again. He gave me the creeps, if you want to know the truth.'

A thought suddenly occurred to James. There was no one better placed than Violet to alert him if the young man did suddenly reappear, for he was likely to choose the same hotel again.

'If you should see him again, I'd like you to let me know,' James said, writing his telephone number on the back of a cardboard beer mat.

Violet looked at the number and fingered the five pound note that was carefully hidden underneath it.

'OK, it's a deal,' she said, mimicking the dialogue she had heard in the local picture theatre.

'And maybe for that,' she said, nodding towards the crisp note, 'you want me to tell you about other people you might know?'

It was a question that hung in the air between them for a few moments.

'What other people, Violet?' he asked, for his only interest had been in the young man claiming to be his wife's half brother.

'Well, I was thinking of Mr Richard Belleville.'

'What about Richard Belleville? Have you been making up gossip about him?'

This accusation was too much for Violet who was indignant at the mere suggestion she would make up stories.

'I don't make up stories, Mr Fitzroy,' she said, her tone defensive and her voice slightly raised. 'It's what I see with my own eyes and hear with my own ears. That's what I know. Not second hand tittle tattle.'

He smiled at her mock outrage, knowing the money and the prospect of more was likely to calm her down very quickly.

'So, Violet, what else do you have to tell me?' he asked, more quietly now, encouraging her to share a new confidence.

Before she could answer, she heard the hotel manager calling her name so she turned and hurried off, back towards the reception desk, where guests were waiting to check in.

'I'll tell you another time,' she called back over her shoulder, as she hurried away.

She almost said, 'And I'll tell you about your own wife and the American too' but she stopped the words as they formed. No point in making trouble in someone's marriage just because she could, she thought. Better to leave that one be.

She slipped the beer coaster and money into the pocket of her skirt.

Money like that was nothing to him, she thought, nothing at all, but she would keep her word and look out for the young man who was intent on causing the Belleville family trouble. It was the least she could do, she reasoned, for she had seen a look in Alistair McGovern's eyes that she did not much care for. There was something about him that spelt trouble and she felt certain that he would be true to his word and exact revenge on the Belleville family at some point in the future.

But just how much she would tell him about Richard Belleville she had yet to make up her mind. In fact to her mind, Richard Belleville was a very charming gentleman who had been badly served by his stuck up English wife, in her opinion.

It was a theory she expounded on at length to any of her friends who would listen. If he was now becoming the subject of local gossip about his romantic links outside his marriage, maybe it was what his wife deserved for spending so much of her time in England. That was the generally accepted view, she decided, because that was her view.

If she, Violet, had managed to lure a man like that into marriage, she was damn sure she wouldn't go roaming off around the world leaving him exposed to the wiles of other women.

With a prize like that, she reasoned, you stayed close and kept him happy and at home. To Violet, any woman who had managed to claim such a marriage prize should take better care of it and she said so often, even as she repeated the gossip she had heard to a widening circle of willing listeners.

Chapter 10: July 1957

Since her return from Brisbane, Jane Warner had been a woman consumed by inner turmoil, a state of mind which did not in any way reveal itself outwardly. Her husband, Tom asked dutifully, but with genuine concern, if her time in Brisbane and her specialist doctor's appointment had been satisfactory.

She had replied that they had been satisfactory and he asked nothing more, for he did not imagine, for one moment, there was anything more to know.

He approved absent-mindedly of the two new dresses she had bought and admired the four new books that sat in the bookshelf. He was not a reader himself but if they made her happy, he was happy to indulge her interests.

Young Tom showed even less interest in his mother's well-being although he was pleased to see her return home, even if it meant he would be obliged to put in an appearance at school. School failed to hold his attention now. He preferred to be with his father, doing the work of a man, and from the age of eleven he had begun to badger his mother to let him leave school, for he said there was nothing more they could teach him. He would learn everything else he needed to know from his father, he said repeatedly. But to Jane's surprise, his father was firm in supporting her that he must complete his schooling before he could work on their property full time.

She suspected that Tom senior did this as much in deference to her opinion as to any real belief he held that extra years at school would benefit young Tom in any material way.

It was Friday afternoon and as usual for any school day, young Tom's school bag was thrown into the kitchen from the back door. He followed the battered school bag seconds later, not bothering even to move the bag out of the way. If it got in his way, he would shove it along with his foot. It was left to his mother to put it carefully against the wall so that no one would fall over it.

Normally, he was straight out the back door in search of his father but on this particular day he stopped, slightly breathless, his eyes bright. It was clear he was bursting to tell her something important.

'Mum, guess what?' he said, giving absolutely no hint of the news he was about to deliver.

'Tom, guess what? What am I to guess about?' she asked, playing along with him, although with a hint of exasperation in her voice.

He ignored her question entirely for he had not really expected her to be able to guess what he was going to tell her.

'I've heard that Mrs Belleville is going back to England for good,' he said, with the satisfaction of someone who knows he has delivered news of great importance.

So surprised was Jane at this sudden and unexpected announcement by her son, who never conveyed any news of anything, that she was rendered speechless for a few moments. He was frustrated then that she had not responded as he had expected.

'You know, the English one with the accent,' he said, as if his mother was being slow to comprehend this big news.

'A big bust up apparently,' he said, adding his own embellishments to the story he had heard on the school bus.

Having recovered her senses, Jane could not resist probing for more information. She had to be sure.

'You mean Mrs Richard Belleville?' she asked, trying desperately to keep her voice even.

'That's her,' he said. 'That's the one. They reckon she's leaving to-morrow.'

Suddenly weak and unsteady, Jane sat down at the kitchen table to hide her confusion. Young Tom did not notice his mother's reaction. Instead he spotted his father beyond the cattle yards and was out the door and out of sight before she could even begin to think of the implications of what she had heard.

Was it true, she wondered? If it was true, what did it mean for her and Richard?

During their few days together, they had not spoken of the future beyond vague promises.

Since his return from the war, they had for years purposefully kept their distance from one another, except on the odd occasion when circumstance had brought them together. On one occasion, they had exchanged angry words and she had remembered that accidental encounter for a long time afterwards. In their brief meeting, she had seen only resentment and hostility. She had presumed that all his tender feelings for her had evaporated.

Yet it proved not to be so. She did not know how but almost without knowing it, they had drifted back into a warm friendship, rekindling their earlier infatuation that had lain dormant for years.

When the opportunity arose to meet him in Brisbane, she had, at first, refused but he had persuaded her and she had gone to meet him.

It was the fact that Richard had not attempted to see her since their return from Brisbane that raised all the old doubts again, the doubts that had consumed her all those years ago. She had felt her confidence in him ebbing away again, as if their relationship was a tide that for a few brief moments reached a high point and then receded, leaving her stranded and alone.

This time she did not know what would happen. Was her future in her hands or his? She had felt confident of him when had they had parted in Brisbane. But that confidence had drained away as the days following her return turned into weeks with no word from him. Just silence.

Now she faced the news of his marriage breakup. Was it true? If it was true, what did it mean for her? Could she really break up the life she had with Tom and young Tom and walk away? She had asked herself that question many times. Only as it came to be a possibility did it become harder to find the answer. Even now, she was far from certain of the answer. She was far from certain in fact that Richard would propose it.

For a long time she sat at the kitchen table thinking through all that had happened. The one thing she was desperate to know but had no way of finding out was whether Richard had admitted to his wife that he had been seeing someone else. She hoped and prayed that he had not brought her name into the argument, for if he had, there would be no way of it remaining secret, and most of all, she wanted her involvement to remain secret. She did not want it to leak out and reach her husband via innuendo or gossip. If she was to break with him, she would be honest and forthright. It tortured her every waking moment that she had gone behind his back with another man. If he should hear it from someone else, she knew he would be devastated.

A wave of anxiety swept over her. If Richard revealed her name, then she knew she would be the one who would pay the highest price, of that she was sure. She clung desperately to the slim thread of hope that he would honour his commitment never to reveal her name to anyone. She hoped desperately he would keep his word.

William had been right. It fell to him to visit his sister to explain the tawdry story of just who Alistair McGovern was and why he was making such a nuisance of himself. It was mid morning and he found his sister sitting at the dining room table writing cheques, which surprised him a little. At Prior Park it was his job to write the cheques, although Alice helped him sort through the bills and keep them in order.

'I see you're helping James out with the paperwork,' he said, planting a perfunctory kiss on her cheek.

'Well, actually no, William, I'm doing what I always do and that is pay the monthly bills,' she said, surveying the neat pile of accounts for which she had already drawn cheques and the other neat pile, still waiting for cheques to be drawn.

He watched as she expertly scrawled her signature on a cheque, blotted the ink carefully and tore it carefully from the cheque book. He could see now that she had done this many times before.

'I didn't know you did it all,' he said, a grudging sense of admiration creeping into his voice. But he remembered of course that his mother had always kept a cheque book of her own but his father had organised with his accountant the payment of all the bills for Prior Park, a task that William had now taken on himself.

He sat down at the table opposite Julia. She looked up, wondering what had prompted his visit. She had not forgotten the purpose of her abortive early morning visit to Prior Park but the opportunity to talk privately with one of her brothers had not yet presented itself. She was still under orders not to ride and in any case she was yet to get a new horse. She could see that James was in no hurry at all to replace Jezebel. So there was no way for her to visit Prior Park that would not immediately attract the attention of her mother.

'I had a chat with James the other day,' William said, as if it was the most commonplace discussion of no real importance.

'He told me you were on your way to Prior Park to ask Richard or me about the unwelcome visitor that came to the house on the night of Mother's birthday party, when you came off your horse,' he said, looking at her for confirmation.

It was a straightforward statement but it surprised Julia all the same. William by nature was more likely to keep information to himself rather than offer it up.

'Yes, that's right,' she said. 'The night of Mother's party, I tried to get into the study because I knew something was going on but Charles Brockman wouldn't let me in. He told me you and Richard were just dealing with some urgent business that had come up and I should go and look after Mother.'

William smiled bleakly.

'Well, he was right in a way,' he said. 'Richard and I were trying to look after some business, well look after the family really.'

He took a deep breath. He wasn't sure why all the difficult matters fell to him to sort out.

'I believe James gave you some inkling of what was going on from gossip he'd heard in town?' he said, waiting for her to acknowledge that she already knew part of the story.

'Yes, he said a young man – I don't know his name – was claiming to be our half-brother,' she said, her voice barely above a whisper for fear of being overheard.

William nodded, his head sunk slightly towards his chest as if to hide a horrible truth.

'Unfortunately, it's true,' he said quietly. 'In fact I don't think you're going to like this story at all but the fact is, our father had another family. He had another son, who, as you say, is our half-brother.'

Shock registered on Julia's face. She had convinced herself that the story was a fabrication. Now her own brother was telling her it was true.

'What are you telling me, William,' she said, all effort to keep her voice low now gone.

'You are telling me that our father was unfaithful to our mother. You talk of another family. I don't understand. I don't understand at all.'

She was shaking her head slowly from side to side, as if her failure to believe what William was telling her would render it untrue.

But William pressed on regardless, knowing that he must not back away now from the whole truth.

'His name is Alistair McGovern. His mother is Muriel McGovern. I would judge him to be about ten years younger than you,' William said.

'The facts are this: our father had Muriel McGovern as his mistress for more than a decade and we did not know about it,' William said, sparing his sister none of the sordid details of their father's other life.

When he had finished telling her all there was to tell, she looked across the table at him. He noticed a maturity about her that he had not seen before as he watched her grapple with this shocking account of their father's tawdry double life.

'I hope Mother doesn't know?' she said finally.

William shook his head.

'No, she doesn't know and she doesn't need to know either,' he said, in case Julia was considering whether she should be told.

William could see the sadness in her eyes as she came to understand the full implications of what he had just told her. Like her brothers, she saw it as a betrayal of the family they had known, as if their father had perpetrated a fraud upon them all. Behind their backs he had supported and shown love and affection to another family and they had never known of it.

'You and James have discussed this since my accident?' she asked, curious now remembering their conversation that had prompted her to try to visit Prior Park very early in the morning.

'Yes, I ran into him the other day in town,' he said. 'James told me what he had heard and that he had told you what little he knew. He felt one of us should tell you the whole story,' William said, by way of explanation.

'Well, I certainly won't be discussing it with anyone,' she said. 'Just make sure you get settled with him, otherwise he'll keep hanging around.'

'That's exactly what we are trying to do,' William said, 'although he hasn't responded yet. I imagine he's hanging out for more money.'

'Whatever it takes, William,' she said, 'whatever it takes, just do it. I keep thinking of Mother and the shame she would feel if she knew.'

'Don't worry, she isn't going to find out from any of us,' he said. 'I think at least we can keep this secret safe from her.'

With that he picked up his hat and was gone, his car leaving a fine mist of dust in the driveway as he headed back to Prior Park.

It was only after William had left that Julia realised she had not raised the other important matter: was Richard's marriage really over?

Now that she had seen William alone there was no impediment to her visiting Prior Park, but she was in no hurry to immerse herself in Richard's marital problems. She liked Catherine but even she could see that her aristocratic English sister-in-law was no longer enthralled by life in rural Australia and the limitations of its provincial society.

Richard and Catherine, wrongly supposing the state of their marriage to be a matter for them and them alone, did not for a moment suspect they were the subject of much discussion in many quarters. While Richard thought his own family might discuss his situation quietly among themselves, it did not occur to him that the secret he vowed to keep buried might find its way out into the open by other means.

He had made no effort to contact Jane since his return. It was only now, as he looked back on the enormity of the betrayal, that he realised he must decide whether to break up the life he had known and in doing so, break up another family or what? Continue their clandestine affair knowing that eventually it would be discovered?

It was late afternoon and he walked quietly in the bedroom he continued to share with Catherine. He had refused her demand that he move out, not wanting to expose their lives to the gossip that would ensue. For the first time he craved the privacy of a home of his own. At Prior Park, the presence of other family members and of staff acted as an unwelcome restraint on their ability to deal with the problems that lay at the heart of their relationship.

He put a hand gently on her shoulder and she turned around. Her face was tear stained. It was clear she had been crying. She was first to speak.

'You know I have really done my best to fit in here, Richard,' she said, her voice trembling with emotion. 'And I have done my best to be a good wife to you and a mother to your sons, but I've failed.'

He hated to see her like this. He was about to speak but she continued, desperate that he should hear her out after their short bitter quarrels of recent times.

'I know I said I couldn't continue to live here indefinitely,' she said, 'but I didn't expect that you would just turn away from me. I had hoped we could work something out.'

She paused, briefly, to regain her composure. He waited for her to go on, conscious now that she needed to say out loud what they had both been avoiding.

'But I know you've been with someone else, even though you refused to give me a proper answer when I asked you again yesterday,' she said, her voice clearer and more determined. She was dry eyed now. Her mood had changed ever so slightly.

'So will you answer me now? Have you been unfaithful to me? Are you in love with someone else, because if you are, I cannot stand to be here with you.'

She did not look at him but she heard his quick intake of breath. Had she looked up at him, she would have seen the look of utter despair that came across his face.

He sank down on the edge of the bed, his head in his hands, knowing full well that the guilt was his and his alone but even so, he did not want to admit it openly. He could see it all clearly, now that it was too late.

He understood now that he had felt abandoned by her long absences and her admission that life at Prior Park was too limiting a prospect for her to continue. Knowing that, a creeping sense of rejection had been the justification in his own mind for his decision to seek out Jane Warner, who, unhappy in her own marriage, had responded once again to his charms, as he had expected she might.

But now he stood at the edge of a precipice, looking into an abyss of his own making and knowing that his reply would determine the course of his life. Could he lie outright and deny it? He could, he reasoned silently, but would she believe him? If he told her the truth, or at least a partial truth, would she forgive him? It seemed unlikely and the issue of her unhappiness at Prior Park remained.

Since her most return from England from her most recent trip, they had drifted aimlessly along, both avoiding a discussion of the topic that remained upper most in both their minds, neither one wanting to be the one to make the first move. Now that almost seemed secondary to the question she was repeating in a louder, more determined voice, as if she was trying to reach him, trying to stir him to respond.

'Well, what have you got to say? Have you been seeing someone else?'

She almost yelled the words at him as she struggled to control her frustration and anger, her refined well-bred composure buckling under the pressure of her emotions.

He looked up at her from where he still sat, his own eyes filled with tears, his hands shaking. The scar on the side of his cheek was more pronounced. Fine lines had begun to form around his eyes, the bloom of his youth beginning to fade just a little.

He ignored her accusation entirely, as if she hadn't said it. It hung in the air between them.

'Catherine,' he said, finally, in a measured almost contrite voice, 'what can I say but that I love you. You are everything to me and I don't want to lose you.'

Tears began to cascade down her cheeks once again. Her dark hair was beginning to unravel. She fumbled for a fresh linen handkerchief from the top drawer of her dressing table and pressed it to her eyes.

'That's not enough. You have to answer me,' she said, almost hysterical. 'I know you've been seeing another woman. I know who it is. I was told …..'

Her words trailed off. Now he appeared offended that she would listen to gossip and immediately believe the worst of him.

'So you've been gossiping about me behind my back?' he retorted, seeking to regain the upper hand in the argument.

'I didn't ask for the information,' she said. 'It was blurted out to me by a well-meaning friend. What I want to know is this, is it true?'

In that critical moment, when it seemed he would have no choice but to tell her, he found he could not admit the gossip she had heard had been right. Instead, he rose from the side of the bed and came up to her. He took her in his arms.

He held her closely and she did not resist.

'There is no other woman for me but you,' he said quietly.

With that, he began to kiss her, gently at first and then with a passion that had been absent between them for years.

'You must not listen to such gossip,' he murmured.

She felt the pressure of his body and his mounting passion. He began to unbutton her blouse but she pushed him away.

'I have to know, Richard,' she said. 'I have to know. You cannot act as if nothing has happened because I know it has.'

He could see she was angry in a way he had never seen before.

'It meant nothing,' he said, finally, in a half admission that told her nothing.

'I'm sorry, really, it meant nothing,' he repeated, as if to render her accusations trivial.

She gave a half laugh, mocking his words.

'I don't believe you,' she said, looking directly at him.

He saw the determined look in her eyes and he wondered then if she was using the situation to her own ends, as if in his infidelity she could find the excuse for the failure of their marriage. The blame then would be his and not hers.

There was such a finality to her words that he did not challenge her. Instead he walked to the door. He paused, his hand on the doorknob, but he did not open the door.

He looked back at her, his face grim.

'If we are to remain married, then you have to accept my apology,' he said. 'That's all I can say.'

He waited for a few moments but she said nothing.

'But I don't think you really want that, do you?' he asked.

She did not reply.

CHAPTER 11: AUGUST 1957

For the second time in his life, Philippe Duval found himself relying on the willingness of an elderly woman to trust the story he was telling only this time he was telling the truth. At the Goulburn orphanage all those years ago, his cover story had been so feeble he had wondered that he had been believed when he had come in search of information about the child Julia had borne him and given away.

Now he sat in Edith Henderson's over furnished living room and with quiet dignity told the story of his affair with Julia Belleville for the first time. He explained how he had come to know that she had borne him a child who he had always assumed was a daughter.

Edith sat impassively through the first part of his story, straining at times to understand Philippe's accent but all the time weighing up the likelihood of his story being true.

She had noted with silent approval the well cut suit he wore. His hair she had noticed too. It was beginning to grey at the temples, which only added to his overall appearance of calm authority. He had hardly needed to establish his credentials with Edith Henderson such was the reassurance of his appearance, although she had earlier taken the card he proffered at her doorstep and studied it intently.

It had taken Philippe some time to decide how to respond to the desperate letter he had received from Pippa, dismissing almost immediately the most obvious course of action in writing back to her. He could not, he reasoned, be sure that a letter with a New York postmark from an unknown letter writer would ever reach her. Nor could he take the chance of an impromptu meeting which would have been difficult to plan and could have had unforeseen consequences.

He had chosen, instead, the only obvious course: to travel to Sydney, only this time the journey was accomplished in far less time.

Finally, Edith Henderson stood up and Philippe followed suit, thinking the discussion was over, but she raised her hand in a friendly gesture, telling him to sit down again.

'Dr Duval,' she said, 'I am forgetting my manners. I haven't offered you tea.'

He sank back in the over-stuffed armchair, grateful that he was not being summarily dismissed. He had been quick to reassure her that he had no plans to attempt to meet Pippa clandestinely. She was relieved, he could see that. It was obvious to him that she was quick to understand how hasty actions could add complications to an already complicated and tragic story.

It was a few minutes before Edith returned to the living room, this time bearing a tea tray containing her best china. He took this as a sign that she was willing to discuss what might best be done.

As they drank tea together, they spoke not of Pippa but of war.

'I've been a widow for nearly 40 years you know,' she said quite unexpectedly. 'I was married just over a year when my husband was killed on the Western Front. I never married again. There were many widows from that war.'

Philippe nodded sympathetically for it was clear that war had robbed Edith of all that she had dreamt of. It had robbed her of a chance to have her own children and then grandchildren. It was only through the death of her niece Anne Jensen that she had been thrust unexpectedly into a role she had never imagined she would be called upon to undertake.

'And other family?' Philippe asked, for there were many things he did not know.

'Anne's mother was my only sister,' she said, 'and Anne was an only child. Sadly, my sister died quite young. Anne had just turned 21 when her mother died. She caught pneumonia and they couldn't save her. Her father died young too.'

Philippe murmured his sympathy at the loss, which had clearly affected Edith Henderson badly.

'I was devastated,' she said, to fill the slight pause in the conversation that this revelation had caused.

The sadness in her eyes betrayed the depth of that loss.

'Then when Anne died, I was completely lost,' she said, 'except that Anne had made provision for me, her only living relative to stand as guardian for the little girl she adopted. The fact that Harry Jensen left his daughter almost nothing didn't surprise me.'

She had answered the one question Philippe desperately needed to ask but couldn't.

'He never really took to Pippa,' she explained.

But it was clear where Edith's sympathies lay.

'He wanted a son. Anne found she couldn't have children. So he agreed to adopt a child, but only a daughter. He left his properties to his nephew Andrew, who was in an unseemly haste, in my opinion, to eject Pippa from her home and be free of her.'

Again she paused, this time to wipe away a stray tear that trickled slowly down her powdered cheek. It was clear to Philippe that Harry Jensen and his nephew did not rate highly in her opinion.

'But Anne loved her daughter passionately. I think it made up for the hollowness of the marriage she found herself in.'

She smiled recalling the memories of happier times.

'When she wrote to me, it was full of Pippa and what she had done and how she had grown.'

She rose from her chair and went across the room to a small sideboard. With some difficulty, she opened the middle drawer and after a few moments, returned to stand in front of Philippe. She held out a bundle of letters towards him.

'Here, read for yourself what Anne wrote. And there are some photos too.'

Philippe accepted the letters, eager to read the story of his daughter's childhood yet sad that he was to become a voyeur of a dead woman's life and hopes.

'Are you sure?' he asked. 'These are very personal and precious to you.'

She smiled, pressing them on him.

'No, you must read them,' she said. 'Then you will know that your daughter was loved and cherished, especially by her mother. When you are finished with them, return them to me.'

He smiled and thanked her.

Edith sat back in her chair. The unexpected arrival of Pippa's father now raised many questions in her mind. Would he want to take Pippa back to America? Was that the best thing for Pippa? Would he be able to by law? Could she stop him?

Philippe could see she was already beginning to try and make sense of everything he had told her and what his sudden appearance would mean to her and her young ward. He could see she had Pippa's best interests at heart so he did not press her for decisions and commitments. Instead he stood up and held out his hand.

'I know this has been a big shock to you. I want you to know that I really appreciate all you are doing for Pippa,' he said, his tone calm and measured.

'I think I should come back tomorrow and we can discuss matters again, once you have had time to think about everything we have discussed.'

She nodded, appreciating his considered approach to the decisions they both faced regarding Pippa's future.

But she could not resist one last question, the question that had been haunting her ever since Pippa had been orphaned.

'But what of Pippa's real mother?' she asked. 'You haven't told me what her circumstances are now. Is there a chance you could finally be the family you should have been when Pippa was born?'

It was an unexpected question and one for which Philippe was totally unprepared.

He paused, uncertain what to say.

'I'm sorry, Dr Duval,' she said. 'Perhaps I shouldn't have spoken so forthrightly.'

He was quick to reassure her. He did not want the goodwill that existed between them to evaporate.

'I don't mind the question, Mrs Henderson,' he said but his head drooped slightly and his bearing was suddenly less confident.

'As far as I know, Pippa's mother is happily married and probably has another family. I don't see that there is any possibility now that we could be a family.'

Until that moment, all his thoughts had been on what part he could now play in Pippa's life. Now he saw the danger, not for Pippa, but for Julia, whose circumstances he could only guess at.

Thoughts crowded his mind. If she had indeed married James Fitzroy and had another family, it was unlikely she had ever told him about the baby she had borne out of wedlock. Philippe knew and understood enough of Julia's mother to know that the existence of Julia's first child would be known only to a very few people.

He resolved then to protect Julia as he had not been able to protect her fourteen years earlier. Understanding that Pippa had written to him without knowing his circumstances, he knew for sure that nothing would stop her writing to her mother, regardless of her circumstances, if she came to know her name.

He raised his hand in a final farewell to Edith as he closed the front gate behind him. Tomorrow he would return and then they would decide what to do. Seeing the warmth and good sense of Edith Henderson had reassured him.

What could he offer a child in New York? Long hours alone while he worked. An unfamiliar school where she would be ridiculed for her accent? He could not imagine it yet he longed to play an important role in her life.

With these thoughts swirling around in his mind, he walked aimlessly for some distance, not noticing his direction nor with any particular plan in mind. It was only the shrill sound of girlish voices that brought his mind back to the present.

He stopped, suddenly aware that he was walking along the boundary fence of Meriden, the school Pippa attended.

He crossed to the other side of the road immediately and then stood beneath a large tree that afforded him some protection yet allowed him to watch the girls as they drifted in groups of two or three into the playground for lunch. At that distance he could not pick out from among all the blonde headed girls the thirteen year old who was his daughter. For the first time he understood how anxious he was for his first sight of her. He had never expected to see her, now, suddenly she was just across the street from him.

He stood watching the playground for some time before he walked away in the opposite direction. He had been tempted, for a brief moment, to approach the girls nearest the fence and ask for Pippa. But he immediately dismissed this fanciful idea, knowing full well that by doing so he would betray Mrs Henderson's trust in him and destroy whatever chance he might have of playing a meaningful role in Pippa's life. He knew he must be patient and yet within him, a sense of anticipation was building that finally, after all these years, he would meet the daughter he had for so long thought he would never know.

To the other residents of Prior Park, Richard's calm outward appearance and Catherine's cool composure betrayed nothing of the precipice on which their relationship teetered.

He had avoided telling Catherine the whole truth yet he knew he had recklessly rekindled his relationship with Jane Warner. In quiet moments, he wondered if it had just been wounded pride that had pushed him to reignite his relationship with her. Was it the fear that Catherine no longer wanted him that had driven him to seek out his first love?

For her part, there was an endless loop of unresolved questions and disappointments that haunted her waking hours yet to all appearances she was relaxed and at ease.

An uneasy truce had settled between them, more because neither knew how to take the next step or what the next step was.

Yet without any decision on their part, this was the day their lives would change.

It was early afternoon when the telegram for Catherine arrived with the mail delivery van.

Telegrams were rare so the arrival of such an urgent missive aroused great curiosity and concern in the household. Seeing the name through the murky window face of the small envelope, Richard picked it up and went in search of Catherine. He held it out to her. She grabbed it and tore it open.

It was brief and to the point:

Father dangerously ill. Heart attack yesterday. Suggest you come back to England. Advise travel plans. Love Mother

She held it out to Richard to read, for her eyes had already filled with tears.

'You must go back immediately,' he said, all thoughts of their recent arguments banished from his mind.

She nodded agreement.

'I'll call John,' Richard said. 'He'll be able to organise the best flight for you.'

Again, she nodded, relieved to leave the organisation of the trip to Richard.

'It's going to take so long to get there,' she said, her frustration at living so far away from her parents bubbling to the surface again.

It was a familiar refrain so Richard did not respond directly, focusing instead on the practical problem of getting Catherine half way round the world in as short a time as possible. The elder of their two sons was suddenly upper most in his mind.

'What about Paul? He's due to come home shortly from school for the spring holidays?' Richard said.

But Catherine was ahead of Richard with her plans.

'Arrange for John to book a stop over in Sydney so I will have an afternoon to see him before I leave for London,' she said, her mind quickly running through the options.

'But I can't take Anthony at such short notice,' she said, noticing immediately the relief in Richard's eyes.

As the younger of their two sons and not yet at school, Anthony had always travelled with her but this time it seemed unnecessary to disrupt his life at Prior Park at such short notice.

'He'll miss you terribly,' Richard said, relieved that he did not have to argue with her about the necessity of leaving Anthony at Prior Park, despite the young boy's attachment to his mother. His older brother Paul, now eleven, and used to the separation from family that attending school had meant, would take the news in his stride.

With the arrangements well in hand, Catherine headed to their bedroom, her thoughts now only on the clothes she must pack to accommodate a very different climate and very different circumstances.

Meanwhile, Richard, having settled Catherine's travel arrangements with a call to his good friend, knew he was of no further immediate use to his wife, so he went in search of his brother, whom he found settled behind his desk in the study.

As he entered, William lowered the letter he had been reading.

'More figures and business stuff, I guess?' Richard asked, without any real interest in the answer.

They had given up hope of a positive response from their new solicitor about the unpredictable Alistair McGovern.

'No, as a matter of fact, it's about the unmentionable person,' William replied obliquely.

'Really? I thought we'd given up hope of a settlement on that front,' Richard said, for it had hardly been the most important issue for him in recent times.

'What does he say? Is there a sensible solution that he will agree to?'

Richard, as ever, was optimistic that money would solve the problem. William, less certain than his brother that it was simply a matter of money, nevertheless hoped Richard was right.

'Henry Baker, our new man, has met with him according to this letter and made him a financial offer, which he writes he is optimistic will be accepted,' William said, waving the carefully typewritten letter with unnecessary vigour.

'Well, I hope so,' Richard stated flatly for he was heartily sick of discussing the matter.

'So do I, Richard, so do I,' William said, although he seemed far less sure of the outcome than his brother.

'When I spoke to Julia about it, she was adamant that we must pay him off, whatever it cost. But I've always felt it wasn't just about money,' William added.

Richard laughed but it was not a pleasant sound.

'You think he genuinely believed he could become part of our family and that's what he really wanted?'

William nodded.

'As bizarre as it sounds, I'm sure that's what was at the back of his deluded mind.'

Richard for once found a point of agreement with his brother.

'You have it right there, William,' he said. 'Deluded he most certainly is. So are you writing back to the solicitor today?'

Again William nodded.

'I am. I am going to say simply that we hope he succeeds with his negotiations but that the nameless young man must sign a document giving up all claims to any Belleville legacy, all attempts to contact us and I've asked for a clause preventing him from changing his name by deed poll, because I thought that was a possibility too.'

Richard shrugged his shoulders.

'I must admit I hadn't thought of that possibility.'

William rocked back in his chair, his hands behind his head.

'It has only just occurred to me, to be honest, but it seems like an extra necessary precaution,' William said, placing the solicitor's letter on the desk alongside his writing pad in order to begin the task of replying.

They were silent for a short time, each of them contemplating the damage Alistair McGovern could do to the family if he chose. To both of them, a legally binding settlement seemed the only way out.

It was William who broke the silence.

'I'm sorry to hear about Catherine's father. Are the travel arrangements made?'

Richard turned away from the window where he had been standing and moved back towards the desk. He sat down in the chair across the desk from his brother.

'Yes, John Bertram has made all the bookings for her. She'll see Paul in Sydney before she flies out. Anthony is staying here with me this time.'

For no reason he could put his finger on, William was pleased that the younger of Richard's two sons would remain at Prior Park. He had never mentioned it to his brother but he and Alice had discussed it on more than one occasion that it was possible Catherine, on any one of her many trips home, would without notice decide to remain permanently in England and Anthony with her.

He was unsure if this scenario had ever occurred to his brother but he wasn't about to ask, saying simply that he was pleased Catherine could get back to England quickly.

'I hope she makes it in time to see her father,' William said, with an almost imperceptible note of sadness in his voice. 'Despite everything that has happened since, I still wish one of us had been there when Father died.'

Richard nodded, understanding all too well the conflicted feelings William now felt towards their father.

For both of them, it seemed that almost all that remained was the anger they felt at their father's betrayal of not only their mother, but of themselves. It was the anger and disappointment that now tarnished their memories and haunted them. It was something that neither of them could speak of, yet both felt a deep sense of betrayal that nothing could change. Yet it wasn't quite enough to wipe out completely the love they both felt for their flawed but charming father.

Charles Brockman and Grace Duffy stood slightly apart from the group farewelling Catherine on the start of her long journey from Prior Park back to Haldon Hall.

First Elizabeth, who admired her daughter-in-law's strong independent character, then Alice and finally Marianne hugged and kissed her while the men stowed her travelling cases into the boot of the car.

Anthony, at first confused, and then alarmed at being left behind, clung to her leg making it difficult for her to move before he was gently but firmly moved out of harm's way by his Aunt Alice.

William, not naturally demonstrative, gave her a quick kiss on the cheek just before she climbed into the passenger seat alongside Richard, who was driving her to the local airport for the first of the flights on the long journey she would make alone.

For just a moment before she stepped into the car, she paused and looked back at the commanding façade of Prior Park. For all that it lacked when compared with the country houses she knew in England, still it had a charm and beauty of its own.

While the short pause went unnoticed by most, Charles and Grace shared a quiet conversation. They were careful not to be overheard.

'I can't help but feel this is the last we will see of her, Charles,' Grace Duffy said.

She turned slightly towards him, to gauge his reaction. He pulled a wry face that spoke much more than words.

'It's possible you could be right, Grace,' he said.

Over the years, they had shared many confidences about the family they both served. Many had speculated that they would one day marry but this had never come to pass, both content, as they were, with the companionship they shared and the trust that had grown between them over the years.

As the family dispersed back into the house and the nursery maid attempted to calm the crying Anthony, Grace and Charles strolled around the house towards the back steps.

'I thought Julia might have been over to see her sister-in-law off,' Grace said, looking to Charles for an answer, assuming that he would know the comings and goings of Mayfield Downs as well as Prior Park.

'Yes, I would have thought so too,' he said, 'but perhaps they spoke yesterday.'

He was always quick to defend Julia from any hint of criticism. The habit of a lifetime was hard to break.

For years, Grace had kept the secret of what she had witnessed on a particular morning in the kitchen at Prior Park when morning sickness had overcome the unmarried Julia and the uproar in the household that had followed.

Eventually, with Julia married, she had shared the knowledge with Charles who had in turn shared his regret at having seen the two young lovers together and done nothing to stop them. These revelations had brought them closer together as friends and confidantes.

So it was an easy decision for Charles to share with Grace the other great secret to which he had been privy: the revelations concerning Francis Belleville's illegitimate son. He knew this was a great betrayal but he reasoned that the Prior Park housekeeper had a

128

right to know, for her own sake. If Alistair McGovern turned up unexpectedly it might be Grace Duffy who would be called upon to deal with him.

'Be very careful of him, should he ever turn up,' he had warned.

'Mrs Belleville does not know about him,' he had added, somewhat unnecessarily.

Grace was about to go up the back stairs into the kitchen but she stopped.

'I heard some gossip about Mr Richard when I was in town the other day,' she said. 'I said I didn't believe it but if it gets around, he'll have an angry husband calling on him any day, I would think.'

This sudden revelation took Charles by surprise. Not for the information it revealed but because it confirmed his worst fears: that Richard's dalliance had become the subject of local gossip, which he knew would eventually reach the very ears it shouldn't.

Did Grace Duffy need to know the truth about this too?

He took a deep breath reluctant now to be the one to confirm the gossip she had heard. She was a good honest woman who would not be capable of dissembling if the question were put to her and she knew the answer so this time he did not share what he already knew to be the truth. Instead, he shrugged.

'I haven't heard that one,' he said, hoping that would reassure her.

'There's probably nothing in it,' he added, for good measure.

He knew it was a lie but he had no idea how far Richard's infatuation with Jane Warner had gone. On this occasion he judged it prudent to remain silent. Grace Duffy, satisfied that if Charles Brockman didn't know about it, it was certainly just malicious gossip, would use the first opportunity she had to pour cold water on the story.

She turned and headed into the kitchen. Charles, anxious to be busy and away from the house, headed towards the stables in search of his horse, yelling as he went for it to be saddled for him. He was suddenly eager to get away from them all. Life had become unexpectedly complicated, not for him, but for the family. As far as he was concerned, the less he was involved, the better. He was no diplomat. He much preferred the cattle and the horses to the intrigues and secrets of the Belleville family.

Chapter 12: August 1957

It was all Aunt Edith could do to contain Pippa's excitement. It was a little after nine o'clock in the morning and it was Saturday, but this was no ordinary Saturday for Pippa. Having waited more than two months for an answer to her letter, her hopes had begun to fade that she would hear from her father.

A thousand thoughts had rushed through her mind almost daily since she had posted the letter, the most alarming of which was that he was dead. Every time this particular thought popped unbidden into her mind she had dismissed it quickly.

After all, she reasoned, he had survived the war. He was a doctor so he shouldn't have suffered any terrible physical injuries. He had been well enough to travel to Goulburn when she was a small child. She had calculated his age time and again and supposed him to be in his early forties, although she could not be sure.

In idle moments, she daydreamed about her father for she knew him to be real. She imagined him in a white doctor's coat. That bit was easy. She could not conjure a picture of her mother for she had no image to guide her. But although she did not know it, it was within her easy grasp to imagine her mother for she had only to look in the mirror. Staring back at her would be the same blue eyes, the same fair skin, and the same blonde hair framing her face. There was no mistaking the likeness.

'Don't fidget, child,' Aunt Edith said, possibly for the hundredth time. But she said it kindly for she knew just what the meeting that was about to take place meant for the thirteen-year-old girl.

'You said he was coming at around ten o'clock,' she retorted, willing the hands of the living room clock to advance faster than normal.

'He will be here soon, Pippa, I can assure you of that,' she said, her hands smoothing the front of her skirt.

It wasn't only Pippa who was nervous. Aunt Edith was nervous too, not so much for herself but for the father and daughter who were about to meet for the very first time.

Just then, the front doorbell rang and before she could stop her, Pippa ran to the door and flung it open.

Then she stood there, as if frozen, uncertain what to do, looking at this strange American man on her doorstep. He wasn't wearing the white coat of her imagination. Instead he was wearing a grey suit. And a hat. He looked like any other well-dressed man she might pass in the street. Behind her, Aunt Edith muttered some words of encouragement.

Philippe Duval, momentarily taken aback by the sudden opening of the door, was rendered speechless by the appearance of the thirteen year old. He shook his head slightly as if he hoped the image of the young girl before him would disappear and the world would be normal again, for the shock of seeing her had been something for which he now realised he was totally unprepared.

He had seen the black and white pictures of her taken by Anne Jensen and passed on to Aunt Edith in numerous letters, but they had not prepared him for the meeting nor for that first moment of seeing her. He was, instead, seeing and remembering the young and beautiful Julia Belleville who had captured his heart so many years before.

The memories long suppressed flooded back into his mind, obliterating the present. But he knew he must say something. All the gentle encouraging words he had rehearsed were forgotten. His very first words to his daughter tumbled out.

'You look exactly like your mother, Pippa,' he said, folding her in a fatherly embrace for the first time. 'I would know you anywhere.'

The young girl relaxed as he released her and they walked into the house arm in arm. Her excitement was matched only by her impatience.

'Tell me everything,' she demanded. 'Tell me everything, every little detail.'

She made no effort to hide her excitement. She could see no potential for disappointment in the meeting, only unbounded joy that she was no longer alone, no longer the orphan she had come to see herself as.

'Tell me everything,' she repeated.

'How you met my mother, what is she like, where do you live, what your life is like. Tell me everything,' she demanded again.

He laughed and smiled across at Edith, who was relieved that Pippa showed no hesitancy at all about the situation.

'I'll tell you everything I can,' he said.

He was calmer now. It struck him that he had been as anxious about it as Pippa although he had not shown it.

'I have lots of time and I know we have lots to catch up on,' he said.

'But first, I have something for you,' he said, and took a jewellery box from his pocket.

Pippa sat down alongside him as if it had been something she had done all her life and accepted the gift with a little squeak of delight.

Inside the expensive looking box lay a beautiful gold chain with a heart shaped locket. He remembered how he had bought such a gift for Julia, never realising that eventually he would buy the same gift for his daughter. 'His daughter'. They were words that were now becoming familiar to him, where once they had been banished from his thoughts altogether.

'I have one like that already,' Pippa said quickly, pulling back her hair from her collar to reveal the gold chain he had given Julia on their last day together.

It was a small detail of the little he knew about Pippa's adoption that Philippe had forgotten. He remembered then that the superintendent of the orphanage had mentioned it yet he was momentarily flustered at seeing the locket again. But Pippa did not notice his reaction.

'So you have,' he said, 'so you have.'

He admired it and remarked its similarity to the locket he had just given her. He was pleased that she did not immediately ask about the significance of the gold locket she had always had for there was much more to tell her before that story.

He was relieved at that point to see Edith arrive with the tea tray, a welcome distraction that allowed him to regain control of his emotions.

Seeing Pippa, he realised, had been like seeing a ghost from his past, yet she was a real tangible living breathing girl.

As they drank their tea, he began to tell her the story of how he served in the war, how he was posted to Australia, and finally, his relationship with her mother and how she came to be born and given up for adoption because he was away and he didn't know about it. It was the simple, factual version of the story he had pieced together from the letter Julia had written him and from what he had discovered on his visit to Goulburn.

He did not mention the determination of Julia's mother to keep them apart nor her role in forcing Julia to give up her baby. In telling her the story, he decided it was enough for her to know the basic facts of her birth. He did not want to burden her with the bitterness and anger that had descended on her mother and the successful efforts of her family to keep them apart. There would come a time, he was sure, when she would understand this for herself. Above all, he did not want to be the one to set Pippa against the family he assumed she would never know, for he could see no purpose in doing so.

Through all this, Edith Henderson sat quietly watching Pippa's reaction, saying little but clearly satisfied that the girl was coping well with the first encounter with her father.

For Pippa, it was a day she would remember forever. She now knew her father, her real father, and he had assured her he would not desert her.

She knew her mother's name was Julia and how her mother and father had met and why she was given up for adoption. She did not press her father for more detail. Knowing who her real parents were had been all that had mattered from the moment she had read the letter he had left behind in Goulburn.

Suddenly life seemed to hold so much more promise. She did not ask about her future for already she was confident that her father would do what was best for her. For the first time since her mother Anne had died, she felt loved and cared for. For the moment that was enough. How the future would unfold she did not know. She knew only that someone loved her and that someone was her father. Her real father. Life was suddenly wonderful again.

It was almost a week before a telegram arrived at Prior Park confirming Catherine's arrival in England. It was short and said little, except that her father remained gravely ill.

Richard handed the telegram to William who read it but said nothing.

'It doesn't sound good,' Richard said, echoing his brother's unspoken thoughts.

'Well, her father is an elderly man,' William said, as if to point out that such an event might well be commonplace once a man reaches his seventies.

'Yes,' Richard said, 'I know that but all the same it will hit her hard.'

William shifted in his seat uncertain whether to change the subject, yet understanding that his brother needed someone to talk to.

'You don't think he'll recover do you?' William asked.

Richard shook his head.

'No, I don't think he'll recover,' he responded. 'And before you ask, I don't know what Catherine will do.'

He ground out the butt of his cigarette in the nearest ashtray with unnecessary force.

'What do you mean – you don't know what Catherine will do?'

William asked the question uncertain as to exactly what his brother meant.

'My wife will feel compelled to stay with her mother for some time if her father dies,' Richard said, in a voice that revealed more than the words he spoke.

'At least that will be her excuse,' he added.

William stood up and began to pace the floor. The conversation was not one of his making and he was uncomfortable with it, yet he wanted to be sure of what his brother was telling him.

'Are you telling me that you are worried that Catherine will use the opportunity to stay in England indefinitely?' he asked, looking hard at his brother for any sign that he was going too far with his questioning.

'If it wasn't for Anthony, I think she would, but I don't think she will abandon him indefinitely to the wilds of Australia,' Richard replied, his tone betraying his concerns.

William remained silent, uncertain how to respond. He and Alice had discussed the situation of Richard's marriage following William's tense encounter with her brother, but discussing it with his brother was quite a different matter.

'She accused me of being unfaithful to her,' Richard said, as he stared out the window at nothing in particular.

William was shocked. He did not want to hear such revelations from his brother. He did not want to share the intimate secrets of his brother's marriage but he felt compelled to ask the obvious question, although he already knew the answer.

'And were you?' he asked, his serious tone betraying the anxiety he felt at Richard's sudden and unwelcome disclosure.

'Yes, I was,' he said, as turned away from the window and faced his brother. It was as if he was admitting to something minor and unimportant, as if the answer no longer mattered.

'Was that wise?' was all William could think to say because the frank admission had been totally unexpected.

'Probably not,' he admitted with a shrug of his shoulders, 'but it will make no difference in the long run. Catherine will be able to use it as an excuse for our marriage failing, but our marriage was doomed from the start.'

'Doomed because she couldn't settle here?'

William asked the obvious question because it was the assumption they had all agreed upon.

'Yes, that's mostly it I believe,' he said, speaking as if his marriage was now a thing of the past.

'What about the boys?' William asked, for they had been upper most in his and Alice's minds.

'I suppose they'll have some long trips ahead of them to spend time with their mother in England,' Richard said, as if he could already see their future.

'But they'll live here,' he added. 'They will be Australians. They will be Bellevilles. They will not be drawing room pansies.'

William couldn't help but notice the sudden firing up of his brother's emotions as their talk had turned to the future of Richard's two sons.

'Don't you think it's for the boys to decide,' he said quietly. 'Anthony is very attached to his mother.'

He wondered if the answer might not be as cut and dried as Richard believed it to be but he could see his brother was in no mood to argue the point.

'William,' Richard said, with a note of exasperation creeping into his voice, 'the child is five years old. Most children of five are attached to their mothers. He'll grow out of it.'

With that, Richard headed towards the door, his sudden desperate need for physical activity overwhelming him. He had had enough of talk and discussion. He and Catherine had done nothing but talk for days before she left.

Through it all he had known deep down that their marriage could not survive. He, wedded to the country life in Australia, could never settle for the type of life she craved. She, conscious of her youth and vitality being sapped by her unhappiness and dissatisfaction, could wait no longer to make the break.

He saw clearly how the news she had so often dreaded had given her the opportunity to walk away with only vague promises as to her return. He felt he knew it was only the separation from the children that caused her deep and lasting concern. He had seen it in her eyes at their final farewell, out of the sight of his family. He had seen for himself that her commitment to him and to their marriage was over. He knew it was now just a formality but he felt no lightness of heart or relief at the knowledge. He felt a sense of emptiness and disappointment that he could share with no one.

Lying prone in his hospital bed, Sir Anthony Cavendish managed a faint smile at the news England had beaten the West Indies by an innings and 237 runs in the fifth cricket test at Kennington Oval in London. It was his last small effort before death engulfed him.

Catherine uttered a faint stifled cry, tears springing readily to her eyes, as she realised the end had come. She sought comfort from her mother who hugged her briefly then turned away from the bed where her husband of forty years had breathed his last. There was to be no public display of grief from his widow nor would he have expected it.

The room was strangely quiet as if death demanded it, the nurse bringing the white sheet up over the lifeless face in a final act of respect. The white coated doctor nodded briefly to the two women, murmuring condolences as he ushered them towards the doorway. For him death was a daily occurrence. His thoughts were for the patients he could help, not for those who were now beyond it.

Together, mother and daughter made their way through the featureless hospital corridor, oblivious to the well-established routines going on around them.

Immediately Lady Marina's mind turned to the practical considerations of the funeral and the relatives and friends who must be informed.

'I must send for the local undertaker,' she said, as if the thought had not occurred to Catherine. 'And there are so many people to advise. Plus the local vicar, of course.'

'Mother, I can help you,' she said. 'Let me make the arrangements. I don't think Father would have wanted a lot of fuss.'

Her mother stopped abruptly forcing Catherine to stop also. She turned to face her daughter.

'I don't think you quite realise that the death of a baronet in the county is of some importance,' she said, with just a hint of rebuke in her voice.

It was as if she was accusing Catherine of having spent too long in the colonies to understand the social expectations of her own father's funeral.

Despite her misgivings, Catherine demurred.

'Then we must do what is expected of us,' Catherine said, for she was unwilling to press her mother further on the matter.

Satisfied with her daughter's response, her mother nodded and they walked on together to the entrance to the hospital and down the few stairs to the car park.

Catherine had at first struggled to drive the Bentley saloon that her father had bought only months before but within a few weeks she had mastered the big car, allaying her mother's misgivings at the lack of a chauffeur in the household.

Following a whirlwind of preparations over the next few days, in the end the funeral was conducted just as her mother expected it should be done.

The respectful service at the local church, the solemn graveside gathering and the hushed and deferential posture of the mourners all satisfied Lady Marina's high expectations.

Together in the hallway of Haldon Hall, mother and daughter, both dressed in deep black, received the mourners who uttered the words expected of them and partook of the refreshments on offer with appropriate decorum.

Yet as Catherine surveyed the scene, she was sure none of them, even her mother, would mourn Sir Anthony Cavendish as she would. It was only then, on the day of his funeral, that she understood what the loss of her father meant to her.

He had always been a moderating influence on her mother and her greatest champion during her childhood. Now she needed him again for his wise counsel and sensible advice, only he was no longer there to offer it. And he never would be again. To Catherine, it seemed as if her loss had been doubled. First her father, now her husband, both lost to her in different ways, but both irretrievably.

Later, in the privacy of her bedroom away from curious glances, she wept for the loss of them both.

It was several days after the funeral before Catherine and her mother had any opportunity at all to discuss the future and Lady Marina was typically forthright.

They were together in the library, a room where Sir Anthony had been most comfortable and his presence was still all around them. Their morning coffee had just been brought in on a tray. Catherine poured coffee for herself and her mother, who sat in her favourite armchair. Neither mentioned the empty chair where Sir Anthony had regularly seated himself, whisky in hand.

'With all that has been going on,' Lady Marina began, 'we haven't had any opportunity to speak about the future at all – your future and my future, that is.'

Catherine set her coffee cup aside, aware that her mother was about to embark on a 'discussion', as she liked to call it.

'No we haven't, Mother, but is there any need?' she asked, in a non-committal way.

She had assumed her mother's life would continue much as before and she was wary of the other questions she thought would be forming in her mother's mind, for there had been little discussion between them since her arrival home, except about her father's final illness and then his funeral. Her mother's deep breath was audible as she began to speak, as if she needed to be fortified for the discussion that lay ahead.

'You haven't asked about your father's will,' she said, without pre-amble.

Catherine was surprised at her mother's opening gambit, because the matter of money was rarely discussed in the household, expect perhaps for an occasional comment on rising costs that she took no heed of.

'It won't surprise you that your father, who inherited Haldon Hall from his father, has left it to you,' Lady Marina said, unexpectedly, 'with the provision that I have the right to reside here during my life-time.'

She paused to gauge the effect of this news on her daughter.

'To me? He left it to me?' Catherine stammered, clearly bemused and not fully understanding what her mother was saying, for she could fathom no reason why her father would do such a thing.

'Yes, he left it to you, with my blessing, because he did not want the estate to endure two lots of death duties in a very short period,'

Lady Marina said simply.

'In fact he left everything to you,' she said, 'with an income for me during my lifetime.'

She was aware of course that this was all news to Catherine, because the decision had been made and enacted very recently. She and Sir Anthony had simply agreed on the move and decided to discuss it with Catherine on her next visit, not expecting, of course, that her next visit would be to witness her father's final weeks.

'Why wasn't this ever discussed with me?' she asked, bewildered. 'How did he ever think I would manage it all from Australia?'

Lady Marina sipped her coffee, delaying her response to her daughter's question.

'We only decided recently, as we have seen some people we know bankrupted by death duties,' she said, aware that was only half the story.

'If I was to be honest, we were both sure you would eventually return to live in England so we did not see it as a problem that you currently live in Australia,' she said. She did not add 'return to live, with or without your husband' but Catherine knew instantly what could not be said between them.

Silence descended on the room. The rhythmic ticking of the clock was all that could be heard, as Lady Marina waited for her daughter's response.

Catherine, no longer content to sit quietly, began to pace the room. She could not help but look at the room more closely, now that she owned Haldon Hall. It was a fine room containing many rare volumes, which she noticed, for the first time, were hardly ever moved.

'You thought my marriage would fail from the start, didn't you?' Catherine said, trying not to let her rising anger betray the hurt she felt at her mother's apparent prejudgement of her hasty marriage.

'Yes, I did, but not for the reasons you suppose,' she countered.

'Richard is a very decent and honourable man from a good family but for you to live happily in a provincial country setting without family or friends, I think was asking too much.'

Catherine said nothing so she went on.

'Be honest with yourself, if you had not been pregnant, would he have married you? Would you have wanted to marry him? Or would you have then seen the circumstances of his life as too different from your own upbringing to contemplate?' her mother asked.

Now, faced with the very questions she had been asking herself constantly, she did not know how to respond. She did not want to appear shallow and self-centred, especially to her own mother.

'I think you already know the answers to those questions, Mother,' she said at last, backing away from a detailed discussion of what had gone wrong in her marriage and why.

'I think if Richard had been willing to live in England, we would still be married but he would have been unhappy,' she admitted. 'And I have said to him I cannot continue to live at Prior Park because I am unhappy there. I feel I don't belong.'

She turned to face her mother, who was eyeing her keenly, as if trying to decide whether there was more to her daughter's marriage breakdown than she was letting on. Satisfied that there was nothing more to it, she moved to the topic that had been worrying her, as it had worried others thousands of miles away.

'And the children?' her mother asked.

'We haven't really discussed the children, except Richard insists they be brought up in Australia,' Catherine said.

Her mother nodded knowingly.

'That does not surprise me at all,' she said. 'Not at all.'

Catherine nodded in agreement.

'I think he was relieved it wasn't practical for me to bring Anthony with me this time,' she admitted. 'In fact, he doesn't expect me to come back, I know that.'

'But you must go back some time, surely, to see the children?'

'I will, Mother. I have a flat in Sydney. I can go during the school holidays and the children can see me there, if Richard won't bring them to England.'

Lady Marina looked up sharply, surprised by Catherine's composure.

'And you are willing to do that, to give up your children without a fight?'

Catherine stopped her pacing and sat down again, her head in her hands, almost the first outward sign of the turmoil in her mind.

'I don't think I have a choice,' she said, her voice wavering.

'I think the courts would side with Richard. The children are Australian, not English. Anthony will be five soon and Paul will be twelve early next year. It won't seem so very long and they'll be off living their own lives. They may wish to attend school or university in England as John Bertram did,' she said, trying desperately to sound rational and unemotional about the decisions she now faced.

Lady Marina could see that there were many uncertainties in the future her daughter described but said nothing more, so Catherine seized the opportunity for a change of topic.

'John Bertram wrote to me, by the way, offering his condolences and apologising for not attending the funeral,' Catherine said. 'He could not change his work roster to be in England at the time.'

'Yes, he wrote me a very nice letter too. It's a wonder he does not marry,' her mother said, almost as an afterthought.

'And speaking of letters, I also received a letter from Edward Cavendish. You met him once, I believe, when you were visiting,' her mother said.

Pleased to have the conversation directed away from her personal life, Catherine relaxed a little.

'Yes, I did meet him,' she said. 'He told me he was a distant cousin but I couldn't remember how he was related. He was very pleasant, as I recall.'

'Yes,' said Lady Marina, 'he is a very pleasant young man. He wrote to me too apologising for not attending the funeral. He's with the Foreign Office and was working in Paris, he said, although he did not say for how long.' Catherine made no comment. She waited for her mother to continue.

'He, above all others, was someone I expected to see at your father's funeral,' she added, without explanation.

'Why Edward Cavendish, Mother?' Catherine asked, bemused. 'I thought he was just a distant cousin.'

'No, Catherine, not just a distant cousin, but the man who stands to inherit your father's baronetcy, as you did not have a brother.'

It was only then that Catherine realised the level of her ignorance of her own family.

'I never thought about it,' she admitted. 'I never thought about Father's title passing on to someone else. It seems unfair that it only goes to sons.'

'Unfair or not, that is the way it is,' Lady Marina said flatly.

'He will have to prove he is in the succession, but your grandfather and his grandfather were brothers, sons of the first baronet. His father Nicholas was your father's first cousin, so Edward has the first – and only claim – on the title. I'm sure he knows it.'

She was impressed that her mother could recite the relationships without reference to any family tree, but remembering her mother's upbringing as the daughter of an earl, she understood the importance of inheritance and blood ties in such families.

It was her own ignorance and lack of understanding that disturbed her for she realised then that there were many questions she had not asked about her own family. Consumed by her own problems, she had not bothered to ask how matters stood with her own parents and now she found herself at a disadvantage, as if she was a young girl again, locked out of the conversations and knowledge of the adult world around her. At that point, she resolved to take a greater interest in the family's affairs.

'Tomorrow, we must see the family solicitor,' Catherine said. 'I must understand what is involved in the estate and Haldon Hall. I must know everything.'

Her mother nodded in agreement, relieved that her daughter showed every sign of accepting the responsibility her father had long thought her capable of undertaking.

Chapter 13: September 1957

Richard grabbed the airmailed letter from the hall table at Prior Park just as soon as it arrived. Through a succession of telegrams he had come to learn the sad news from the other side of the world but he looked through the mail every day for a letter from Catherine.

Now that she had finally written, he craved privacy in which to read it so he mounted the stairs two at a time and headed to the bedroom he had shared with his wife until her departure the previous month. He tore at the envelope impatiently anxious to read what she had written.

It was as if there was a part of him that refused to believe their marriage was over. In quiet moments, he felt an emptiness at her absence yet in his rational moments he knew she had tried and failed to make a fulfilling life for herself as his wife in Australia and that he had failed her.

Had he really tried hard enough to help her settle or had he left her too much to her own devices? He found these thoughts worried him more and more. He could understand her yearning for the social life she missed and for the friends who had all but forgotten her but had he really ever given himself totally to the marriage? It troubled him that the failure was as much his fault as hers.

He read quickly through her account of the funeral for the names she mentioned meant nothing to him. It was the second page of her letter that contained the biggest surprise and one he had not expected. He had not known, nor even considered, that his wife would inherit Haldon Hall. Like her, he had expected Lady Marina to be the beneficiary of Sir Anthony's will but as he read on, he understood the explanation she offered.

Yet it was clear she did not yet understand the extent of the responsibility and what it entailed, only that she was meant to take her father's place in running the estate, for which, she wrote candidly, she had received no preparation at all. There was just a hint of panic in her words yet she did not reach out to him for help, as she might once have done, and he felt a sense of disappointment at her failure at least to seek his advice.

Beyond the news of her inheritance, she did not speak of the future, only that she would write again very soon and that she sent her love to him and the children.

He folded the letter carefully and put it in a drawer.

He sat for some time on the edge of the bed, pondering the news. Her letter had reminded him of one thing: the unresolved issue of his and William's wills. It was something he decided could be left no longer.

With this in mind, he went in search of his brother who was himself reading a long letter but this letter was from their solicitor, with news that would make neither of them at all happy.

William looked up as Richard entered the study. Richard could see immediately that the contents of the letter William had just thrown carelessly on the desk were not to his liking and Richard guessed the reason immediately.

'I take it there is no good news from Henry Baker?' he asked, almost not expecting a reply.

'No, there's no good news from Henry Baker,' William said, with an exaggerated sigh.

'After four months of negotiations and just when we thought we had a deal, the unmentionable person has decided we don't have a deal. He's decided he wants more of everything. He feels he is entitled to a third of Father's estate; he wants to be recognised as a family member and he wants to be invited to visit.'

William picked up the letter he had discarded and began to read it to Richard.

' "I think this young man is prone to bouts of erratic behaviour and he is not to be trusted." That's what our solicitor writes,' William said, his anger and frustration rising with every word.

Richard did not respond immediately. The solicitor's words worried him but he did not want to add to William's concerns. Instead, he offered William his opinion. Like his brother, he was tired of the cat and mouse game they were playing.

'I think we tell Baker to up the offer by a thousand pounds and indicate that all the terms we offered are final and not negotiable,' he said.

'We could use some of the money from the sale of the shares in the woollen mills,' he added, somewhat unnecessarily, because he knew William monitored their cash position very closely.

'What if he won't accept?' William countered.

Richard turned to face his brother. He was grim faced.

'If he doesn't accept, there is actually nothing we can do,' he said with some force.

'We must take our chances with him. If we appear weak and willing to give in to him, he has the upper hand. If we play a hard game with him, if he has any sense, he'll know we will always win.'

William looked unconvinced, for his preference was to tie up any loose end in a watertight agreement. He did not relish conflict or un-certainty.

'What's the worst he can do?' Richard said, challenging his brother to face his worst fears about the situation.

In the end, Richard answered for him.

'I'll tell you what he can do and what he can't do,' Richard said, the harshness of his voice betraying his determination not to give in to the hated interloper.

'He can spread gossip and turn up here and make trouble,' he said, 'but we will make sure that he never reaches the front door.'

William, seeing the determination in his brother's face, grew more, not less anxious.

'How can we be sure of that?' William said. 'You and I can't always be here, in the house, as if we are guarding it.'

Richard smiled.

'No, we can't but we can hire a couple of men for that specific purpose. It would make us feel safer,' Richard said.

'Like security guards, you mean?'

'Well, I wouldn't call them that, but a couple of former soldiers who know how to handle themselves would be useful around the place.'

The idea had not occurred to William but apart from the extra expense he could see some merit in it. Most of all he worried that Alice might be forced to deal with Alistair McGovern if he and Richard were absent. The tone of the solicitor's letter had made him feel distinctly uneasy, without really knowing why. Was Alistair McGovern a danger to them? It was hard to imagine but William was not one for taking chances.

William's natural instincts to protect his own family overrode any commonsense objections he could mount to Richard's plan.

'OK, then, I'll write to Baker to put our final offer but you will have to organise the other aspect,' William said.

'Don't worry, William, I will,' he said. 'Leave that part of it to me.'

Richard was almost out the door before he remembered his real reason for seeking out his brother.

'By the way, I've heard news from Catherine about the funeral,' he said.

'How was it?' asked William, out of politeness rather than any real desire to know more.

He knew that Catherine's father had been an important man in their county and he imagined the funeral would have been well attended. He was, in some ways, surprised that Richard had not made the attempt to get there, but then it was probably an impossible thing to do, he supposed, although he had not asked.

'The funeral? Much as you might have expected – a big turnout of local dignitaries, and, according to Catherine, some of them very curious to see the daughter of the house who'd married a wild colonial,' he said, in an attempt to lighten the mood.

'They probably expected to see the wild colonial himself,' William replied.

'Probably,' Richard said, 'but the big news in her letter is that she has inherited all her family's wealth, with her mother only having a lifetime interest.'

He could see that William was stunned at the news for, like his brother, he had not considered the possibility.

'Did you know this was likely?' he asked, as if there had been secrets he had not been privy to.

'No, I did not know it was likely and neither did Catherine until after the funeral,' Richard explained.

'It seems they wanted to avoid two lots of death duties, which are pretty steep over there,' he added.

'That makes sense,' William said, for it appealed to his commonsense not to waste money and to protect a family's assets.

'Yes, it does make sense,' Richard said, 'but it also shows that her father had a lot of faith in her ability to run the estate and their business interests.'

For the first time, William realised how little he knew of his sister-in-law's family. He could not resist the obvious question.

'Are they very wealthy?' he asked, his curiosity getting the better of him, for it was unlike him to ask such a prying question.

Richard laughed at his brother's obvious embarrassment in having asked such an improper question.

'I don't think you would regard them as very wealthy but they do have some tenant farmers and some investments in commercial real estate in London, I believe,' he said. 'That's really all I know. It's what I gleaned from my few conversations with Sir Anthony. Money was a vulgar topic never discussed at the dinner table.'

William mulled over the response for a minute or two.

'Pretty well enough off, then, by the sounds of it,' William said, satisfied with Richard's answer.

'I'd say so,' said Richard, 'but hearing that news from Catherine reminded me that we never did resolve the question of our wills, because there have been too many other things to think about.'

In fact, William had thought about it often but was unwilling to raise it again for fear of provoking the same forceful and intransigent response from Richard, so this time he was non-committal, waiting instead for his brother to speak.

'I think we should sign the draft wills that have been lying in the safe since I returned from Brisbane,' Richard said.

'I've changed my mind. If Catherine can inherit all her family's property, then your daughter can share in the Belleville inheritance.'

It was a concession William had not expected yet he was relieved at Richard's unexpected change of mind. He stood up from the desk and walked across to where Richard was standing. He put his hand on Richard's shoulder in an awkward gesture.

'Thank you, brother,' he said. 'Thank you for seeing it my way. I think that's what Mother wants too. We should sign them without delay and send them back to the solicitor.'

Richard nodded but said nothing further. It had only begun to dawn on him since he had read Catherine's letter that he had not exhibited the same faith in her judgement that her own father was prepared to do. He cursed the missed opportunities, for he realised now, had she been more involved in their business affairs, she might have felt a greater sense of belonging. He realised too late he had mentally consigned her to the role he thought women played in the household, never realising that Catherine had been capable of much, much more.

Afterwards, as William lay beside Alice, he told her everything that had been discussed between him and his brother. It was Alice who attributed Sir Anthony's confidence in Catherine as the major reason for Richard's softened attitude.

William was less sure so Alice did not press her point of view. Whatever had brought about the change of mind they could not be sure but it was Alice who slept that night with a greater sense of contentment for her daughter had now been recognised and given the same standing as Richard's sons. Until the change of heart, she had not realised how important it had become to her.

Alongside the letter from Catherine, another letter, the handwriting unfamiliar, had been waiting for Richard on the hall table. The contents of this letter he discussed with no one, certainly not his brother William. He was, in fact, relieved that he had been the first to examine the pile of letters shortly after they were delivered by the mail van.

The letter was short and signed only with an initial but he could not mistake the sender. He had spent weeks in a private turmoil, most of the time sorry that he had rekindled his relationship with Jane Warner, but that was by no means a constant thought.

If anything, his thoughts were confused, but if he tried to imagine her with him, as his wife, he could not. He could imagine no other person in place of Catherine, and to him that was a problem too difficult to confront. He knew he owed Jane an explanation of his actions yet he could not seek her out for fear of reigniting the gossip that he suspected might be circulating about their relationship.

Jane, knowing that Catherine had left for England, was emboldened to write a note to him, yet she did not beg him to make a decision about a future for them. She simply asked that he honour his promise not to reveal her name and to stay out of her life.

'Your silence', she wrote, 'tells me everything I need to know so do not contact me again.'

The words stung him with their barely disguised bitterness. He knew he had hurt her deeply, just as she had hurt him years before, but he did not feel any satisfaction in that knowledge. Nor could he write back to her to explain his actions for fear her husband would intercept the letter. Even keeping her letter was a risk. Yet he could not bring himself to destroy it.

He remembered the pleasure of being with her, but in the cold light of day, the disruption to their lives, should he press her to leave her husband, was a responsibility he could not take upon himself.

He replaced the short letter in the envelope and hid it away. He understood, now, that he wanted desperately to give his marriage with Catherine one last chance. He wanted to keep the door ajar. He was not ready to install another woman in her place. It was only then he began to think deeply about his insistence on living at Prior Park full time. Was that really the only option, he mused silently? Was it too late for him to reach a compromise with Catherine?

Elizabeth Belleville, to whom the advancing years had not been especially kind, had much to tell her daughter on her usual Tuesday visit. Elizabeth had demanded to know the full story of Catherine's inheritance after Alice's startling news that Richard had changed his mind about the disposition of the Belleville family assets to include Marianne, a decision which Alice artlessly attributed to Sir Anthony Cavendish's decision to make his daughter his sole heir.

'What do you think of that?' Elizabeth Belleville asked Julia, with a smugness born of greater knowledge.

'Well, it was obviously a surprise to Richard, and to Catherine, I shouldn't wonder,' she said, without adding that she wondered if this did not complicate matters further between Richard and Catherine.

'Alice and I think that's why Richard changed his mind about including Marianne as one of the heirs to the Belleville interests,' her mother said, forgetting that Julia herself had been excluded, but for other reasons.

'Well, since it doesn't affect me, Mother,' she said tartly, 'they can do what they like with it, but I am pleased that Marianne is to be included. John gets on very well with his cousin. She seems a very sweet and clever little girl.'

Her mother nodded in agreement.

'Yes, she is very bright, and a very good little girl too. Alice has brought her up very well,' Elizabeth said.

Julia wondered if this was a slight against her own son, for he was generally regarded as a tearaway but she decided to say nothing to provoke an argument.

'Is Richard going over to England?' she asked, for it seemed an obvious course of action for him.

Her mother shrugged her shoulders in a gesture of uncertainty for Richard had confided nothing of his plans to her.

'I don't know if he is or not, but I think he should go,' she said, 'not that he will take any notice of me. He has been very withdrawn and somewhat moody and unsettled since she left, I know that.'

'Perhaps he has other things on his mind,' Julia said, without being specific, for James had shared the titbit of gossip with her he had heard about his brother-in-law.

'I know he is worried about what investments to make, now that the family's interest in the woollen mills has been sold,' Elizabeth said.

She did not add she was interested in what Richard would decide for she too was facing decisions in her own investments, that she discussed with no one within the family.

'James thinks he was right to sell,' Julia said, unexpectedly, for it had not occurred to Elizabeth that such matters would be discussed between Julia and her husband.

'You seem to know a lot about these matters,' she said, looking more closely at her daughter.

'Well, I do run everything with James,' she said, as if the fact should come as no surprise to her mother. 'He values my opinion on business matters and we make joint decisions.'

Elizabeth was silent for a few moments, thinking back to the poor decisions her own husband had made, knowing that her opinions had made no difference to his lack of judgement, for he had not valued her advice at all.

She sighed, the sound she made a mixture of disappointment and resignation for she knew nothing could change what had gone before.

'I'm thinking, once Richard is more settled, I might spend more time in Melbourne with Jean Dalrymple,' she said, trying to gauge her daughter's reaction to the suggestion.

'That is an excellent idea, Mother,' she said, 'you would enjoy that. And I am sure she would enjoy the company too.'

Julia, happy to have the conversation move to neutral ground, was keen to encourage her mother's latest idea.

'I would,' Elizabeth admitted, 'and Alice is very capable. Even if Catherine stays away for a few months, Alice is very good at looking after young Anthony as well as Marianne, and Paul, when he is home on holidays.'

'Has Anthony settled down?' Julia asked, wondering how the child would cope without his mother for such a long separation.

'I think he cries for her occasionally,' Elizabeth said, 'but that's to be expected. Most times he plays contentedly and when Marianne is here, he follows her around like a little puppy.'

'And will Catherine come back when everything is settled over there?' Julia asked, hardly expecting that her mother would know the answer to that question, but it was the question everyone was wanting to ask, yet no one was prepared to ask Richard himself.

'I don't know. I don't think Richard does either, but I do know he is miserable without her,' she said. 'I do hope some solution presents itself soon.'

With that, Julia rose and kissed her mother on the cheek. It had been some time since she had seen her mother in such good spirits, despite the domestic problems, and she was pleased for it. Deep down, she nursed a grievance that would always come between them, but she could not hate her mother for it.

Catherine could only imagine the impact of her news on Richard and his family in Australia. It was news that simply added another layer of complexity to the situation as far as she was concerned. She had not sought to have such responsibility thrust upon her and had certainly never expected it, but now that it had occurred, she was determined to meet the challenge head on.

In the days that followed her mother's revelation that Catherine had inherited all the family's property and wealth, Catherine found herself, reluctantly at first, in long meetings with the family's solicitors and, one by one, with the tenant farmers who came to pay their respects, as soon as it became widely known that she was the new mistress of Haldon Hall. Most expressed the private view that it was a pity Sir Anthony had not had a son to inherit, but overall, they expressed themselves satisfied with the young woman now in charge, all the while wondering when her Australian husband would arrive to take the daily decisionmaking off her delicate shoulders.

It was only during her third meeting with the solicitors that the issue of her husband was raised.

Maurice Langton, a man who, at twenty-five had looked forty, seemed very old at fifty yet he was clever and capable.

As Catherine sat across the desk from him in his best visitor's chair, he leaned forward, in a way designed to stress the confidentiality of what he was about to say.

'Mrs Belleville,' he said, pursing his lips in an unusual fashion, as if the words were being manufactured as he spoke. 'We haven't spoken about your marital situation or your own family situation.'

Catherine glanced up at him quickly for she had been studying the latest documents he had just handed her and had hardly been paying attention.

'What is it about my marital situation, as you call it, that you wish to know, Mr Langton?' she said, in a tone designed to discourage unnecessary questioning.

'Well, I know your husband is Australian; I know you generally live in Australia,' he said, by way of explanation. 'I know you have two sons. What I don't know is whether you plan to stay in England permanently to live at Haldon Hall and if you do, does your husband plan to come and live here with you?'

The questions were equally unexpected and unwelcome but before Catherine could ask why he wanted to know, he anticipated her question and began to explain.

'Taking over Haldon Hall is a big responsibility, Mrs Belleville,' the solicitor said. 'As it stands, if something was to happen to you suddenly, your husband would inherit everything. We need now to consider how you would want to dispose of the assets in the event of your untimely demise, if I may put it so bluntly.'

'Your children, after all, are still minors by some years,' he added before she could begin to answer.

Having had only a week or so to adjust to the news that she had been the main beneficiary of her father's will, she was totally unprepared for the solicitor's pointed reminder that she too must consider her will and how the property would be left. It seemed absurd to her even to be thinking about it so soon after her father's death yet think about it she must.

She rose from the chair and extended her hand. Maurice Langton took her gloved hand in his and bowed ever so slightly. He had been in awe of her father for he had been the firm's most important client. Now he extended the same deference to the young woman who had suddenly become his most important client but was almost unknown in the local community.

She did not know her hasty marriage to an Australian immediately after the war had been much discussed locally. Nodding knowingly as to the reason, the local gossips had conceded that her husband had fought valiantly for England but nevertheless he was now treated with some suspicion for having deprived local society of the daughter of the big house around which the social life of the village centred. Knowing of her sudden elevation in importance, the gossips now agreed it would be good to see her and her family settled back where they belong.

Maurice Langton shared those views although he was careful never to express an opinion to those who broached the matter with him.

CHAPTER 14: SEPTEMBER 1957

Violet Cunningham stood half concealed by the doorway into the lounge bar of the Criterion Hotel. Beside her, her niece Sharon followed the direction of her aunt's gaze. Thanks to her aunt's intervention, Sharon had recently come to work alongside her at the Criterion, where the standard of clientele was much better than other places she had worked before.

'A regular is he?' Sharon asked, for she could tell her aunt was familiar with the tall, dark haired man who strode through the bar with a calm air of natural authority.

'Yes, sort of,' she replied.

'Remember I told you about the odd young fellow who was talking out of turn about the Belleville family of Prior Park, well the man who just came in is James Fitzroy,' she said. 'He was the one who gave me some money to keep an eye out for the strange young man, in case he should come back.'

Sharon was about to say 'he's married to Julia Belleville, isn't he?' but her aunt never failed to fill in unnecessary details.

'His wife was Julia Belleville,' she said. 'They've been married about ten years.'

Sharon, who, at twenty-four, clung tenaciously to the romantic idea she was destined to marry a wealthy man and live happily ever after, was immediately disappointed to know the object of their discussion was already married. She turned her attention back to her aunt.

'But you haven't seen the strange young man since, have you,

Aunt?' she asked, sure that if she had, Sharon would have heard about it.

'No, I haven't,' she conceded, 'but I saw a letter requesting a booking for later in the year and I think it could be the same man but I just can't remember his surname for sure.'

Sharon noticed that her aunt looked worried, more worried than usual, beneath the carefully made up face.

'You think there'll be trouble don't you next time he turns up?' Sharon remarked.

'You're right,' she answered. 'I do think there'll be trouble, big trouble, in fact.'

At that point, Violet decided not to engage James Fitzroy in conversation. It would be less complicated, she thought, to wait and see if the young man turned up again rather than cause unnecessary alarm.

She moved back towards the hotel reception desk as her niece headed out the door having finished her work for the day.

From her reception desk, Violet had a view through the front door of the hotel towards the river. It was late afternoon and the light was fading fast. It had been a perfect spring day and part of her wished she could leave her desk and go for a stroll in the cooler air of the late afternoon. As she sat in a quiet reverie thinking of nothing in particular, she saw James Fitzroy walk slowly along the riverbank after leaving the hotel.

Alert now to the direction he was taking, for she knew it was in the opposite direction to where his mother lived, she noticed him greet a young woman she did not know and slip his arm around her waist in an intimate gesture that suggested they were more than mere friends. Then he pulled the girl into the shadows of the trees. Violet could hear the girl's high-pitched laughter as he wrapped his arms around her. Violet did not know the girl but she knew for certain that it was not his wife he had greeted so lovingly.

She shook her head slowly wondering what promises James Fitzroy had made to the young woman. She doubted the girl would know he was married. It would come as a shock, she thought, when she came to realise she'd been duped by promises he could never keep. But she was not surprised. She had known from the first time she had met James Fitzroy that he could charm any girl he wanted. Even, as it turned out, Julia Belleville, who had been so in love with the US Army officer during the war.

Had his marriage been such a disappointment to him, she wondered? Or was it simply his nature to be casting his eye around after ten years of marriage? She had wondered if his wife had ever really loved him or had he been second choice for her? Violet suspected correctly that her mother had pushed her into the marriage. Perhaps that was the problem at the heart of it, she mused. Perhaps James Fitzroy, knowing all along he had been second choice, had finally decided to seek a woman for whom he was first choice. Who could know, Violet thought, but she was disappointed all the same for the betrayal she saw taking place before her very eyes.

Given as she was to gossip, she could easily have spread this delicious titbit among her tight circle of friends. But she decided against it. Instead she felt a twinge of sympathy for Julia Belleville, or Julia Fitzroy as she was now, who, she guessed, had taken a long time to recover from her doomed wartime romance. To have to face a husband's disloyalty would, Violet decided, be a double blow.

She returned to her work but despite her determination to forget the incident, the image of James Fitzroy and the girl she did not know haunted her for the rest of the day.

Her last thought, as she drifted into sleep that night, was that there was trouble coming for the Belleville family but exactly where it would start and where it would end, she could only guess. She hoped, for Julia's sake, the trouble did not extend to her.

With Catherine absent, a new routine had developed at Prior Park. Most days, an insistent Anthony Belleville demanded his father's attention in the late afternoon.

With Marianne now at school in town during the week, the young boy was at a loose end so Richard was called upon to entertain his son. With infinite patience, he would bowl slow gentle looping balls towards the five-year-old budding cricketer. Any number of tennis balls had been lost in the undergrowth but Richard made sure he had a constant supply. It was little enough he could do to make up for the absence of the boy's mother, for Anthony still asked daily when she was coming home. To that question, Richard had no satisfactory reply for his young son. As the light faded and they were about to head inside, Alice appeared on the back steps.

'There's a telegram for you, Richard,' she said, holding the yellow envelope aloft. 'I'll take Anthony now. It's time for his bath.'

Richard, not for the first time, silently thanked God for the calm good sense of Alice who had taken over the management of his children, Anthony in particular, without even being asked. Both of his boys loved her and she in turn lavished attention on them as if they were her own children.

He had noticed how quiet Paul had been during his recent school holiday visit. It had only been Alice and Marianne who had been able to get him to join in their games and their outings.

Richard had struggled to reassure his older son that his mother would return very soon, for the words had sounded hollow and unconvincing, even to his own ears. He did not know if Catherine was writing regularly to Paul, but he hoped so.

As he watched Anthony take his aunt's hand and head for the bathroom, Richard turned his attention to the telegram. It read simply:

'Having many meetings re estate. Suggest you bring Anthony over to visit soon. Please cable your response. Love Catherine'

It was a simple telegram that might have lifted his mood had it suggested it was him she wanted to see, as well as her young son. But he could not ignore the summons. He went inside in search of his brother who had spent the afternoon paying bills and ordering supplies.

William did not mind the interruption and gladly accepted Richard's suggestion of a drink, although he waved away Richard's offer of a whisky in favour of a beer.

'So Catherine wants you to go over and take Anthony?' William said, relieved that at least some news from Catherine had finally raised Richard's spirits, if momentarily.

'Yes, I guess she is missing Anthony perhaps more than she thought,' Richard said.

'And missing you, too, I don't doubt,' Alice said as she opened the door to bring in William's beer, having anticipated his preference. He liked that about her. She knew what he liked and almost always turned up at precisely the right moment with what he wanted, before he even knew himself.

'Well, that might be stretching the truth a bit far, Alice,' Richard said, 'but of course I will go and take Anthony with me.'

'When will you leave?' Alice asked, for she was the first to consider the practical question of packing clothes for a young child for a totally different climate.

'I'll get on to John Bertram as soon as I can to do the bookings for me,' he said, 'but I guess it will be in a week or so.'

Alice nodded, pleased that Richard would be heading to England to see Catherine. Both she and William were of the same opinion: if Richard went to England to see Catherine, everything might turn out all right.

'I'd better go and see if Anthony is out of the bath,' she said. 'He's been known to miss important bits, but I'll leave it to you to tell him about the trip, Richard.'

Both men laughed, fully aware of the lack of interest of five-year-old boys in the daily bath ritual. After she had gone, Richard turned back towards his brother.

'I am so grateful to Alice, the way she has helped with my boys. You are a lucky man, William,' Richard said, paying his brother's wife an overdue compliment.

'I know,' William said. 'Alice is a wonderful wife. I couldn't have chosen better. And she doesn't mind at all looking after the boys.'

Alice's successful management of the Prior Park household was something that had almost gone unnoticed, William had often thought, so he was pleased his brother had finally spoken of it.

'Make sure you tell her how grateful I am,' Richard said. 'It has made my life so much easier since Catherine left. I don't know what I would have done without her help.'

William smiled and nodded, at the same time, pulling open the left hand drawer of the desk.

'I will tell her,' he said.

As he spoke, he opened a red jewellery box he had retrieved from the drawer, holding it open for Richard to inspect the strand of neatly matched pearls and delicate pearl and diamond earrings that nestled in the satin lining.

'I've bought her these for our wedding anniversary next month,' William said, a satisfied smile crossing his face.

Richard looked quickly at the opened box, surprised at William's good taste.

'Very nice, I'm sure she will love them but isn't that a bit premature?' Richard asked, remembering that the pearl anniversary was much later than the thirteen years of his brother's marriage.

'Maybe,' William said. 'But I wanted something really special for her. I think she will like them.'

'I'm sure she will,' Richard said, as he watched William return the box carefully to the drawer.

It occurred to him that he and Catherine would also celebrate their wedding anniversary very soon, but unlike William, he could not be certain there would be any reason to celebrate. Nevertheless, he decided to take his cue from his brother and acquire a suitable gift before he left for England. He realised then it would have to double as a birthday gift for he had missed that too.

James Fitzroy's late arrival home that evening did not cause Julia even momentary alarm or raise her suspicions about her husband's whereabouts. She was used to his erratic hours which he explained away because he had called to see his mother and stayed for dinner or that he had got caught up drinking with the other men after the weekly cattle sale. It did not occur to her to question him further. Having added another car to their household following her riding accident, she was no longer dependent on him being home to be able to go out.

Often, although he did not know it, she was in town on the very same days that he was, but she chose to go alone at a time that suited her rather than him. Even though their household was smaller than *Prior Park*, Mrs Fry was always on hand to look after John when he came home from school if she was out. For the first time in her life, it seemed, she had the freedom to come and go as she pleased. It was a freedom she relished.

She had not regretted her marriage to James Fitzroy but as the years progressed and their life together settled into a well-established pattern, the small spark that had brought them together, fuelled by Julia's desperate need to get away from her mother's suffocating control, had been all but extinguished.

They did not argue or disagree about very much but there were times she wondered if there should be more to life than the familiar routines that comprised their life together. Were there to be no highlights, she wondered? It was at such times she imagined a life with Philippe and pondered what might have been. And inevitably her thoughts drifted at such times to the daughter she had lost. The pain of the memory was sharp and almost physical yet she could not stop it in the quiet moments. It tore at her very soul to remember what had happened and yet she could share the grief of that loss with no one.

There was no way for Julia to know her daughter's future was being discussed almost at the exact moment her mind had most recently drifted to the events of March 1944. Having become used to the idea of having a father again, and this time a real father, Pippa had begun to pepper Philippe with questions about her future each time they met, before he was even ready or able to answer them.

Having already decided that a lonely apartment in New York was no place for a teenage girl to grow up, Philippe had then begun to think more deeply about Pippa's future and his own future and more importantly, his role in her future.

How was he to tell her he was already planning his return to New York? For this he was grateful for the sturdy commonsense of the girl's Aunt Edith, who saw the dilemma immediately and was the one to propose a solution.

'You know I am happy for Pippa to stay on with me,' she said, without prompting. 'I enjoy having her and she is no trouble to me.'

Philippe had called specifically to see Aunt Edith while Pippa was at school, hoping she would volunteer such a solution.

'We haven't really discussed it all properly since I arrived so unexpectedly on your doorstep a few weeks ago,' he said, 'but I must admit I couldn't see how Pippa would fit into my life in New York. Not the way it is now, anyway.'

Edith Henderson nodded, aware without needing to be told that Philippe's role as a leading neurosurgeon would be a demanding one, both in terms of time and dedication. He had told her too about his brief failed marriage. She knew, as well as he did, that a thirteen-year-old girl could not be taken to live in a household of one busy man, even if that man was her father, with no one to look after her, in a city where she knew no one.

'I think you should talk to her sooner rather than later about what is best for her,' Edith said, 'before she has time to create an idea in her mind of what she thinks her life is going to be and then be disappointed.'

He smiled, grateful for the older woman's insights.

'You're absolutely right,' he said. 'She may have already built a fantasy life that is all about the bright lights of New York, which of course she will see some day, but just not yet.'

Edith laughed.

'She isn't the only one who can create fantasies of the bright lights of New York.'

She looked away, slightly embarrassed at the gaucheness of her admission, but Philippe simply smiled and nodded.

'You will see it one day, I guarantee it,' he said. 'Pippa won't be old enough to travel by herself for many years. She will need a companion to come with her. I hope you will do that for her.'

Edith got up and began stacking the teacups onto her best tray to cover her confusion. She had not intended to manoeuvre him into such an offer.

'Well, we will see,' she said, 'that time is some way off I imagine.'

He nodded, not realising her discomfiture.

'Yes, it probably is some way off, but she will, if I know her at all, be demanding to come and visit me when she finds out she is to stay on with you here.'

On that point they were both in agreement.

163

'So when are you returning to New York?' Edith asked, for he had not previously mentioned how long he planned to stay in Sydney.

'I plan to leave early next week,' he said, 'but there is a medical conference starting in a couple of months and I will come back for that. I will come by on Saturday to see Pippa and explain everything to her.'

Edith was relieved. She did not want to have to be the one to tell the girl that she could not live with her father. Although no one had ever suggested it, she suspected Pippa might have assumed it would be the case.

Edith closed the door behind him and went back to the task of washing the tea things. She felt reassured by Philippe's sensible approach.

The one thing in particular they had both agreed on was that Pippa should not be told anything more about her real mother. As much as she might press them for information, they both knew Julia must be protected, for they did not know what her circumstances were. Yet they knew for certain a headstrong thirteen year old would not hesitate to write a letter, as she had done to her father, if she discovered her mother's full identity.

For a few moments, Edith Henderson reflected on how much her life had changed in the past few months, yet she was not unhappy for the change, except that it had come about in such a tragic way.

Despite the years that divided them, Pippa had begun to feel more like a daughter to her. She did not know how the young girl felt and could not guess, but Edith had found a new purpose in her life that for so long had lacked any real meaning. She hummed quietly to herself as she went about her household chores, satisfied that Pippa's future was now secure.

As it turned out, Pippa was far less enthusiastic about the arrangements proposed for her future than either her father or her Great Aunt Edith had bargained for. Her tears flowed copiously as her father gently but firmly insisted that the arrangements that he had agreed with Aunt Edith were in her best interests.

'But I may never see you again,' she said, between sobs, 'and you've only just found me.'

Repeatedly he tried to reassure her that he would come back. In fact, he told her, he would be back in a couple of months for a week or so for a medical conference.

But such a promise was too general and too far in the future to satisfy Pippa so he eventually reached into his jacket pocket for his small diary, to satisfy her that the conference was indeed taking place, for he had marked the dates carefully.

'See,' he said, pointing to the diary entries, 'the conference runs from the 6th to the 9th of November. I will promise to take you to lunch at my hotel on the 10th of November, which is a Sunday. How does that sound?'

She counted the weeks out loud on her fingers, satisfied then that she could endure the weeks until she saw her father again.

'But what then?' she asked.

It was the question Philippe had hoped she wouldn't ask. Foolishly he had thought she would be satisfied with knowing when he next visit would be. He spoke gently to her, once again, his voice and manner patient and sincere.

'We will discuss it when I come back in November,' he said, 'but of course you will see me often, and when you are finished school, you will be able to visit New York and stay with me for weeks at a time.'

It was all he could think to say, for her future so many years into the future had not been discussed. She was still a child and what she might do beyond her high school years was still to be considered.

Eventually they parted. Pippa stood at the gate watching the taxi depart until it turned the corner and she could no longer see it. By the time she went back inside to Aunt Edith, she was composed and dry eyed. She was sure that her father would come back for she now understood he was not a man who gave his word lightly.

CHAPTER 15: OCTOBER 1957

It was Saturday and Edward Cavendish was expected for lunch at Haldon Hall. As the hall clock struck twelve and he had still not arrived, Lady Marina became anxious, first surprised at his late arrival and then slightly annoyed, once she had convinced herself he had come to no harm and was simply a poor timekeeper.

She and Catherine sat together in the library awaiting his arrival, the quietness of the room accentuating the air of expectancy that hung over them.

'You have the right day I assume, Mother,' Catherine asked, almost as an after thought.

'Of course I have the right day,' Lady Marina retorted. 'He told me he was back from the Paris trip and available to come and see us this weekend.'

Catherine, still struggling to understand all the workings of her father's estate, had only found out that morning that Edward Cavendish was to visit them.

'Has he received word about the baronetcy?' Catherine asked, when her mother announced his visit that morning.

'I'm not sure,' was all that Lady Marina said in response although they both expected the result to be a formality.

Now, waiting for him, Lady Marina could not help but point out the obvious to her daughter.

'If you hadn't got yourself tied up with an Australian,' she said, 'perhaps you could have married Edward. Just imagine what that would have meant. The baronetcy would have remained with the estate.'

Catherine looked up, rather taken aback by her mother's sudden declaration. Not wanting that particular conversation to continue, Catherine rebuffed the idea.

'I think he is several years younger than me, Mother, in case you hadn't noticed,' she said.

But Lady Marina was not to be so easily put off.

'Two years at most,' she said quickly, 'and that is nothing. It's just that the war got in the way and before we could launch you properly, you were off marrying Richard.'

At least this time she hadn't referred to him as a colonial and she had softened the distain in her voice. It was not that she disliked her daughter's husband. Far from it. Had he been an Englishman she would have reconciled herself to the marriage even though there was no title involved. At least there was property and money, she had said on more than one occasion to her late husband who had been far more sanguine about his daughter's choice of partner than his wife.

'Well, it's too late for regrets of that kind,' Catherine said, hoping to bring the conversation to an end once and for all.

But Lady Marina was not to be silenced on the subject about which she had worried endlessly despite the fact she could do nothing about it at the time.

'Maybe it's not too late,' she said, 'depending on what you plan to do about your marriage to Richard.'

This time Catherine felt her mother had gone too far but she did not want to start an argument so she did not answer, preferring silence instead.

At that precise moment Myners, now slightly stooped and moving very slowly, announced their guest, who was immediately apologetic for having arrived late due to a flat tyre that had to be mended.

A faint tinge of colour appeared on Catherine's cheeks as he bowed extravagantly over her hand and commiserated with her on the death of her father.

She in turn searched his face for any sign he had overheard her mother's words but she found none, so she relaxed. As his attention turned back to Lady Marina, she looked more closely at him. She could not help but compare him with her absent husband.

He wasn't quite as tall as Richard nor as well built but there was an athleticism about him despite his pale skin and carefully manicured hands. He sat opposite her in the chair to which Lady Marina had directed him.

'Was it something interesting that took you to Paris?' Lady Marina asked, automatically assuming that he was free to talk about his work.

'Not frightfully interesting really, Lady Marina,' he said. 'We were getting briefings about the establishment of the European Economic Community. Six European countries signed a treaty earlier this year which will reduce tariffs on trade among them but the treaty doesn't include the United Kingdom.'

Lady Marina considered this information for a moment or two before expressing her opinion.

'I don't suppose we will ever want to be part of a European union,' she said, as if the idea was unthinkable. There were things she admired about Europe such as Paris fashions and the south of France but the rest of Europe she viewed as a foreign place of little interest.

'Well, I'm not sure that is right,' Edward said, for he doubted that Lady Marina had her finger on the pulse of Foreign Office work.

'Do you mean that we might want to join with them at some future time?' she asked, for it seemed an impossible notion to her.

'Yes, I think Britain may want to join at some future point, but I think we will find some opposition from the French,' he said, realising that he may have already said too much but feeling safe that his faux pas was unlikely to be reported to his superiors.

'Well, that I should live to see such a thing,' she retorted.

'You may well live to see it, Lady Marina,' he said laughingly, for she did not give the appearance of dying any time soon, he thought.

'And you are continuing with your Foreign Office career, even though you have inherited Grantham Manor from your father?' she asked.

'Well, my mother as you know still lives at the Manor but she is pressing me to give up my career and come back and manage things,' he admitted.

'And are you going to?' Lady Marina could not resist the question.

'Probably at some future point,' he said. 'We have a very good agent but there are decisions to be made, as I am sure Catherine is finding out, that really require a great deal of thought and my mother no longer feels she is up to it.'

'Yes, I understand exactly how she feels,' Lady Marina said. 'There is so much to deal with and so many decisions.'

He had been surprised when he had learned that Catherine had inherited the estate from her father because he had expected Lady Marina to be Sir Anthony's sole beneficiary, despite the fact that his own father had done exactly what Sir Anthony had done.

Both he and Catherine were only children. He had always known that the estate and the baronetcy were not tied so he had harboured no expectations on his own behalf. Yet, unlike his own mother, he thought Lady Marina more than capable of making all the decisions regarding Sir Anthony's estate, had she wished to exert herself.

'I remember when we last met, Catherine, you were on your way back to Australia,' he said. 'It was only some months ago, wasn't it? Circumstances have certainly changed for you.'

Realising he was treading on delicate ground, he did not come straight out and ask her if she planned to return to live in England permanently.

Catherine nodded, aware of the question he was wanting to ask but couldn't.

'They have changed,' she said, without elaboration. 'I'm still coming to grips with everything. I didn't know my father had so much business to deal with as he almost never discussed it.'

Edward finished his pre-lunch sherry and put the glass down on the table in front of him.

'My father was the same. I think he thought he had more time to show me the ropes, but as it turned out, he didn't, which is a pity.'

It was then that Catherine realised they had much in common, both inheriting estates and both being totally unprepared for the sudden responsibility thrust upon them; she because she did not know it was to happen; he because he had not taken the time to spend with his father, thinking there was plenty of time in the future.

'I assume your children are back in Australia?' he said, avoiding the mention of her husband because he had been warned on the

169

telephone by Lady Marina that Catherine's relationship with her husband was strained.

'Yes, and I miss them terribly,' she said. 'Paul is at boarding school in Sydney but Anthony, who has only just turned five, is at Prior Park with my husband and his family.'

She hesitated but did not add that she expected her husband and younger son to arrive in England in the next couple of weeks.

Her mother, ever alert for insights into her daughter's state of mind, noticed Catherine avoided using the word 'home' in describing where her children were.

She took it as the first real sign she had in fact begun to distance herself from her Australian life. Edward said nothing more as he offered his arm to Lady Marina to walk into the dining room for lunch.

They were seated in a small group at one end of the long table, which Catherine thought very unsuitable for small lunch parties. She wondered idly if she could change this routine while her mother was alive, for it seemed as if it belonged to another age entirely.

'We must see more of you,' Lady Marina said. 'I'm sure it would be a great help to Catherine to have your advice.'

She did not notice Catherine bridle at the insinuation that she could not manage the affairs of her father's estate without a man's help, but Edward noticed and sympathised.

'I'm not sure I have much practical advice to give Catherine,' he said, using his diplomatic skills to calm the atmosphere between mother and daughter, 'but you must come and visit me all the same and have lunch with my mother and me, now that I am back home for at least a month.'

Seeing Lady Marina's need for reassurance that he was not proposing a long tedious drive for her, he repeated the invitation.

'It's only twenty miles from here with the new road,' he said.

Lady Marina nodded, saying she would be delighted to hear from his mother, as if he needed reminding that Lady Marina could only properly respond to an invitation issued by his mother.

'I'm sure Catherine can manage to drive that distance very well,' she said, 'although if she goes back to Australia, I will most certainly need to hire a new chauffeur.'

It was a none too subtle form of blackmail that Catherine had begun to recognise: the many things her mother claimed only Catherine could do that would be a problem if she did not live permanently at Haldon Hall. Edward was surprised that Lady Marina did not have a chauffeur and said so.

'Oh, the last one retired and Sir Anthony got it into his head that he preferred to drive himself,' she said, as if the idea had been a foolish one from the outset.

Edward caught Catherine's eye and smiled, understanding the small irritations of daily life with a widowed mother all too well.

'Well, I'm sure there are many good men around, probably some former Army drivers, who would be grateful for the job,' he said. 'I could ask around if it would help.'

Catherine mouthed a 'thank you' to him as Lady Marina ignored the offer, concentrating instead on the meal in front of her.

'Our vegetable garden has been yielding wonderfully this year,' she said, noticing the spread of vegetables on her plate. 'It was Sir Anthony's pride and joy, you know.'

'Then let's drink a toast to Sir Anthony and his vegetables,' Edward said, in a bid to lighten the mood.

'And to the new baronet, if I'm not mistaken,' Lady Marina said, for she had been keeping this news from her daughter.

'Yes, I'm Sir Edward now,' he said, 'but I would have much preferred the title to pass to Catherine once her father passed on. It doesn't seem right, really, to switch to another branch of the family, just because there was no son to inherit.'

'I'm sure you will do the title great credit,' Catherine said, not wanting to spoil the moment.

'Well, there'll be pressure on you to have a son now,' Lady Marina said.

'You don't have to remind me of that, Lady Marina,' he said, chuckling almost to himself.

'My mother has reminded me daily of my obligations since it became clear that I would inherit the baronetcy from Sir Anthony. I feel sure she wants to advertise in The Times for a wife for me, if only I would let her.'

At this, they all laughed, even Lady Marina, who was known to take matters of succession very seriously.

'I sympathise with your mother,' she said. 'I hope you don't disappoint her.'

'I'll try not to, Lady Marina,' he said. 'I'll certainly try hard not to.'

Out of sight of Lady Marina, Edward and Catherine exchanged knowing glances, his eyes holding hers for the briefest of moments.

Richard's final act, before setting out on the long journey with his young son to England, was to sign his will which was witnessed by his sister Julia and her husband James.

Julia, curious as to how the matter had finally been settled, was pleased that her niece was accorded the same status as Richard's two sons. William, at the urging of his brother, signed his will too so that the matter could be resolved before Richard set off.

After the formalities had been completed and William returned the documents to the envelope ready for mailing back to their solicitor, it was Richard who was first to speak for he knew it was a disappointment to his sister that she had not shared in the Belleville inheritance. The value of the Dalrymple trust she would receive one day from her mother was little consolation against the lack of any future stake in Prior Park.

He tried to reassure her.

'I am sure the money Mother will leave you will be more than compensation for not having a share in Prior Park,' he had said.

Only then did she speak frankly to him, that the issue was not money but her love of the place that had been her home that was at the heart of her disappointment.

How could she explain she had no ownership of anything?

'You don't understand, do you?' she said finally. 'Mayfield Downs belongs to James, and after James, it will be John's. I have no real ownership of it just as Alice has no stake, except through William, in Prior Park.'

He was about to say: 'how could it be any different' but he stopped mid sentence. Of course it could be different.

It was then Richard understood how few women really had a

stake in the place where they lived and worked. It was their husbands' names on the title deeds. He wondered how he would feel, if the positions were reversed.

Only then did it occur to him that if he went to live at Haldon Hall, the positions would be reversed. He would have no ownership whatsoever. Just as for years Catherine had felt she didn't belong at Prior Park, he wondered if he too would feel like he didn't belong at Haldon Hall, even though it now belonged to his wife.

His life was now in a state of confusion. He did not know what he really wanted. Could he live without Catherine? Could he live without his beloved Prior Park? For it appeared very much as if he could not have both, yet there remained in his mind a lingering sliver of hope that there would be a solution awaiting him on the other side of the world.

The signing of the will had not in fact been Richard's final task before readying himself for the trip to England. Later that same afternoon, he pulled his brother aside with the news he had hired two men to be general labourers around the house and sheds, doing whatever jobs Charles Brockman assigned them, but in fact their real jobs would be to keep an eye out for unknown outsiders coming to the house.

William was relieved by the news but concerned also that two strangers would be arriving the next day and within hours Richard would be setting off on his long journey.

But Richard reassured his brother, for the security of their families was something that was upper most in their minds. Neither man considered that Alistair McGovern would make good his threat, but they were not prepared to take the risk.

With Richard away, he knew it left the house and its inhabitants almost completely dependent on William and Charles Brockman, should trouble of any kind occur. Above all, William wanted to protect Alice and Marianne.

William carefully wrote down their names. Jack Finch and Ted Lambert.

'How did you come across them?' William asked, for the men

were totally unknown to him.

'Through a contact who had seen army service with them,' Richard said. 'These two men stayed on in the army after the war for a few years. One was a sergeant and one was a corporal. They've been doing contract fencing work but they fancy something easier now, I think.'

William considered this information for a moment.

'Not too old are they?' he asked.

'No, they're only late thirties and both have done some amateur boxing up until a year or so ago,' Richard said. 'I think that makes them ideal candidates for what we want.'

'So have you told them what it is they'll be doing?'

'Yes,' said Richard, without elaborating. 'And I'm leaving Charles Brockman in charge of them. He can handle them. There's room for them in the single men's quarters.'

William nodded, relieved that Richard had been as good as his word, but wary of strangers in their midst. He would caution Alice to make sure Marianne stayed clear of them. They did not sound like suitable people for his young daughter to know but still he was reassured that, should trouble occur in Richard's absence, there were men he could call on to deal with it.

Alistair McGovern knew for certain that he would be the main topic of conversation at Prior Park between his two half brothers, given his reluctance to accept any settlement offered to him.

His mother Muriel regretted his decision to decline the substantial offer of money he said he had been offered.

'It's a very generous offer,' she had said when he told her the details of the latest offer but she could tell immediately from his contemptuous attitude that he had no plans to accept it.

'They think they can buy me off with trifles,' he said bitterly. 'And they want me to agree never to contact them again. And I must never take the Belleville name.'

His mother's tone was conciliatory. She could tell he was becoming obsessed with the issue. Above all she wanted him to move on with his life and forget about the Belleville family altogether, just as she had done. But she could not help reflecting on how the news must have been received by her lover's family.

'It must have been a shock to them to learn about your existence,' she said, 'but I understand what it feels like to be betrayed.'

He threw his head back almost violently, a strange sound emerging from the back of his throat. It was not reassuring.

'Betrayed? You talk about betrayal. I've been the one who's been betrayed the most, Mother,' he said, his voice becoming louder and more belligerent.

'Francis Belleville betrayed us both, and I want what rightfully belongs to us, to me, and that isn't a few pounds doled out every year as if we were some faithful old servants who should be grateful for the pittance they deign to give us.'

But his mother refused to join in his tirade, for her anger and disappointment were long spent.

'I still think it's a good offer and you should accept it, or at least continue to negotiate,' she said, her tone more measured now, for she could see how close to hysteria her son was.

'You may end up with nothing and how does that help your future?'

But he refused to listen to her good advice.

'This is about more than just money, Mother, it's about my name and my place in the world,' he said, the menace in his voice unmistakeable. 'If they don't make me a decent offer that says they respect me, then I will make them pay, make no mistake about that, I will make them pay.'

Muriel McGovern, not for the first time, shook her head slowly from side to side but said nothing more, for she knew there was nothing she could now say to influence him. He would make his own choices, good or bad, and all she could do was stand by and watch. It was beyond her now to cajole or urge him towards a sensible decision. He was beyond her influence and she could do nothing more for him.

CHAPTER 16: OCTOBER 1957

Edward Cavendish was as good as his word. A matter of days after his visit to Haldon Hall, an invitation to lunch arrived in the form of a handwritten note from Edward's mother Louise.

Lady Marina held it out to Catherine who scanned the short letter briefly. They were asked to lunch on the following Tuesday.

'Have you met Edward's mother previously?' Catherine asked, for she could not recall her name ever being mentioned.

'Once or twice, I believe, although I don't remember exactly how long ago,' Lady Marina said. 'Your father didn't care much for Edward's father Nicholas, as I recall, so our paths rarely crossed.'

Catherine's interest was piqued at this admission, for her father had hardly ever expressed a dislike for anyone, certainly not someone they knew.

'Why didn't Father like Edward's father?' she asked. 'That seems very strange since they were related and he must have known after a while that side of the family would inherit the baronetcy.'

Her mother was uncharacteristically silent, reluctant to respond to the question. Catherine, correctly interpreting her mother's lack of response, provided the answer she felt her mother did not want to say.

'He didn't think that side of the family was suitable, did he?' she asked. 'That's why he didn't seek them out.'

Her mother let out an audible sigh, as if it was unseemly to be discussing it now.

'I don't know why you've jumped to that conclusion,' she retorted, 'but yes, your father didn't see eye to eye with Nicholas. He thought he was a bit, you know, flashy.'

Catherine laughed out loud, for she could easily imagine that such a person would not meet her father's high standards.

'And was he flashy?' she asked, trying to imagine the settled country squire Edward had described as unsuitable to know.

'Well, I think he kept some unsavoury company at times when he was young but he wasn't disreputable,' she admitted. 'But I have to say his son seems very level headed and sensible by comparison.'

Having up to this point avoided any discussion of Edward beyond the commonplace, Catherine was in no mood to encourage her mother's unspoken presumption that her daughter was on the lookout for a new husband.

'Yes he does,' Catherine said, without elaborating further.

Her mother, sensing some further explanation was required about their lack of contact with Edward's family, looked up at her daughter.

'If you must know, we didn't move in the same circles,' she said, which was hardly an explanation at all. 'And when Nicholas died, your father was unwell so we wrote apologising for our absence at his funeral and explaining our reasons for not attending. We received a short note in acknowledgement. That was all.'

'So that was that,' Catherine said. 'No more contact until I met Edward a few months ago, quite by chance as it turned out.'

'Well, I'm pleased you did,' her mother said, 'for it saved us some embarrassment if you want to know the truth. We knew we should have invited his family over, for as you say, it became certain that the baronetcy would move to that side of the family. Your coming out would have been the perfect excuse but of course that never happened because of the war and then you headed off to Australia.'

Catherine nodded, aware that her years in Australia had left a gap in her parents' lives and, if she was honest, a gap in her own life. Only now was she beginning to reacquaint herself with the local families she had known as a girl.

Twelve years had brought a lot of change, to them and to her, but she was surprised at how many people in the local village remembered her, but now of course the men were doffing their hats and the women were, if not dropping curtsies, then certainly treating her with an unspoken deference she did not feel was her due.

The news that she had inherited everything from her father had circulated locally more quickly than news of Hitler's defeat. It was the speculation about what she would do with her hastily acquired Australian husband that split opinion although the idea that she would return to live permanently in Australia was dismissed out of hand.

'When I first made Edward's acquaintance, he spoke about going to Ascot races yet he works for the foreign office,' Catherine said. 'I'm surprised he had the opportunity.'

Lady Marina smiled.

'I don't think men like Edward are necessarily restricted by the same rules as the ordinary office clerk,' she volunteered although she did not know for certain.

'I think he has made it his business to be on good terms with the more illustrious parts of his father's family,' she continued. 'I think him rubbing shoulders with them at Ascot would be seen as good for his job and his prospects, if you ask me. And of course he excelled at Oxford.'

Catherine immediately understood what her mother was trying to tell her, without spelling it out in great detail. She could see that people like Edward, connected to the old influential families who once ruled by right, were ideal candidates for the Foreign Office. He was not an outsider. He was one of them. In the same circumstances Richard would have been treated, if not with outright suspicion, then with a reserve bordering on condescension.

'Anyway, shall we go to lunch next week at Grantham Manor?' Catherine asked, knowing full well that curiosity alone would be enough to get her mother to accept the invitation.

'Yes, of course, it would be churlish to refuse. I will write a note this afternoon accepting the invitation,' Lady Marina said. 'We have no good reason not to go.'

With that, Lady Marina headed out through the door towards the stairs. She was in the habit of doing all her correspondence at a small desk in her private sitting room on the first floor, which left Catherine the opportunity to take over her father's desk in the library, where she remained sitting for some time.

There were still many outstanding matters she was being asked to attend to, but at the top of the list the solicitor had marked in red pen in the margin of the most recent letter the necessity of her making a will, now that she was in possession of her father's entire estate. She understood the urgency but she was stalling, all the same, for she did not know what the future held for her and Richard.

He had admitted to her that he had been unfaithful but was that really the biggest stumbling block to them continuing to be together? In her heart she knew it was not. If she loved him she felt sure she could forgive him in time, but the question she could no longer answer with any certainty was exactly that: did she still love him? And even if she did, what compromises were they both prepared to make to continue their marriage?

Above all else that was the question to which she no longer knew the answer. She hoped and prayed his visit would settle the issue for her.

Just as it had surprised Catherine to learn of her husband's infidelity, it would not have surprised her in the least to learn that James Fitzroy had turned his amorous attentions elsewhere. On more than one occasion she had known him to overstep the boundaries of convention when he had greeted her on family occasions.

At times she had felt a faint frisson of excitement at the nearness of his body in those fleeting intimate moments but she had actively discouraged him. She had known right from the start that he would have needed little encouragement to go further and she felt for Julia that it should be so. Richard had never noticed and she had said nothing, for fear of a family row. It seemed harmless enough when examined rationally.

It had taken Susan Crawford just a matter of days to succumb to James Fitzroy's charm and flattery. At twenty-two, she felt she had endured the attentions of awkward, inexperienced boys her own age too many times. They were boys who lacked the social graces and the imagination to romance a girl. She had guessed that James was different and she had fallen quickly under his spell.

'You look lovely tonight,' James whispered, his lips against her hair.

'Thank you,' she said, as she tried to wriggle from his grasp.

'Where are you going?' he asked, for he was already desperate to pull her back into bed.

She held the slender wine glass aloft.

'I want to refill my glass,' she answered with a smile.

He watched as she walked across the bedroom and out into the living room, where he had opened a bottle of wine earlier in the evening.

He was disappointed she had quickly wrapped her dressing gown around her for he had hoped for an extended view of her naked body which he had been caressing only moments before.

But he need not have worried. She was back in the room very quickly, sipping the wine as she walked, the gown falling around her feet, his eyes feasting on her young slim body.

He reached up and pulled her down to him. As he did so he felt a small splash of the cold clear liquid on his chest but he ignored it.

She managed to place the wineglass on the bedside table just as he pulled her head down towards him, his lips hungry again for hers and she responding with a passion she had never felt before.

Later as they lay together, their bodies entwined, she asked the question she had wanted to ask from the beginning but hadn't, for fear of the answer.

He had not lied to her. He had simply not told her he was married, but she knew the truth now, for he was too well known for her not to be able to find out about him.

'I know you're married,' she said, but there was no accusation in her tone.

'So you think you know all about me now, do you?' His tone was teasing, for her knowing did not bother him in the least.

'I do wonder if your wife suspects anything,' she said, for she could not imagine that his wife could be anything but jealous and possessive of such a husband.

'I don't think I'll discuss my wife with you,' he said frostily. To James such a discussion was entirely off limits.

'What if she finds out about us?' Susan persisted.

James sat up, wondering if this was a threat for if it was, the girl would find herself quickly dumped and probably unemployed. She worked at the local stock and station agent of which he was a major client. They would do almost anything to oblige him.

But he laughed off the suggestion.

'Well I certainly won't tell her, and I don't expect you will either,' he said.

'No of course I won't tell her.'

She laughed nervously at the suggestion. One thing though had been made abundantly clear to her in that brief exchange. Whatever their relationship was or wasn't going to be, it would be on his terms. She was disappointed then for she had hoped for more. Like any girl, she hoped for marriage, even a marriage to a divorced man if he was wealthy enough. But she quickly sensed that James Fitzroy would not be that man.

For James what had started as a casual affair would end as a casual affair. The seduction had been almost too easy for him. If she wanted to end it now, he would be disappointed, nothing more.

He could never imagine another woman taking Julia's place as his wife. He hoped Julia never discovered his occasional dalliances or if she did, she would choose to ignore them. To him, they were largely meaningless. Julia would always be the love of his life. It was the sexual challenge of having another woman that he could not resist. He hoped they all understood that for there would only ever be one Mrs James Fitzroy and that was Julia.

Julia, meanwhile, would have remained entirely unaware of her husband's dalliances had it not been for an uncharacteristic lapse on his part. Asked by his wife what had delayed him in town until late in the evening on the most recent occasion, he had replied without thinking that he had attended a committee meeting of the Cattlemen's Union.

Julia thought nothing of it until later that day, knowing her brother William was on the same committee, she asked him, out of no real interest, how the meeting had gone. It was William's reply that caught her attention.

'There was no meeting this week,' he had said. 'The meeting's next week.'

He did not ask her why she had asked the question and she did not venture an explanation.

It was the first hint she had that her husband had not told her the truth about his whereabouts, but she did not immediately jump to the obvious conclusion, thinking perhaps that he had mixed up one committee name with another, because he seemed to her to be involved with so many these days.

Instead, on her way home from her weekly visit to Prior Park, she had instead turned her car in the direction of Springfield. She did not know why exactly or what she expected to find, but she did know her husband was away from home. Springfield was not a big city, she reasoned. It should be possible at least to find his car for he mostly parked on the riverbank.

With nothing more than this vague plan, she set off for the city, arriving mid afternoon. It did not take her long to locate her husband's brand new Holden, which was an unusual shade of pale green. It was parked, as she expected, on the riverbank in the shade of a tree. Having spotted the car, she did not know what to do next, so she parked further along the street and sat quietly in the car, thinking what her next move should be.

It was perhaps twenty minutes later she noticed a familiar figure in the distance. It was James, walking towards his car. He appeared to be alone. She was relieved for it seemed as if her suspicions were entirely baseless and her husband had made a genuine mistake in explaining his lateness.

'There must have been another committee meeting,' Julia thought. 'He was tired and he just got confused.'

She was about to head home when suddenly she noticed a girl approaching him. She did not know the girl and it was difficult to see her clearly at a distance, but she could not mistake the greeting the girl received from James. Aware that it was a public place, she noticed James look around cautiously before he enveloped the girl in his arms and began to kiss her.

Julia's head slumped forward, her arms cradling her head on the

182

steering wheel. Tears crept down her cheeks. She had always known that her husband was attracted to other women but she was sure it would go no further than a harmless flirtation. What she witnessed on the riverbank told her a different story.

She did not know how long she sat there. She did not know what would happen as a result of what she had seen. All she could remember, later, were the words constantly and repeatedly flashing through her mind: to love, honour and betray, for that was what it amounted to.

How many men did she now know who had taken their wedding vows and when it suited them, had betrayed those vows with other women? It hurt her to think the list of men had begun with her own father, included her elder brother but now, worst of all, her own husband.

Only by believing her marriage to James had been successful and they were happy could she feel the greatest sacrifice of her life had been worthwhile. It was only then was she able to believe the repudiation of her first born child had been worth the price. If her marriage ultimately proved to be a sham, what had she left? A son who would grow up in the image of his father; a marriage rendered worthless by the betrayal; and a daughter she had abandoned.

Tears cascaded down her cheeks unchecked. It was in that moment her world began to fall apart.

Edward Cavendish proved to be an excellent host and Grantham Manor proved to be a charming, if somewhat small, house, at least compared with Haldon Hall. Louise, his mother, was an agreeable, if nervous, hostess.

After lunch, Edward had taken them for a quick tour of the house, pointing out items of interest, including the portrait of his great grandfather, the first baronet, who was said to have profited handsomely from selling opium grown in India to the Chinese. It was an early portrait, much earlier than the one that hung in Haldon Hall, as Catherine remarked.

Standing together before the portrait, Edward remarked the likeness to his own father. On learning that a later more important portrait existed at Haldon Hall, he simply smiled.

'Such is the lot of younger sons, I'm afraid,' he said to Catherine. 'Younger sons inherit the items of lesser value or the things that are not esteemed at the time. No doubt your father possessed the most important silver too as well as the most important paintings.'

Catherine smiled in return, nodding in agreement, for she had recently inspected the silver cupboard at Haldon House and found it to be surprisingly full of exquisite pieces, but she did not mention it, nor did she mention the two J M W Turner paintings among the inventory of artwork belonging to her father's estate.

'You don't seem to have suffered too greatly for being from the line of the younger son,' Catherine said, her eyes moving around the room in unspoken appreciation of the obviously valuable artefacts adorning the room.

'You're right. We haven't suffered at all for it but you must remember both my grandfather and my father made, shall we say, propitious marriages.'

Catherine laughed.

'You mean they married for money?' she said boldly.

Edward demurred.

'That's not quite what I meant but they were both encouraged, I understand, to marry girls with considerable dowries.'

She realised then she knew very little about Edward's mother but her nervousness in hosting them suggested the role did not come naturally to her, as it did to Lady Marina.

'Tell me about your mother. Was she considered a good catch then?' Catherine asked in a forthright way, only later realising that she had perhaps been a little too forward in her quizzing of Edward. But he had not seemed to mind the question.

'Well, I was given to understand that her father was determined she would make a good marriage so he was quite strict about admitting possible suitors. But she did fall in love with my father and so the marriage eventually had her father's blessing,' he said, obviously recounting the story he had been told. 'My grandfather, I believe, relented when the size of the dowry was mentioned.'

They both laughed together for it seemed ludicrous to them now that marriages could have been as much a matter of business as of love.

Catherine was still curious though about his mother's family.

'So what did your mother's father do to make his fortune?' she asked, for she could not recall Edward's family ever being discussed in any detail at Haldon Hall.

'He started a business supplying automotive parts just as the car manufacturing business was getting going. It proved to be a stroke of genius,' he said. 'Of course during the war the factory was turned over to war work.'

'Obviously your mother didn't run the factory when her father died?' Catherine asked, for there had been no mention of other family.

If Edward was surprised at her curiosity, he did not say so.

'No, my mother had a younger brother, George, who was running it,' he said.

'After the war, it was taken over by a bigger firm. My mother had always been a silent partner but she was sad to see it slip out of family control. It was for the best though as it turned out. George, sadly, died in a boating accident in Monte Carlo only three years after the sale. He wasn't married so everything then went to my mother.'

'So your mother turned out to be quite the heiress?' Catherine said, attempting to lighten the mood.

'You could say that,' Edward said. 'We certainly haven't had to resort to selling off the paintings or the silver, or the land for that matter.'

'And that's a good thing too,' Lady Marina said, for she had been standing directly behind them. They had forgotten her presence but she had been listening intently nonetheless.

'And your career, Edward? Have you thought any more about that?' Lady Marina asked. It was more a statement than a question.

'As you know, my mother is pressing me to leave and manage the estate,' he said guardedly, 'but I haven't yet made a decision.'

She nodded, appreciating the dilemma he faced but sympathising with his mother.

'Yes, I understand the problem entirely,' Lady Marina replied. 'It's all very well relying on agents and lawyers but you must have the finger on the pulse yourself, as Catherine is finding. It's a complicated job. I'm sure your mother doesn't want to be burdened with it all.'

He smiled but said nothing. If this was another hint that Catherine might need his help in managing her father's estate and it would be better if he was close by, he guessed it would not be at all welcome.

But Lady Marina's conversation had moved on.

'On another matter entirely I assume you have received an invitation to the Duchess's birthday party?' Lady Marina asked.

He nodded.

'Yes, I've suddenly found myself in more demand than previously,' he said with a smile.

'And you, Lady Marina? I assume you also received an invitation?' he asked in turn.

'Yes, of course, but I declined,' she said quickly. 'I'm not inclined to go down to London for the sake of a birthday party but you should take Catherine if you are not escorting anyone else. It would be good for her to meet some people.'

He knew exactly what Lady Marina meant by 'meeting some people'. He noticed Catherine's embarrassment at her mother's audacity but he did not mind at all. In fact, he had been on the verge of suggesting it himself.

Each time he met her it was with a growing sense of anticipation mixed with unease. He knew he was becomingly increasingly and ir-revocably attracted to her. Was she likely to divorce her Australian husband, as Lady Marina had hinted? He found the answer to this question was becoming more and more important to him with each and every passing day.

CHAPTER 17: OCTOBER 1957

James Fitzroy remained blissfully unaware his wife had discovered his secret for several days. If he noticed her coldness towards him, he did not remark it. Instead he went about his days as usual.

With a measure of self-control she had previously lacked, Julia decided she would confront her husband at a time of her choosing. She longed to confide in Alice and ask her advice but that was impossible. How could she tell Alice what she had seen? She would be asking Alice to side with her against her own brother and she knew instinctively Alice would never do that. Alice would simply not believe her.

To confide in her mother was to risk a conversation that might stray into dangerous territory. She knew her mother would quickly condemn James, not realising that her own husband had been guilty of the same treachery. Nor could she discuss what she had discovered about her husband with either of her brothers. William would be outraged but he would tell Alice. Richard was about to leave for England and had troubles of his own. She realised then how much she missed Catherine, for she felt that only Catherine would be sympathetic and understanding.

For the first time in her life, she felt very alone. She had not expected such a betrayal from her own husband. Had she not seen it with her own eyes, she would have dismissed any gossip about him as merely the output of malicious tongues. But she had seen it with her own eyes and it had been devastating. Having seen his betrayal, she could not ignore it.

In the cold light of day, she wondered how many others there had been. She tried to remember how many times he had been unaccountably late home. In fact she realised it was something she had grown used to in recent times. The thought that this was all to cover his casual affairs brought on another wave of despair.

He would deny it, she knew that. He would try to charm her and reassure her. But the evidence of her own eyes could not be denied.

Her mind was in turmoil. If she confronted him, was she prepared to push for a separation and the end of their marriage? If she did that, where would she go?

The thoughts tumbled through her mind, one after the other, until she could make no sense of them. But she could not, she knew, continue on as before, with him not knowing she had discovered his dirty little secret.

It was late afternoon. She had been waiting for him for some time, an unread magazine on her lap, her untouched drink beside her, her body rigid with an anger that had built slowly but inexorably over the preceding days.

It was nearly dark before she heard the unmistakeable sound of his footsteps on the verandah. She knew he would first walk along the hallway to the bathroom and then to the living room. It was a well-established habit each evening he was at home for dinner. The crystal decanter was kept filled with his preferred single malt whisky for his pre-dinner drink.

'Ah, there you are, darling,' he said, as he headed towards the sideboard to pour his own drink. 'What are you doing, sitting in the dark like this?'

He reached down first to one lamp and then another. The room was suddenly almost ablaze with light. Still he did not look directly at her, instead walking back to the doorway to shout down the hallway to the housekeeper Mrs Fry who came bustling into the room. He handed her the empty soda syphon which she hurried away to replenish.

Julia watched all this in silence. She did not trust herself to speak. She knew everything, even the most banal words, would come out in an angry tirade. Instead she waited until the housekeeper had returned with the soda syphon and left the room once again. Only then did she begin to speak, slowly at first, before the deep well of anger within her rushed forth in a string of accusations.

As she was speaking, she got up and walked across the room to confront him. They were close together now. She could see his face. She could see the struggle within him as to whether he should admit anything to her or go on lying. In the end he went on lying.

'What's this? You think I've been playing around with another woman? What gave you that idea, darling?' His tone was joking, condescending, almost as if he was talking to a child.

Julia was angered afresh by his casual dismissal of her accusations.

'I saw you,' she blurted out. 'I saw you three days ago on the riverbank near your car. I saw you kiss another woman. Not just any kiss. A passionate kiss. The kiss of a lover.'

He reached out to her, trying but failing to pull her into his arms. He wanted to silence her. He didn't want to hear anymore, but she wasn't finished. In fact she was far from finished.

'Who is she? Are you going to tell me?' she demanded, her face flushed with anger.

He too was angry now. More with himself for being so careless than with her for finding him out. But having already denied it, he could see no way forward but to continue to do so. He drained his glass.

'I don't know what you're talking about,' he said, his voice more serious, as if she was being unfair to him in not accepting his denials.

Julia laughed. It was a hollow unhappy laugh. She had expected him to deny everything so she was not surprised. Now she must go further. She must push him towards an admission. Towards the truth.

'Her name is Susan Crawford, in case you need reminding, and she works at the stock and station agent's office,' Julia said, almost triumphantly.

The revelation silenced him momentarily.

'If you really wanted to go after another girl, I'd have done it less

189

publicly,' she said finally, the sarcasm in her voice unmistakable.

'So you don't accept my denial, then, I take it?' he asked.

He poured himself another drink. Julia noticed the slightest tremor in his hands.

'You think I'm involved in another relationship that means something to me?'

Julia seized on his words. It was the first hint he had given that she was right. It was not quite an admission of his guilt for he had carefully sidestepped that.

'I don't know if it means anything to you,' she said quietly, 'but you will need to decide what means the most to you.'

He could not mistake the emphasis or the carefully chosen words. There was a greater threat now, he understood, in her ultimatum than in her earlier accusations.

'What do you mean?' he asked, playing for time, as if he didn't already know.

'Let me put it plainly,' she said. 'You can have all the girls you like, if that's what you want, but you can't have them and me.'

She had not planned to say it quite that way, but now she had said it, she saw it was the only possible way to deal with the situation, even if it felt overly dramatic and clumsy.

'Are you threatening to leave me?' he asked, wanting her to spell out her threat.

He was suddenly alarmed as the prospect of his marriage disintegrating before his eyes became very real.

'It's what I said,' she replied. 'I will not play gooseberry to your fancy girls. I deserve more. You end it, or I end this marriage.'

She had said it now. He had goaded her into the final ultimate threat.

His face had grown pale. He had never seen her like this. Determined, in charge, mature and decisive. He glanced at her. For the first time, he was certain she meant it. He could see it was useless to attempt to charm or cajole her. It had all gone very badly. It had never occurred to him that he would have this particular discussion with his wife. He had been totally unprepared for it.

Julia had crossed the room to put some distance between them.

She was now hovering in the doorway onto the verandah, as if she was preparing to walk out of the house that very moment.

She was trembling with anger and nervous tension for the words had forced themselves from her. She had not meant to go so far but the enormity of the betrayal and his reluctance to admit to it had left her no choice at all.

'I hear you,' was all he said. 'I hear you.'

She nodded but said nothing more.

'You are the only woman for me, you know that, don't you?' he said finally. There was almost a pleading note in his voice. 'You'll never have cause to doubt me again.'

He avoided looking directly at her for fear his dramatic declaration would be rendered false by the slightly superior smile hovering on his lips. He felt a small sense of triumph that he had endured the emotional storm, which now appeared spent. He was sure an expensive gift would bring the unhappy episode to a satisfactory conclusion.

Julia nodded but said nothing more, for she felt there was nothing more to say that would not inflame the situation further. She did not want to hear the sordid details of his casual adultery.

But she had wanted to say, 'You have a strange way of showing it' but she did not for it seemed such a predictable thing to say. She knew him well enough to know that goading him would simply bring forth another meaningless declaration of his commitment to her.

She brushed past him.

'I must see how the dinner is going,' she said, as if they had been having a mundane conversation of the kind that happened almost every day.

He turned back towards the sideboard. As she left the room, she heard him unstopper the decanter and pour himself another whisky.

Was that to be the first of many such conversations, she wondered? Next time, he might be more discreet but she doubted his ability to remain faithful to her, despite his easily given promises.

It was only then that she began to wonder if it really mattered to her at all. She felt a creeping sense of disappointment engulf her. Not with his infidelity but with the fact that, deep within her, she wondered if she really cared enough for it to matter.

Had her mother been better served by her blissful ignorance of her husband's infidelity? It was a shocking thought but one that came unbidden to Julia's mind. Had she turned away from the riverbank a few moments earlier, she would never have seen her husband's passionate embrace of another woman. She would have thought that her suspicions where totally unfounded.

Was it just her pride that had suffered? To the outside world, they appeared happy, contented and still in love. Their daily life together had been comfortable and even companionable. She did not know when the passion faded from other marriages. Did it just dwindle away as theirs had done? She did not know that either but she knew she would be the one who would be judged a failure if it became known she had failed to keep her husband by her side.

Had he known without being told that he would always take second place in her heart? Had that pushed him towards other women? Or was that making excuses for him that he did not deserve?

She did not know the answers to these questions. But she knew for certain she would never trust him again.

Haldon Hall sparkled in the late autumn afternoon light as the taxi approached. Inside the taxi an excited little boy craned his neck for the first sight of his mother. His father, less certain of his welcome, merely smiled at his young son's eager little face pressed against the car window.

As the taxi stopped, the door of the house opened for their approach had not gone unnoticed.

Richard opened the car door and five-year-old Anthony almost fell out, his keenness to see his mother overwhelming him. Within seconds, he was wrapped in her arms, his face smothered with kisses. He was examined and fussed over. At first he clung to his mother's skirt, not wanting to let her go. Then he proceeded to explore the garden where he had often played. For him it was like a second homecoming.

Then it was Richard's turn to be welcomed.

He held his wife briefly in his arms. He thought the quick kiss she bestowed was as much for the audience behind her, especially her mother, as it was for him. Their eyes met briefly but she averted her gaze, as if uncertain now how to treat him.

As they walked together into Haldon Hall, he could see that she had changed in the months they had been apart. He could see too with his own eyes just how her circumstances had changed. While outwardly Lady Marina remained in charge of the household, he was quick to notice the subtle changes in how the household staff treated his wife. There was a little more deference in their approach. He sensed their anxiety to win her approval, even in the small things.

At Haldon Hall, she was now mistress of all she surveyed. He knew then, as if he had not known it all along, that she would never return with him to Prior Park. This was her destiny. This was where she belonged. Haldon Hall was where her future lay.

Within his heart, he knew then their marriage was doomed, not because of his unfaithfulness for she might have eventually forgiven that, but because she belonged at Haldon Hall and he did not. He could not imagine a life without the wide horizon and the bright blue sky of the Australian bush. Looking at the lush green countryside and the lowering grey skies of England, he felt a sense of deep melancholy that only the sun on his back and the smell of the eucalypts could cure.

'Did you have a good trip?' Lady Marina asked, breaking into his reverie.

Richard, standing at the bottom of the stairs, suitcase in hand, replied politely.

'We did, Lady Marina, and Anthony wasn't sick at all, which was a blessing.'

'And young Paul and the rest of your family are well?' she asked, again hardly interested in the reply, except to hear reports of her favourite grandson.

'They are, thank you. And Paul is doing well. He will be home in early December at the end of the school year,' he volunteered.

'You should send him over here for his final school years,' Lady Marina said, without preamble. 'I'm sure I can get him into Eton.'

Richard suspected the idea had been taking shape in her mind for some time. He wondered if she had discussed it with Catherine. It was an idea he was keen to quash before it had taken root.

'He's happy where he is and doing well at Shore in Sydney. I don't think I would want to disrupt that arrangement,' Richard said, with an air of finality, as he headed upstairs to unpack.

Lady Marina said nothing more on the topic. She did not want to have a disagreement with her son-in-law on the first evening of his visit but she certainly meant to raise the topic again with her daughter.

If Edith Henderson had hoped her young charge would be more settled following the discovery of her real father, she was to be disappointed.

Pippa had certainly changed for the better. Her sunny outlook on life had returned, replacing the morose and emotionally distant girl of a few months before. But she pestered Edith almost daily for news of her father. Every day she returned from school, her first question was: has there been a letter?

On the days that she found a letter from him propped up on the sideboard, she was almost delirious with excitement. Today was one of those days.

Edith waited patiently while the girl read the highly-prized letter.

'So what does he say?' she asked finally. 'Is there any news I should know?'

In truth, she was as anxious as Pippa was to have news of him. Not for her own sake but for the girl's sake. She was certain he was not the kind of man to let his daughter down but even so, as each letter arrived from him, she was reassured that her faith in him had not been misplaced.

Today, the girl's face shone with joy and expectation.

'He's booked his ticket to travel to see us next month,' she said, excitedly waving the letter.

'Here, read it, Aunt Edith,' she said for she always shared the letters with her great aunt. There was no guile or cunning about the girl now. She wanted to share her happiness with the woman who had taken her in and cared for her.

Edith scanned the letter quickly.

'Well, that's not so long now,' she said, 'and you'll be seeing your father again.'

'It's wonderful,' Pippa said, retrieving the precious missive from Edith. 'I can't wait.'

The girl danced excitedly around the room, almost knocking over a precious vase. But Edith did not mind. To see the girl's spirits restored was worth almost anything.

But still, she exerted a firm but loving hand on the girl.

'Well, one of the first questions he will want to know is how you are doing at school,' Edith said, 'so I suggest you get in and do your homework.'

Pippa slumped into a chair. Homework was obviously the furthest thing from her mind, but she did not bridle at the advice.

'I'll do it directly,' she promised.

Her aunt nodded, happy with the response. Pippa was a good student and in recent months her results had begun to improve beyond even her expectations.

Was it possible that she could go on to university after she finished school? It was only in the past month or so that Edith had begun to harbour such ambitions for her young charge.

In writing the letter, Philippe had been careful not to raise expectations, saying only that he expected to stay for two weeks, and some of that time would be taken up at the medical conference where he was to present a paper.

What he did not say, for fear of later disappointment, was that he had applied for a teaching post at one of the major Sydney hospitals.

For the first time in years, the prospect of a new city and a new professional challenge had raised his spirits. New York now seemed less important to his own future. His discovery of his daughter had given his life outside his work real meaning and he was determined to do as much as he could for her. If that meant moving to the other side of the world, then he would do it gladly for the guilt he felt at her having been abandoned as a baby to an unknown fate continued to haunt him, even though he now knew her entire history.

Finding Pippa had brought back memories of Julia he tried hard to suppress. Now, in idle moments, he found himself speculating on how her life had turned out. He wondered if she was happy. He wondered if her attachment to him had become a memory revived only occasionally by thoughts of the child she had given up. Without knowing for sure, he was convinced it would have been the defining event in her life. He was sure she would look back with sadness and guilt, just as he had always done since the chance discovery of her letter telling him of her pregnancy. A letter received too late for him to help her.

James Fitzroy, of course, knew none of this about his wife of ten years. Instead he had put her occasional sullenness down to temperament. Now of course her unhappiness had a reason that he understood. He was angry with himself for his carelessness for he did not want his marriage to founder. It was the bedrock around which his comfortable life functioned. She was the mother of his son. He did not berate himself for his infidelity, only for his stupidity in being found out.

It had been a week since Julia's revelation that she knew about his affair. There had been chilly silences between them for days following their argument. He knew that he had to make amends. He wanted his life to return to what it had been.

He hoped that a gesture would win her forgiveness so he surprised her with news that he had booked a trip to Sydney.

'I've booked tickets for us to travel to Sydney next month,' he said, holding the tickets aloft as if she might need proof.

He was momentarily afraid that she would not want to go, but the prospect of a change of scene and a visit to Sydney was enticing enough for her to unbend a little towards him.

She took the tickets from him and read through the travel itinerary.

'Well, that will be nice,' she said, without any real enthusiasm in her voice.

She was beginning to discover how hard it was to pretend everything was as it had been. Yet it was clear to her that was exactly how James wanted it to be, and indeed, believed it to be.

'Am I coming too?' asked a still childish voice from the doorway.

'No,' James said to his son, 'you are not coming. You are staying right here and going to school as you always do.'

With that the three of them headed towards the dining room where Mrs Fry, the housekeeper, was beginning to fret about the hot meal already set out on the table that was beginning to cool.

CHAPTER 18: NOVEMBER 1957

It was several days before Richard found the opportunity to be alone with his wife. He had suffered the humiliation of being shown to a guest room on his arrival in silence.

Catherine had not engineered the meeting; in fact it appeared to him she was deliberately avoiding it. But Richard, desperate to discuss their situation, suggested they take advantage of an uncharacteristically fine day and walk towards the village. Anthony, renewing his acquaintance with the elderly gardener, was happy doing the small tasks allotted to him and did not notice his mother and father walking together down the driveway.

Richard had rehearsed his opening lines to Catherine so many times the words had begun to sound stale to his own ears. They were the very words Catherine both dreaded and expected to hear.

'Catherine,' he said as they walked together slowly along the path to the village, 'I think we should both admit this marriage is over. I don't see a way forward for us now. I think you've made that pretty clear.'

They stopped and she turned to face him. For his part he had never imagined it would come to this. He had always thought there would be a solution that would bring their two worlds harmoniously together but being at Haldon Hall, now that she owned the estate and had responsibility for it, the idea seemed fanciful. Here she had the status she lacked in Australia. At Prior Park, despite her best efforts, she had hardly seemed more than a guest. He could see that more clearly now.

She looked up at him, taking in the sun bronzed face and the tall athletic build that had first attracted her. She still liked him but the spark had gone. He was a good father to her children. But now their worlds had divided irrevocably she was no longer willing to give up her childhood home and all the responsibilities she had inherited to return with him to live in Australia. She had tried, and failed, to imagine herself back at Prior Park.

Yet she hesitated before she spoke. She did not want to hurt him despite the fact that he had betrayed her with another woman. She believed in her heart that his infidelity had been a predictable response to the cooling of their marriage and her growing dissatisfaction with her Australian life.

'I did try, you know, to make a life with you in Australia,' she said quietly, with a touch of genuine sadness.

He noticed she was already speaking in the past tense.

'But I belong here. This is where my family ties are,' she said, as if he hadn't already known that.

'And mine are not,' he added, unnecessarily.

'And yours are not,' she said, echoing his words. 'I just couldn't see you being able to settle here.'

She glanced around, mentally comparing the traditional English landscape that surrounded them on all sides with the vastness of the Australian bush she knew he loved.

There was a hint of wistfulness in her voice but he could see that she was prepared to face the truth about their marriage. He was glad she was honest. He would have admired her less if she had tried to persuade him to settle at Haldon Hall and travel backwards and forwards between the two countries, never quite settling in either place.

She had faced up to the fact there was no practical solution for them. Their two different worlds had come together briefly but now they must separate, each of them returning to where they belonged.

'I agree with you,' he said. 'You belong here and I belong 12,000 miles away.'

His head and shoulders slumped just a little, as if in defeat. She noticed it but chose to ignore it. Instead she steered the conversation towards the practical matters that had been occupying her mind.

'And what of the children?' she said. 'What do you propose?'

She was cautious, waiting for him to say something. It was clear to both of them it was the only topic left to discuss. On the subject of their marriage and its failure, there was nothing more for either of them to say.

Richard did not answer immediately but he could see that she wanted him to declare what his plans were. He knew instinctively then that she harboured hopes of Anthony staying with her.

'You want Anthony to stay with you, don't you?' he asked, without preamble.

She nodded. She held her hand up to her eyes. Just then the sun had come out so she had to shield her eyes from the glare.

'You're right,' she said. 'I do want him to stay with me. He's only young. He's just turned five. He really needs me.'

She was making a strong case, as he knew she would, but he ignored her plea for the moment. He wanted to make sure it was Anthony's best interests she was protecting, and not a sudden surge of selfishness on her part to deprive him of his children.

'And what about Paul?' he asked.

In a level voice, she spoke reasonably and sensibly, knowing that was the only way to influence him.

'Well Paul is much older. He'll be twelve early next year,' she said, 'and he's been away at school for several years now. I don't think we should disrupt that arrangement, do you?'

He nodded, relieved that he did not have to mount an argument for Paul to be kept in Australia. But he had to be sure that she was being entirely truthful with him.

'You know your mother wants to bring him across here to finish his schooling at Eton,' he said, anxious to see if she had known of her mother's proposal.

Surprised, Catherine looked up at him.

'Really, did she say that?' she asked. 'Paul is a favourite of hers since we brought him over as a one year old, but she hasn't suggested it to me.'

He was relieved then that he was not fighting a battle on two fronts. Setting aside the question of Anthony for a moment, he asked the obvious question.

'And when would you see Paul?' he asked. 'He's too young to travel alone and will be for another few years yet.'

She had already worked it out. The fact that she had ready answers to his questions did not surprise him.

'I'll come across a couple of times a year to Sydney to see him,' she replied. 'If I have Anthony with me, then I will bring him too.'

It troubled Richard that the two brothers were not to be brought up together but, in the end, he could not deny Catherine her younger child. With an age gap of more than six years, he doubted the two boys would form a close bond until adulthood, and perhaps not even then. He and William were very close in age, which had made them natural companions, but he knew the gulf between a five year old and an eleven year old was a big one.

Knowing that he had repeatedly stated that his children would be brought up in Australia, Catherine was anxious for his response.

'If I agree to Anthony being brought up with you for the time being,' he said, attempting to qualify the arrangement, 'if he decides when he is older that he wants to come back and live in Australia, you must respect that.'

Again, she nodded, relieved that he was not going to be obstinate. She knew without his cooperation, her hopes of keeping Anthony with her would be doomed.

'I would agree to that,' she said, without any hesitation, 'although I'm surprised, if I may say so, that you will agree to it.'

He smiled then. She could see the remnants of the charm that had captivated her years before.

'You must think me very hard hearted,' he said, 'not to be influenced by the sight of a gleaming young face pressed up against the car window desperate to see his mother.'

She laughed quietly at the mental image of her five year old. She knew exactly what Richard had described.

'Thank you, Richard, for agreeing to the arrangement,' she said.

She reached up and kissed him on the cheek. This time he could sense genuine affection in the gesture.

'I will do my best to bring him up as you would want. He will be a son you will be proud of,' she said.

He could see the look of relief on her face that she was not to be denied both her children.

For him the separation from his small son would be painful but he was an adult who understood the reasons for it, reasons of his own making. He found he could not deprive the child of the unconditional love of his mother to satisfy his own ego. He knew it was right to put Anthony's interests above his own, as hard as it would be for him.

They walked on in silence for some way. They both knew there was one further step ahead of them. Who would initiate the divorce?

But in the companionable goodwill that existed between them as they walked along, it seemed that further discussion about the dismantling of their marriage could wait for another day.

Three days later, Richard stood in the driveway of Haldon Hall, bags packed and ready, waiting for the new chauffeur to bring the car around to drive him to the station, from where he would begin the long journey back home.

He stood awkwardly beside Catherine. He noticed how Anthony clung desperately to his mother's skirt. He and Catherine had little more to say to each other, apart from the reassurances that both children would be looked after. The expensive necklace and bracelet he had planned to give her as a reconciliation gift remained ungifted in his suitcase.

'I guess we need to get the lawyers started?' Richard said finally, although he was unsure as to the jurisdiction in which their divorce should occur.

'I will get the proceedings started,' Catherine said, in a moment of decisiveness for which he was grateful. 'We married in England so I guess it should be an English divorce. The solicitor will write to you about it.'

He nodded in agreement. To him it was just paperwork. He would simply do as she asked.

At the last moment, Anthony seemed to understand that his

father was going away but he and his mother were staying behind. The child did not know how to respond but his father picked him up and gave him a quick hug.

'Now, you be good for your mother, and your grandmother,' he said, as he put the boy back down, and dropped down to his level.

'You won't be seeing me for a while but you will live here with Mummy,' he told his son.

The boy nodded warily as if he understood what his father was saying.

Richard got into the car and the door closed behind him. Within minutes, he was gone from their sight and they had turned to walk back into the house.

In the car Richard slumped back into the seat, emotionally and physically spent. Even the prospect of returning to Prior Park could not lift his spirits for he had begun to realise what lay ahead of him. He knew he would take time to adjust to a life without Catherine. Deep down, he still loved her. The certainties of his life had been ripped asunder. He did not know as he began the long trip back home what life would hold for him, but he knew he could not return to Prior Park and resume his life as if nothing had happened. Such was the price of a failed marriage.

John Bertram was one person who could be relied upon to lift Richard's spirits, so it was with a mixture of relief and surprise that Richard greeted his old friend in the cocktail bar of the Savoy Hotel.

'John, I wasn't expecting to see you here,' Richard said, as the two men greeted each other warmly. 'I thought you were to be in Sydney by now, based on your schedule.'

John smiled broadly.

'A little birdie told me about your plans so I took a few days off so I could be here to see you,' he said. 'In fact Catherine told me you would stay overnight in London before heading back home so it was more than a lucky guess. And where would I find you but in the bar?'

Richard signalled for the waiter, his low spirits suddenly lifting at the prospect of an evening in John's company. Two large whiskies were quickly produced. Richard sipped his appreciatively.

'I take it Catherine's told you what's happening then?' Richard asked.

John nodded, his mood suddenly less buoyant.

'Yes, she has, old man,' John said. 'How are you about it all? She told me that Anthony is staying with her. That was considerate of you.'

Richard looked across at his friend, aware now that Catherine had discussed their situation with John in some detail. But Richard did not mind. John had, after all, been the only relative at their wedding and a good and loyal friend to both of them so it did not surprise Richard that he knew so much already.

'I thought about it and in the end I couldn't deprive her of Anthony,' he said. 'I think he really needs his mother at his age. I know I could have fought it, but I didn't want the marriage to end in bitterness and recrimination.'

John could see how much the decision had cost Richard. He wanted to reach out to his friend, to make some friendly gesture, but the moment was gone. Instead, he tried to reassure him.

'You did the right thing, mate,' he said. ' You know you did. There's no reason why the children should suffer. Like you I think the boy is better off with his mother at his age.'

John sat back in his chair to gauge the effect of his words. He drained his glass and looked around immediately for a waiter but there was none to be seen just then.

'Paul, our older boy, is in school in Sydney so he'll stay in Australia,' Richard continued. 'I'm just sorry the boys won't grow up together, but it can't be helped now.'

'Yes, it's a pity,' John said, 'but hopefully they'll spend time together in the holidays. Did Lady Marina attempt to put her oar in?'

Richard laughed at John's perceptive question, for she had indeed attempted to influence the arrangements for her grandsons and she had not taken failure well.

'As you probably expected, Lady Marina had some plans for Paul to come across to England and finish school at Eton, which I quickly scuppered,' Richard said.

John chuckled. Lady Marina had turned out to be as predictable as he had expected in trying to influence the arrangements between Richard and Catherine.

But there was one question that remained unanswered. He knew now was the only time he could get to ask it.

'Did Catherine actually suggest you stay on at Haldon Hall with her?' John asked, for he was uncertain as to whether it was Richard who refused to stay or Catherine who didn't suggest it.

Richard shook his head, somewhat surprised at the question but prepared to answer his friend truthfully.

'No, she didn't. I don't think she thought it was worthwhile asking,' he admitted. 'I think she felt my feelings about where I wanted to live were already well known and it wasn't England.'

John felt keenly the internal tug of war of loyalty that was playing out in his head. He was torn between supporting his best friend and defending his cousin.

'It can't have been easy for her, living in Australia for all those years,' John said, suddenly aware that he wanted Richard to know he understood both sides. 'She wasn't born to the Australian way of life.'

'No, I know that, and I do wonder if she had not been pregnant whether we would have ever got married,' Richard said, his mood suddenly growing reflective, 'but it's all water under the bridge now. She has a new life ahead of her now, back at her childhood home and mistress of all she surveys.'

There was just a hint of bitterness and disappointment in his voice.

It was then John Bertram remembered an article from the social pages of a newspaper he had carefully cut out and folded into his wallet. He pulled it out to show Richard.

'Your wife's good fortune in inheriting all her family's wealth has not gone unnoticed,' John said, handing over the small clipping.

Richard read the small article carefully:

Mrs Richard Belleville (pictured here) is expected to spend more of her time in England now that it has been confirmed she is the sole beneficiary of her father's substantial estate. Sir Anthony Cavendish passed away recently after a short illness, leaving his daughter as the mistress of the family's fine country house Haldon Hall in Derbyshire. It is as-

sumed her mother Lady Marina Cavendish will continue to live at the Hall. Mrs Belleville was photographed here alongside her distant cousin Sir Edward Cavendish, who has inherited the baronetcy from Sir Anthony. They were attending the recent birthday celebrations of the Duchess of Devonshire. Both Mrs Belleville and Sir Edward are distantly related to the Duke of Devonshire. It is known that mothers with eligible daughters have taken a renewed interest in the unmarried Edward Cavendish, whose Foreign Office career is said to be flourishing, following his elevation to the baronetcy. Mrs Belleville, the former Catherine Cavendish, married the Australian Bomber Command hero Squadron Leader Richard Belleville, DFC, at the end of the war and has subsequently been living in Australia, apart from regular return visits to see her parents.

Richard read the small article through carefully. He was surprised that Catherine had not mentioned the event to him. To him it simply served to illustrate the gulf between them. He was equally surprised at the knowledge the gossip columnist had about what he regarded as private family matters. He squirmed at the description of himself as a Bomber Command hero, for he had only done what thousands of others had done alongside him, many of whom had paid a much higher price.

He handed the clipping back to John, who folded it and returned it to his wallet. John knew better than to comment on the description of Richard's war exploits so he was silent on that front.

'Did you meet the new baronet?' John asked.

'No, Catherine told me about him, of course, but I believe he was busy with his Foreign Office work while I was there,' he said.

He was thoughtful for a moment.

'She did not tell me though that he was young and good looking and that she'd been photographed alongside him at a society event,' he added.

There was a hint of jealousy and just the faintest hint of suspicion in his voice. It suddenly struck him that Sir Edward Cavendish would have been seen as a far better suitor for Catherine than an Australian intent on dragging her half way around the world.

The same thought had occurred to John Bertram but he did not say as much. He realised then that Catherine had been very cautious in what she had told him about Edward Cavendish. He thought Richard would have to be blind not to see that they were two young people enjoying each other's company.

He wondered then if he had been right to show him the clipping, but it was only as they looked at the article together that the full implications of it had dawned on John and by then it was too late. All he could do was reassure his friend that Catherine was simply being kind to her most recently discovered, not to mention recently elevated, family member.

But he could see Richard was far from happy at seeing his wife written about in such a gossipy way. He said nothing more about it but it was plain it had caused him more heartache than he was willing to admit.

'Let's have some dinner,' John said, in an effort to brighten Richard's mood.

Richard nodded and together they headed towards the hotel dining room, where they were shown immediately to a table. The process of ordering dinner and drinks was a welcome distraction for them both and their talk became more general, reverting to the lively banter of their earlier more carefree days.

CHAPTER 19: NOVEMBER 1957

It was only a matter of days later that Richard found himself enveloped in the warmth of the late spring sun in Sydney. He noticed how the harbour sparkled as it stretched away to the east and west on either side of the bridge. But his taxi took so little time to make the journey across the expanse of water he almost wished he had asked the driver to slow down so he could take in the view, which never ceased to amaze him.

But sightseeing was not his purpose today. He was headed to his elder son's school on the northern side of the harbour, not far from the famous bridge. It was the school both he and William had attended and while they had both said they would have preferred to go to school locally, when it came time to choose a school for Paul, he had not hesitated. He knew it was important for his elder son to mix in social circles that were only available beyond the narrow confines of Prior Park and its surrounds. He reasoned that when it came time for Paul to manage the Belleville inheritance, which, as the eldest heir, Richard fully expected him to do, the contacts he would make at the elite school could help him in the task.

But none of this he reflected upon today. He had telephoned the school in advance requesting permission to take his son out for the day and it had taken much persuasion on his part for them to agree to it.

So he was pleased to see his son waiting for him in the gravel driveway. He hugged the boy briefly and together they got back into the taxi.

'Where shall we go?' Richard asked, for he wanted the day out to be a treat. Paul did not yet know his father was the bearer of bad news.

'Let's go to Bondi,' Paul said suddenly, for the novelty of being given the choice of destinations had made him bolder in his choice. He was not used to seeing his father like this so he was keen to take advantage of the situation.

'Bondi it is,' Richard announced to the driver, who was happy at the prospect of a good fare. He had quickly sized up his passenger and decided he wasn't a man to quibble about the size of a taxi fare. Anyone who could afford to send his son to a posh boarding school was certainly able to afford a few quid for a taxi, he reasoned.

Forty-five minutes later, father and son were strolling along the seafront, where wave after wave pounded the sand. They stood together for a while marvelling at the skill of the surfboard riders on their long balsa boards. Then they moved along the beach to a quieter area where they stopped and leaned against the railing over-looking the beach.

It was only then that Richard found the words to tell his elder son that the family he had known as the bedrock of his young life was to be split asunder and that his younger brother was to live permanently in England with their mother, who would not be returning to live in Australia.

Paul was silent at first, for he had not expected such terrible news. He did not know how to respond. It was a new and totally mystifying adult world that he was being dragged into unwillingly.

'So when will I see Mum again?' he said, for he had been looking forward to the end of term in a mere five weeks. He had expected her to be back from England by then.

'And Anthony?' he added, almost as an afterthought, for his younger brother had only lately begun to engage his interest.

'I will write to your mother and ask her when she plans her first visit,' he said. He was sorry now that he had not insisted on her naming a date before he left. It seemed a vague promise to give an eleven year old.

But Paul helpfully filled the gap.

'Do you think it will be for my birthday in February,' he said, 'if she isn't coming for Christmas?'

Richard was relieved because he had not thought of that himself, but he did not want to make a firm promise.

'That's probably going to be her plan,' he said, without knowing for sure.

He hoped Paul did not notice his uncertainty for he did not want the boy to suffer further disappointment. But Paul's thoughts had moved on.

'Do I have to tell them at school?' he asked. 'I don't think anybody else has divorced parents, well none of the boys I know.'

Richard shook his head, understanding immediately that Paul did not want to be singled out as different from the other boys.

'No, you don't have to tell them if you don't want to, although I should, as a courtesy, tell the headmaster,' Richard said, although he thought afterwards perhaps that wasn't strictly necessary either.

It was only then he wondered if there had been gossip about Catherine in the Sydney newspapers as there had been in England, but as he had no way of knowing, he decided Paul could take a chance on secrecy.

With a maturity Richard had thought beyond his son, Paul attempted to reassure his father.

'It'll be all right, Dad,' he said. 'We're still a family - you, me and Anthony even though Anthony is over in England. And that's what's important.'

Richard gave his son a quick hug as much in appreciation as acknowledgement. The boy had seen just how his father had struggled to put the bad news into words. In that moment father and son were closer than they had ever been and they both, for different reasons, cherished the moment.

At about the same time Richard was breaking the bad news to his young son Paul, Henry Baker, the Belleville's family's new and much more assertive lawyer, was having a final terse conversation with Alistair McGovern in an attempt to get him to settle with the family.

'You have no rights, you know,' he said to the nervous young man sitting opposite him. 'Francis Belleville never recognised you as his son in any legal way. It was only his two sons who made a kind gesture to your mother when their father died that paid for your living and your education.'

This was too much for Alistair McGovern. He had long since ceased to see himself as a charity case that the Belleville family helped out of the goodness of their hearts.

'I believe, and your predecessor did too, that my father was going to recognise me and make provision for me,' he said, his voice rising in anger. 'But he died before he could do it. That's what I believe. That's what my mother believes. And that's what I want now. To be part of the family.'

Alistair got up from the chair and began to pace the small room which had grown warmer as the morning advanced. His agitation alarmed the solicitor. Yet in the face of the young man's disquiet, Henry Baker remained measured and calm, for there was no proof to support the young man's belief.

He knew his predecessor had been expecting Francis Belleville to make a small amendment to his will but there had been no suggestion that it was to recognise and provide for his illegitimate son. Such a thing had never been spoken of, as far as he knew, for he had meticulously reviewed the notes of meetings the firm had conducted with Francis Belleville and could find no reference to him.

So he refused to enter into discussions based on what might have been said and what might have been done. He concerned himself only with the facts.

'Let me be plain, Mr McGovern,' he said, with a firmness and finality to his voice that he hoped would convey the message that what the young man sought was impossible.

'You will never be recognised as Francis Belleville's son. That is the fact of the matter and you should get used to the idea,' Henry Baker said.

He paused to gauge the effect of his words on the troubled young man, then he went on.

'You are fortunate the family is willing to make you an offer. I am authorised to make that offer and I must say it is a generous one,' he said, almost as if he was reluctant to explain the details, for he thought it was overly generous to the young upstart.

He pushed a document across the desk towards Alistair.

'You will have an income for life,' he said. 'A generous income for life in fact, but you must agree to certain provisions that have been explained to you previously and are set out here. Principally, you cannot contact any member of the family in any way and you can never change your name to Belleville.'

But Alistair McGovern was no longer interested in offers. He did not bother to pick up the document, for it did not contain what he really wanted most of all: recognition that he was in fact one of them. That he was a Belleville.

Without that provision, any settlement they offered was simply about money, money to buy his silence and his acquiescence. And he would not take it. However much he was tempted, not just for his own sake, but for his mother's, he would not take their money.

'I don't want their thirty pieces of silver,' he said flatly, as if by accepting, he was betraying his legitimate claim to his birthright.

'They can keep their money. Until such time as they offer me what I am due, they can keep their filthy money.' He almost yelled the words.

He rose from the chair, agitated and aggrieved. He said nothing further to Henry Baker who was by this time was on his feet, unsure of what Alistair McGovern would do next. He was not used to such behaviour. Generally, his clients were respectful and polite. He was uncertain how to respond.

But in the end, no response was necessary. Alistair McGovern grabbed his hat and flung open the door to the outer office, which he closed with a bang as he left without uttering another word.

Within moments, Henry Baker's secretary Janine put her head around the door, for she had witnessed the final moments of the meeting.

'Is everything all right, Mr Baker?' she asked, for she too had been stunned by the behaviour she had just witnessed.

'It's fine, Janine, it's fine. But come in. I must dictate a letter immediately to Richard and William Belleville. They must know about this final rejection and how the meeting transpired.'

Quickly, Janine picked up her freshly sharpened pencil and her notepad and sat down in the recently vacated chair opposite her boss. If he was keen to dictate a note and a letter quickly, she was just as keen to find out what had gone on.

The letters to the Belleville family and her employer's file notes had been a source of much interest to her, for most of her work was routine and dull. But to be in the middle of a real life scandal involving one of the firm's most important clients had given her much to think about. The story, she thought, was as good as some of the true romance stories she had read recently. Perhaps she could try and write a short story for the magazine, she pondered, with different names of course.

She sat patiently while Henry Baker assembled his thoughts. And then he began.

Dear Messrs Belleville ......

Almost as soon as Richard had departed, Edward Cavendish had manufactured an excuse to call on Catherine and her mother. Having assisted in the appointment of Lady Marina's new chauffeur he now had a reliable source of information on the happenings at Haldon Hall so Richard's departure was not news to him.

To his feigned surprise, he was greeted by a slightly reticent five year old who had quickly warmed to him when he discovered the sugary treat that lay in store in the pocket of his overcoat. Edward's years in the Foreign Office had sharpened his diplomatic skills, even the skills required to deal with a wary child.

With Anthony happily devouring the small packet of sweets, Edward turned towards Catherine, pleased to have her to himself for a few moments.

'I hope you enjoyed the duchess's birthday party?' he asked, for they had not spoken since that evening.

She smiled and nodded.

'It was very grand,' she said, 'but I must say everyone seemed to be very well informed about my affairs.'

He held out to her the very same newspaper clipping that John

Bertram had shown Richard. She read it quickly and laughed.

'How exotic they make me sound,' she said, handing it back to him.

'I hope your husband has arrived back in Australia safely?' he asked, tentatively.

He felt the topic of her marriage had almost been off limits between them. He hoped the simple polite enquiry about Richard, whom he had not met, would not be resented. So he waited, in some trepidation, for her answer.

'Yes,' she said, quieter now as she reflected on the enormity of the change in her life. 'He did send me a telegram to tell me he had spoken with Paul, our elder son, who's at school in Sydney and that he was then heading home to Prior Park.'

Edward wanted to say: and I assume that means you are getting a divorce and remaining here at Haldon Hall and that Anthony will grow up here, but he was careful not to presume he had any right to know about Catherine's private life. He was disappointed she did not elaborate further.

Still he took the news of Richard's departure without Anthony as confirmation that her marriage was over. He did his best to hide the little frisson of pure joy that he felt at the news as they entered the library to be greeted by Lady Marina.

As it transpired the solicitor's letter arrived at Prior Park at almost the same time as Richard walked through the door to a warm but subdued greeting from his family. William was grateful for the distraction of his brother's return for he had made the mistake of opening the letter in front of his mother whose natural curiosity was piqued by the sight of the firm's address on the outer envelope.

He was about to give his mother an offhanded and probably unconvincing reason for the long letter, when Richard flung open the door. He had opted for surprise, hiring a taxi to drive him out to Prior Park, rather than arrange for William to pick him up.

Under cover of the greetings, William slipped away to his office to place the letter in a locked drawer, safely away from prying eyes, for he had become more alert to the danger that carelessly exposed letters could present.

Richard had forewarned his family by telegram that he would be returning alone, but still the sight of him walking into the house without his young son and without his wife dampened the spirits of those who gathered to greet him.

But it was Elizabeth Belleville who was first to broach the almost forbidden topic as the family headed towards the drawing room.

'So you agreed to her keeping Anthony with her?' his mother said, without preamble and with an emphasis that already lay some uncontested blame at the feet of her estranged daughter-in-law.

'Mother,' Richard said, his voice even and calm, 'the boy is five. I really believe in my heart he is better off with his mother at the moment. I could not deny him that for my own selfish reasons.'

But she was not easily convinced.

'So I am to be denied my grandson because you don't want to appear selfish?' she countered, as if to make the point her wishes had not been considered at all.

It was Alice who came to his aid.

'I can see Richard's point,' she said, in the hope her mother-in-law would see reason. 'Anthony needs his mother at his age. We will all miss him terribly but he would miss his mother more than he would miss any of the rest of us. She is the most important person in his life right now.'

Richard was grateful for Alice's support. William, who had rejoined the group, did not want to get caught up in the tense conversation between his brother and their mother, but he was inclined to support Alice, for she always spoke good sense. It had been Alice, after all, who had been called upon to look after Anthony when his mother had travelled back to England at short notice. She, above them all, was the one, apart from his father, who had developed a deep attachment to the boy, so if she thought the decision was the right one, then it must indeed be right by William's reasoning.

'Thanks, Alice, I'm pleased someone agrees with me,' Richard said, smiling a friendly acknowledgement towards his sister-in-law.

'It's not like you won't see him again,' Richard said, turning back towards his mother.

'Well,' Elizabeth said, knowing she had been outflanked on the subject, 'I hope she doesn't just come to Sydney to see Paul and ask you to go to Sydney when they are there.

'That is quite likely, you know,' she warned her son.

But Richard would not be drawn in to a pointless discussion of what ifs about the future of his two boys.

'I will make sure both boys know that Prior Park is their home and I will make sure both of them spend time together here,' he promised, although just how that promise would be fulfilled in the future he did not know.

There was a lull in the conversation. Neither William nor Alice were inclined to discuss the other issue that was concerning them all, so it was left to Elizabeth to ask the questions no one else would.

'I assume a divorce is planned?' Elizabeth enquired, in a very matter of fact tone of voice. She might well have been asking a mundane question about the management of the household.

Richard grimaced at his mother's forthright question but he answered her all the same.

'A divorce is planned, Mother,' he said, without elaboration.

And with that, she had to be content for at that moment, Mrs Duffy opened the door, juggling a heavily laden tea tray on her right arm. Alice jumped up to help her and the conversation turned to the general pleasure of Richard's return and the routine happenings at Prior Park he missed out on in his absence.

After the tea was drunk and the tray stacked, William managed to get Richard to one side. Despite the obvious fatigue in his brother's face, he was keen to share the latest news from Henry Baker so together they walked the short distance to the office.

Richard, closing the door behind him, sat down in one of the armchairs while William read the letter, dictated a matter of days earlier, by Henry Baker following his final meeting with Alistair McGovern.

The news was not good. Despite the cost of the settlement, they had both wanted Alistair McGovern to accept it and slip quietly out of their lives but there was now no hope he would do so. Money had simply not been a sufficient lure to silence him.

But it was Henry Baker's final words that caused them fresh alarm. William read them slowly and then again, so he was sure that Richard had heard him.

"I believe the young man in question is not entirely of sound mind. Had I the opportunity I would have counselled him again against contacting you, but he left my office in such a rush that I did not get to say anything further to him. He seemed offended by the offer, which I do not understand. He is very fixated on wanting to be part of the family but I told him flatly that this would never happen.

I am sorry not to be able to bring you better news but I believe I have done my best to persuade him to accept your very generous settlement, which he said if he accepted, would be like him accepting 'thirty pieces of silver' which I take to mean a betrayal of his claims.

I can do no more in the matter but I caution you to take care should he ever approach you personally or present himself at Prior Park. Who knows what he is capable of?"

Richard, restless from the days of travel, began to pace the room, although it took him only a few strides to the traverse the length of it. The activity helped him think.

William sat, lips pursed, in the chair behind the desk.

Neither of them drew any comfort at all from Henry Baker's letter, both recalling the ugly scene on the night of their mother's birthday party nearly six months earlier.

'I take it Jack Finch and Ted Lambert are still about the place?' Richard asked, for he had hardly thought about them since they had arrived.

'Yes,' William said. 'Charles has had them rebuilding the stockyards and adding to the sheds. As it turned out, they're quite good at the work so they've been very useful.'

Richard nodded but said nothing.

'I'd kept Charles informed about developments,' he said, 'or the lack of them up until now, but it might be worth reinforcing things with them now that we have this letter.'

This time Richard responded.

'Good idea,' he said. 'Tell Charles about it so he's alert.'

'Can the other two be trusted to keep quiet about it all?' he asked, although he knew it was probably far too late for such a question.

'Well, I haven't heard any gossip but then perhaps I wouldn't,' William said. 'Any gossip would be behind our backs.'

'That's true,' Richard admitted. 'But sometimes it's a look or something not spoken that gives it away.'

'Well, I haven't noticed anything,' William said, 'and I've been to some meetings and to the cattle sales as usual.'

Richard smiled. He did not say he thought his brother was probably the least likely person to detect any undercurrent of speculation or gossip in the circles they moved in.

'Well, I hope those two prove their worth should this young upstart come around the place,' Richard said. 'I don't like Henry Baker's description of him as not being of entirely sound mind. I do wonder what that makes him capable of?'

The question hung in the air between them for neither of them knew the answer. They did not know it then but it was to be only a short time later they would have their answer and bear witness to its devastating consequences.

CHAPTER 20: NOVEMBER 1957

Shortly after Richard returned to Prior Park, James and Julia set off on their planned trip south. James had co-opted Alice to drive them to the airport and she arrived promptly on the morning of their departure. She was her usual self, bright and cheerful.

It was James who pressed her for details about Richard and Catherine, for he had heard only the briefest details from Julia, who had heard the news from her mother. As it turned out, Alice was no more forthcoming.

'I don't know what his plans are, James,' she had said, in response to his question about what Richard would do now.

'We were surprised he agreed young Anthony could stay in England but the boy is only five. Catherine persuaded him he needed to be with his mother,' she added.

She was really only repeating the generally agreed reaction at Prior Park.

James digested this news, silently wondering whether another woman might now be featuring in his plans but he did not share this thought. Instead he finished stowing their suitcases into the boot of the car and held the door open for Julia.

'Well, we will see him when we get back from Sydney,' James said, as he displaced his sister behind the wheel of her own car, relegating her to the back seat.

She did not mind. She was a very competent driver but she would have been nervous at the wheel with James as a passenger. Far better to let him do the driving, she decided. She was not about to change the habit of a lifetime and stand her ground against her brother. It simply wasn't worth the effort.

He glanced at his watch impatiently as he started the engine. He did not want to risk missing the daily flight to Brisbane where he had planned they would stay for several days before travelling on to Sydney, so he pushed his foot further down on the accelerator. It was a move that silenced his passengers and demanded his full attention as the car left in its wake a shower of dust and gravel as its speed steadily increased.

After watching their plane taxi across the flat open space of the airport, Alice relaxed and set off to visit her mother, with whom Marianne now stayed during the week to attend school.

The arrangement had worked better than either she or her mother had imagined. Amelia Fitzroy had found the task of looking after her granddaughter much more rewarding than nursing a sick husband who in the prime of life had been difficult but charming but towards the end of his life had simply been difficult, although in her loyalty to him, she would never have said as much.

But now she was much more relaxed and talkative and she was keen to hear the gossip from Prior Park. She and Alice agreed between them that Richard's marriage had been doomed from the start. Not because they did not like Catherine, but because the circumstances of her upbringing and expectations were at such odds with their life at Prior Park.

'How you could you expect an elegant, upper class English lady to adapt to life in country Australia?' Amelia said to her daughter, not for the first time.

Alice nodded in agreement, again not for the first time.

'I feel sorry for the children,' she said, as she watched her mother busy herself around her small kitchen.

Alice could not imagine being separated from Marianne for more than a few days. She did not know how Catherine could stand to have her son at boarding school for most of the year. To Alice it seemed entirely wrong and her mother agreed wholeheartedly. So there was no more to be said on the topic as they sat down together to share a pot of tea.

If Alice sensed a reserve about her mother that morning, she did not remark it. She did not know that her own mother could not find the right words to tell her what she had heard about Alice's brother.

She had been horrified to learn that James had been the subject of gossip among her friends, one of whom had been over loud in recounting the details of his latest indiscretion. She had pretended not to hear it at the most recent gathering but she could not avoid it.

She had noticed how some of the women seated close to her had shifted uncomfortably in their seats, well aware that she was overhearing gossip not meant for her ears. The story she heard had troubled her deeply, all the more because she feared that it was most probably true, for she had no illusions about her son. She loved him dearly, too much perhaps, but she was not blind to his faults.

In the end, she could see no point in sharing the gossip with Alice, who had decided against saying anything to her mother about the tension she had noticed between James and Julia when she had seen them together that very morning for the first time in weeks. She hoped the holiday would sort out whatever it was that lay at the heart of the trouble between them.

Her mother held out a similar hope that her son would come to his senses before it was too late.

So they both remained silent about James and Julia. In a way Alice would have been quietly relieved to hear her mother's story for she feared it was Julia who had lost interest in the marriage.

Knowing Julia well, she feared that her interest, once lost, might never be rekindled. She would have been oddly reassured to have a reason not of Julia's making for the tension.

Only time would tell, she thought, as she absentmindedly ate another slice of her mother's excellent chocolate cake and chatted on about inconsequential matters.

Julia was relieved the trip, first to Brisbane, and then to Sydney had been uneventful. She found she did not like flying very much and even less when turbulence buffeted their small aircraft. It seemed such a fragile thing to be kept aloft by a couple of engines and the lethal looking propellers.

As she looked around the elegant foyer of The Australia Hotel, she suddenly began to feel just a little out of place, for it had been years since she had visited such an establishment.

James, following her gaze, reassured her.

'Richard told me about this place,' he said. 'He always stays here when he is in Sydney so I thought it sounded just the place for us.'

The beautiful marble entrance, the slick professionalism of the staff and the superbly dressed clientele had made the right impression on her. Suddenly she remembered staying in the hotel with her mother but she had been a young girl at the time and she could not remember any of the details. Still, she mentioned it and James was not surprised, although he had hoped it would be her first visit.

'You probably don't remember much of it anyway,' he said, 'it would have been well before the war.'

She smiled for he had forgotten that she had attended school in Sydney and she reminded him.

'Of course, no second rate local schools for the Belleville children,' he said, with just a touch of sarcasm.

'And tell me, what did you learn at SCEGGS that was to equip you for later life that you could not have learned closer to home?'

She ignored his sarcasm for it was true that much of what she had learned had hardly proved useful, but even so, there had been some things she had enjoyed.

'I learnt French. Very useful, you know, for when we travel to Europe,' she said, although they had never discussed a European holiday. 'And we studied English literature.'

'And what would that be useful for?' he asked, although of course he had done the same and would have struggled to answer the question himself.

In the end she ignored his question. She had no ready answer for him. Her education, she now realised, had almost no specific purpose beyond the need to be educated. Neither she nor her mother had ever expected her to work for her own living. It was strange, she thought, how the idea had never crossed their minds. Her future had been seen as that of a wife and mother, supported by a husband, never by her own efforts. In the heat of the argument with James, she had faced the awful truth that she lacked the skills to earn a living. Leaving him would have meant returning to Prior Park and being dependent on her family's goodwill. In this realisation, she had felt humiliated, as if full adulthood had eluded her, as if she was some child-woman always needing the protection of a husband or a family.

All of these random thoughts occurred in rapid succession, as if she had never before had the time to consider her life and the choices available to her.

It was certainly the first time she had wondered if her education might have been put to better use.

Just then, James broke through her reverie.

'I have the key to our suite,' he said, holding it aloft. 'Let's go and settle in and then we can go off sightseeing. We should go and see the site of the proposed new opera house down on the harbour. It's currently a tram shed, can you believe it? I think there's mixed feelings about the design. The winning designer is Danish.'

Julia merely nodded at this information. She had not expected her husband to be interested in the site of an opera house. Her first instincts had been to head a short distance south towards the leading department stores for which Sydney was well known, especially David Jones, where she, like her mother, shopped by mail order. But that would have to wait.

As the lift doors closed behind them, it was the merest chance she avoided seeing Philippe Duval. The doors of the lift alongside the one they were stepping into were opening just as their lift doors closed behind them.

Philippe Duval, intent on his own mission, scarcely looked around him as he strode through the foyer of the hotel and out onto the street. He had been busy finalising his presentation for the medical conference the following day. But now satisfied with his speech, he was intent on visiting his daughter for she would not happily wait until the weekend to see him. For his part he was keen to see how she had progressed in the months since his first visit. The concierge raised his arm and a taxi slid into the driveway of the hotel. In a moment, he was gone, heading out to the suburbs to visit his daughter.

Pippa was anxious. She had been home from school for half an hour and there was still no sign of her father. She had already changed out of her school uniform, washed her face, combed her hair and now there was nothing left for her to do but wait for him.

She would not sit down. She began to pace the living room, her anxiety growing by the minute until she became dissatisfied with waiting inside the house. She flung open the front door and walked the short distance to the gate, scanning the roadway in both directions for any sign of him. She ignored Aunt Edith's pleas to settle down, that he would be along directly as he promised.

Just then, she spotted the taxi slowing down as it approached the house. Almost before he could pay the driver, she was hugging her father, for there was no reticence at all in her nature. She had loved him with the unsullied trust of a child from the first moment she had met him. He in turn had embraced and revelled in her warmth for he had never known such unconditional love before, except from his mother.

In quiet moments he knew he had not always returned the same affection to his mother and he was sorry for it. He could only blame the callowness of youth. It was no consolation to him that his mother had understood and excused his occasional dissatisfaction with their life together. He knew she had done her best for him and he berated himself when he thought of her for his lack of understanding of her daily struggles.

But that was all in the past. At least he could make amends in some way by securing the future of his daughter and that he was determined to do.

He held her at arm's length, noticing how she had grown in just a few months. Before his eyes, she was changing from a child to a young woman.

'You look wonderful, my dear,' he said, as they walked together into the house. He had almost said 'child' but he sensed she no longer viewed herself as a child.

He greeted Aunt Edith warmly and the older woman beamed at his flattery, for he had noticed how much care she had taken of her appearance too. He did not arrive empty handed.

Edith Henderson gasped at the generosity of his gift. Nestled in a bed of blue satin lay a necklace of cultured pearls. She had never received such a gift before and was rendered speechless by his largesse. But to him, she had given him a priceless gift, the care and love of his daughter. He had thought that worth much much more than the gift he gave her but he was happy that she liked it.

For Pippa he had chosen a gold bracelet to match the gold chains she already possessed. He had been careful in his choice and she was delighted, displaying it proudly on her slim wrist for them both to admire.

'And school is going well?' he enquired, just as Aunt Edith had predicted.

'Yes,' Pippa replied, 'it's fine.'

She shrugged her shoulders. She thought school was too boring to spend time discussing it but her aunt was quick to reassure Philippe.

'She's doing very well, Philippe,' she said, for she knew he would want more details.

'She is in the top two or three girls in her class now,' she added, her pride in her young charge's improvement very evident.

'That's very good, Pippa,' he said. 'I'm pleased to hear you are doing well. We will have to discuss your future education soon. We will have to think about what you might like to study at university.'

She did not immediately respond. She did not know why adults always wanted to know how you were going at school. It's boring, she wanted to say, but she did not want to disappoint him, if it was important to him. Instead, she nodded in silent agreement. If he wanted her to go to university, then of course she would go to university.

But the most important thing to her was being able to see and be with her father. To her, everything else about her life was secondary and less important; his approval and his love was all that mattered to her. His sudden presence in her life had begun to heal the hurt of first losing her parents and being evicted from her home and then discovering that she had not been their real daughter after all.

It had all been such a lot to take in that she was now simply

225

content to bask in the security of knowing who her father was and knowing that he loved her and would be a part of her life forever. That was as much as she wanted from life. To know she was loved and to know that he cared.

For his part, Philippe did not mention the possibility that he might come to live in Sydney. He did not want to raise their hopes until he was absolutely sure of his new job. But in the coming days, he expected the job offer to be confirmed.

And what better way than to treat Aunt Edith and Pippa to lunch at the Australia Hotel and announce his news then.

So the invitation was extended and accepted with alacrity for the coming Sunday. Until then he told them he would be busy with his work. Pippa was satisfied for the promise of a special Sunday lunch with her father in a grand hotel was something to look forward to.

As he left, she clung to him for a moment, but he gently untangled himself and got into the taxi. He began to wonder how it would all turn out. He had not planned his move beyond the necessity of being accepted for a top surgical post. Once that happened there would be many other things to consider, not least of which would be the question of where Pippa would live. But that was a question for the future, he decided, as he waved to her from the taxi.

Not for the first time did he look back with regret. If only he had not been posted, if only he had been there to support Julia, then they would have been a family from the very beginning. Instead he was left to make amends for the past as best he could and yet he felt he had to protect Julia. He could not in all conscience reveal her name for he knew Pippa would not rest until she had contacted her. That at least he could prevent for he knew he could not expect a child to understand the consequences of such a move. To Pippa, everything was simple and uncomplicated. To him, his discovery of his daughter had brought with it complications he had never imagined, but he was not sorry for them.

The small anxieties he felt were not for himself but for that future time when it would no longer be possible to dissuade Pippa from going in search of her real mother.

CHAPTER 21: NOVEMBER 1957

It was Sunday. After several days of non-stop sightseeing and shopping, Julia was in no rush to dress for the day ahead. Instead she lay sprawled across the bed reading the latest women's magazine while James finished the breakfast that had been brought up to their room.

Looking up from the Sunday newspaper, he noticed she had paused in flicking through her magazine. She sat up and he noticed the cover. It was the summer bridal issue. His curiosity got the better of him.

'Looking for a dress for your next wedding?' he asked, only half joking for relations between them were still cool.

He was unhappy that the extravagant gift of jewellery he had given her at dinner the previous evening hadn't achieved quite the response he had hoped. She had admired the jewellery but somehow he felt her response was more polite than effusive. So he was relieved when she laughed good humouredly at his remark.

'No,' she said, holding out the magazine page to him, 'one of the girls I went to school with here in Sydney is pictured in the social pages. Her name is Sally Macpherson. I thought she'd be married by now, but it appears not.'

James read the photo caption. There was a collection of black and white photos on the page. He knew none of the people pictured. They were mostly women in expensive frocks and hats.

'It looks as if we should have gone to Melbourne instead of Sydney,' he said. 'It seems all the action is in Melbourne with the spring racing carnival.'

He handed the magazine back to her.

He and Julia occasionally attended the local races in Springfield, but she was not enthusiastic about the sport, which had surprised him, because she enjoyed horse riding. She preferred the balls that accompanied the major events but there were few enough of those.

'Perhaps you should have chosen a husband from the upper echelons of Sydney or Melbourne society,' he said. 'Then you would have had a chance to appear in the social pages.'

It was an opportunity for her to say she had the husband she always wanted, but she did not. Instead, she scoffed at the suggestion.

'And just how was I going to meet such a man?' she asked.

She did not add that her mother, seeing her as 'damaged goods', opted for a less ambitious marriage for her only daughter.

'Your mother came from Melbourne as I recall,' he said. 'I always wondered why she never took you down there, but then I suppose you spent so much time there when she was ill, she was reluctant to return.'

It had been years since he had even referred to her absence from Prior Park alongside her mother years before they married. She had thought he had most likely forgotten about it.

She could feel the blood drain from her face. She hoped, in the muted light of the hotel room, he would not notice.

The memory of her time in Melbourne was seared in her mind. Each time she thought about it, it took almost a physical effort to shut the memory away again.

It was some moments before she was composed enough to respond.

'I think, as you might recall, she decided she had a good prospect in you, without having to go hunting further afield.'

She tried to make her answer sound light hearted.

'And so she did,' he said.

He came across to her and she allowed him to embrace her. He began to kiss her, lightly at first, then passionately. He got up abruptly and went to the door. He hung the 'do not disturb' sign on the outside. His intentions were clear.

It had been months since he had made love to his wife despite his tentative overtures on many nights. This time he was not to be denied.

Later, as she lay in his arms, her eyes closed, she knew for certain she no longer loved him. Had she ever really loved him or had she just tried to will herself to love him? She did not know for sure. She could not recall now because there had always been the shadow of another man between them. He had not known of the shadow of Philippe but she had.

She had quickly discovered how hard it was to give herself fully to a marriage with the knowledge there were things about her he must never know. Especially that she had borne a child to another man.

She had wanted to shout out, 'how are these lies the basis for trust in a marriage' but her mother had silenced her.

Now there were his lies to contend with, his lies and duplicity to forgive. At least she had not broken her marriage vows, but he had. And how many times, she wondered?

And what lay ahead of them?

Could she continue the fiction that she loved him? Would they grow old together, with less and less to say to one another? Would she find herself looking back, wondering what other life she might have led when it was all too late?

She was suddenly restless. She got up from the bed and headed to the bathroom. She turned on the shower until it was steaming hot. She stood there letting the water run over her body as if it would wash away her problems.

Later, wrapped in a towel, she returned to the bedroom.

'Let's go for a walk in the gardens,' she said, 'and then we can come back here for lunch. I believe Sunday lunch is special here.'

She had a sudden desperate need to get out into some fresh air. She had to see the sun and feel the breeze on her cheek.

James rolled off the bed and headed to the bathroom. She watched his retreating figure. He was still strong and muscular, his exposed skin brown from the sun. Wherever she went with him, she felt the envious glances of other women whose husbands did not quite measure up to his looks and physique.

But she did not feel any secret pleasure in their envy. She had tried to build on her girlish attraction to him but failed. She knew, despite his protestations, that he would drift off again into the arms of other women.

She did not know who or when. But she knew he would betray their marriage again and again.

Aunt Edith almost tripped over Pippa as they made their way through the foyer of the hotel. The girl had stopped suddenly to admire the grand sweeping staircase, the like of which she had never seen before, on their way to meet Philippe in the dining room. She gave the girl a gentle push towards the restaurant, for she could see Philippe waiting for them at a table.

'It's really beautiful here,' Pippa said as she approached the table. Everything was new and exciting to her.

'I haven't been in a proper hotel dining room before,' she said artlessly, as she turned back towards her father. 'Do you eat your dinner here every day?'

'Most days,' he said, 'unless there is a conference dinner.'

He was amused by her questions. He found it refreshing to see everything again through the eyes of a child. He had told her about his own childhood which had certainly never included visits to high class hotels.

'Were you very poor?' Pippa had asked at the time.

And he had replied honestly that his mother had worked as a cleaning lady to support them. She had not asked about his father so he had said nothing, hoping she would believe his father had died. He did not want her to know he too had been deserted by a father who wouldn't lay claim to him.

'I'm pleased you chose a table near the entrance,' Aunt Edith said. 'It is quite busy today and we might have had difficulty finding you.'

He smiled and nodded in agreement.

'I'd thought of that too so I came in a little earlier so that I had a good choice of table.'

There was silence for a few moments while they each studied the menu, which seemed incomprehensible to Pippa, but she followed her father's example. In the end, her meal was chosen for her, as she expected it would be, but she had at least had the pleasure of appearing grown up.

Once the waiter had taken their order, it was Philippe who broke the silence.

'I have something very exciting to tell you,' he said leaning forward and looking from one to the other.

He noticed Pippa's eyes light up, excited at the prospect there was some special secret he were about to share.

'I'm going to be moving to Sydney,' he said simply. 'I have been offered a surgical post at one of the major teaching hospitals and I have accepted it.'

He waited to gauge the effect of his announcement. Aunt Edith's face broke into a wide smile, for she had not been expecting the news at all. Pippa jumped up and down on her chair excitedly, so that she attracted the attention of the people near to them.

He laid a hand on her arm to steady her.

'I won't be moving until next year,' he said. 'They want me to start next February when the academic year starts here.'

She could not contain herself at his news. She threw her arms around his neck and hugged him ferociously.

'That's wonderful. That's so wonderful. That means you'll be here all the time not just coming for a couple of weeks at a time?' she asked, uncertain now as to whether he meant he would be here all the time.

He nodded, smiling, reassuring her.

'Yes, I'll be here all the time,' he said, laughing at her exuberance.

They began to chat excitedly about his news. Aunt Edith wanted to know how he had got the job and all the details.

Just then, something made him look up for he was facing the entrance to the dining room. Later, he could not recall if it had been a sudden movement or a voice that had caught his attention.

And then he froze, speechless, oblivious to everything going on around him. Just a few feet away from him stood a young woman he would have known anywhere.

Older, certainly, and more mature but all he saw was the young teenage girl he had been forced to leave behind all those years before.

Then he noticed her companion. Dark haired, suntanned, smiling confidently his hand guiding her through the door, he knew instantly he was looking at James Fitzroy. Julia's husband, he guessed.

In that split second, he prayed she would not see him but it was too late. The chatter from their table had caught her attention and she glanced towards them.

And then she looked away.

And then she looked back and this time she saw him.

Her hand flew to her mouth to stifle the quick intake of breath that was her only visible reaction to the shock of seeing, before her very eyes, the man she had loved, the man to whom she had borne a child, the man she thought was dead in the war.

Philippe pushed back his chair and half rose from the table. He did not know what to do. He wanted to rush to her side and embrace her. But he faltered. If he did that, there would be no going back. There would be awkward explanations. For those brief moments, it seemed to him that time stood still.

And then he watched helplessly as she crumpled to the floor.

Philippe was first to react. His professional training asserted itself. He took command of the situation and understood instantly what he must do. He spoke in an urgent undertone to Aunt Edith who seemed to understand what was happening without being told.

'Get Pippa away from here. Take her home,' he said, his words just above a whisper. 'I'll explain later.'

Aunt Edith grabbed the child, who was looking on wide eyed but without any understanding of what she was seeing, and hustled her out of the dining room to the front door of the hotel to hail a taxi.

Philippe, relying on his natural authority as a doctor, ordered the still unconscious Julia to be carried to a quiet room. The hotel staff milling around the unconscious woman were only too willing to be told what to do. He did not make eye contact with anyone.

He fervently hoped she would not regain full consciousness until she was safely away from the crowd that had formed a ragged circle around them. Only he understood the reason for her collapse. The shock of seeing him had simply been overwhelming.

It took just a few moments to move her and then Philippe hustled the hotel staff out of the room with his reassurances that he would take care of her. While all this was happening he had chosen to ignore James Fitzroy, who now grabbed his shoulder with some force to get his attention. There was just the three of them now in a small private room off the main dining room.

'I know who you are,' James said, without preamble. His voice was not friendly.

'I know who you are,' he repeated more loudly, for he did not think he had been heard the first time.

Philippe turned to him, having first made sure that Julia was comfortable and likely to recover without intervention. She was already beginning to stir. Philippe was cautious in his answer.

'How do you know who I am?' he asked.

Philippe's voice was deliberately quiet and controlled, giving no hint of the turmoil he felt inside.

'You're that American doctor she was seeing during the war. And then you left suddenly,' James said. 'Back then I saw you with Julia.'

It was more a statement than a question. Philippe did not bother to deny it. He did not want to engage in a conversation with Julia's husband. There was too much at stake now for Julia. So he said nothing. He merely nodded.

'And who were those people you were with?' James asked, out of curiosity for he did not suspect any connection between them and his wife.

'Friends,' Philippe replied, for he did not want to elaborate or to lie outright.

'I'm here for a medical conference,' he said, as if that would explain the presence of an elderly woman and a young child at his table.

For the moment, James seemed satisfied with Philippe's responses and they both turned back towards the sofa where Julia had been laid.

She was struggling to sit up, shaking her head from side to side as if to clear it. Philippe began to help her until James pushed him away. Within moments, she was fully conscious again. Bewildered,

233

she looked from one man to the next.

No one spoke. The room was so silent it was as if none of them was even breathing. Then she broke the silence.

'Philippe, I can't believe it. I thought you were dead. I never heard from you. You never wrote …'

The words tumbled over one another before her voice trailed off. There were so many questions she did not know how to ask. She did not know how to give voice to the disappointments she had suffered in never hearing from him. The memory of her broken heart flooded her thoughts.

Ignoring James, he sat down beside her and took her hand in his.

'I wrote you many letters,' he said gently, 'but I never got a reply from you. Not once. I thought you had decided you did not love me.'

Julia opened her mouth to say more but she was suddenly cautious too, realising her husband was standing above them. He would be an unhappy witness to any revelations.

It was James who interjected.

'This is all very touching but since my wife seems somewhat recovered, I think we should go up to our room so she can rest,' James said, leaning forward as he spoke to help her up off the sofa.

He put his arm around her waist to haul her to her feet but she pushed him away, shaking her head from side to side.

'No, no,' she said repeatedly. 'I must speak with Philippe.'

James hesitated, unsure what to do.

'James,' she said, 'I must speak with Philippe alone. Just for a few minutes.'

He still hesitated. But then he looked at her and he knew instantly that he must retreat or face the undignified prospect of dragging his wife out of the room against her will.

He said nothing further. He turned on his heels and strode to the door which he closed behind him with a bang.

For a few moments after James left, Julia and Philippe sat together in silence, neither one knowing how to bridge the gap of years nor to understand the subterfuge that had kept them apart. In the end it was Philippe who spoke first.

'I wrote to you often in the first eighteen months,' he said, remembering how he had searched in vain for a letter from her.

'Did you not get any of my letters?' he asked. But in his heart he already knew the answer because of the one letter she had written to him.

It was only then the enormity of her family's treachery began to dawn on her.

'I was right,' she sobbed. 'I believe you. I always believed in my heart that my mother must have intercepted your letters.'

Tears began spilling in a rapid stream down her cheeks

'But I asked my mother many times if there were any letters from you and she said there were not. She lied. She must have lied,' she said, her voice a mixture of utter despair and bitter disappointment. She knew then she had been betrayed by the people she had loved the most.

He moved towards her, wanting desperately to hold her.

'I wrote to you often,' he said, remembering his own disappointment, 'until I lost heart.'

She glanced at him.

'And I couldn't write to you because I didn't know where to write to, but I did write to you once care of your mother. Did you ever get that letter?'

She waited now, anxious as to whether he knew her big secret. He nodded slowly.

'I got the letter but only several years after the war, when she died. I found it among her things. She never sent it on to me,' he said. 'By the time I read it, it was far too late to help you. I could do nothing.'

She could see the sadness in his face.

'I know you had a baby,' he said quietly. 'I'm sorry I wasn't there for you, wasn't there to protect you.'

Tears were now coursing down her face uncontrollably as she remembered the misery and the loneliness she had felt, bearing his child alone and in secret.

'She made me give up our daughter,' Julia said, her voice now almost hysterical. 'I was only nineteen. She made me go away to have it so no one would ever know. She made me discard my baby.'

He reached out and drew her into his arms. She was sobbing. He struggled for composure. He could only guess what she had suffered.

'Had I known you were pregnant, I would have come back somehow and married you,' he said. 'You know that, don't you?'

He held her at arm's length, searching her face for the answer, wanting to be sure that she believed him.

She nodded but there seemed to be no way to console her just then. It was as if the effort of keeping the secret had become too much. The flood of emotion, once released, could not be stemmed.

But he was being careful now. She had already suffered one great shock in seeing him again and realising the extent of her family's deceit. He tried to gauge how she would react when she found out the child at the restaurant table was her long lost daughter.

But she still focused on the past.

'You might have come back to see me after the war,' she said, forgetting that her silence had convinced him that she was no longer in love with him.

'But I didn't hear from you,' he reminded her, 'and when I did find out what had happened, it was all too late. But that's another story.'

She looked up at him then.

'What do you mean another story?'

She had been listening after all, he thought, and he regretted the words immediately. But he knew he could not stop now. She had to know the whole truth. She had been denied the truth before through her mother's intervention. She was entitled to know everything now, and so he began.

She listened intently as he described his journey to find their child and his attempts to ensure she would know the name of her real father when she grew up.

He described his disappointment at not being able to be part of his daughter's life and she saw for the first time that she had not borne this grief alone. His voice faltered as he grew closer to the revelation that he had received a letter from their daughter quite unexpectedly.

He took a deep breath.

'There is more you must know,' he said. 'It will be a shock too. A very big shock.'

But she shook her head.

'Nothing can be as big a shock as seeing you today. My mother convinced me you were dead. I never challenged that idea. I never said to her: how do you know for sure?'

Her voice was angry and bitter.

'If you are sure, then I will tell you the rest,' he said gently.

'I am sure,' she said, now more composed. 'What else do you have to tell me?'

He could see she had not thought any more about the people he was with at the restaurant table. And then it struck her in a moment of revelation.

Before he could say anything further, she burst out.

'The child. The young girl at your table,' she said, her voice rising in excitement as the realisation of what he was about to tell her dawned on her.

'The child with you was our daughter. Tell me I'm right,' she demanded, her hand pressing on his arm.

He smiled for she had made it much easier for him.

'You are right,' he said, pleased that she had come to the conclusion herself. 'The young girl at the table is our daughter Pippa.'

Julia was shocked into silence momentarily and then she began to bombard him with questions. When did he first meet her? How often has he seen her? Where is she living? Where does she go to school?

Suddenly, she realised she would now get the chance to meet the child she had given up. The child she had never expected to see again. The child she had thought about every single day since she had given birth to her.

'I must meet her. I must see her,' Julia demanded as Philippe recounted the story of her adoption, the loss of her adoptive parents, the letter he received and the part he had begun to play in her life.

He told her about Aunt Edith and the happy circumstance of having such a sensible mature woman to guide his daughter's life.

But Philippe was being cautious too. It was not only Julia who had been shocked. He began to imagine how and when he would break the news to Pippa.

'Of course, you can meet her, but I have to ask one question first? Does your husband know you had a child before you married him?'

She shook her head.

'No, he doesn't. My mother insisted, and I agreed with her, that he must never know. Richard doesn't know either, only Mother and William. My father died years ago.'

He smiled ruefully.

'I know your elder brother does not know about your child,' he said. 'You obviously don't know I met him in Goulburn after the war when I was looking for Pippa?'

She was suddenly alert, understanding for the first time the extent of her mother's iron grip on the family. She could imagine her mother discussing it with William and the two of them agreeing she must never be told of the encounter.

'He must have been warned not to mention your name because he never said anything at all,' she said, more painfully aware now of the depth of deception that had been perpetrated to keep her and Philippe apart.

'And will you tell your husband now?' Philippe asked quietly. 'I think he is at least owed an explanation of what has happened today.'

Julia sat very still for a few moments. There was much to consider but she suddenly felt a lightness of heart that she had not felt in years.

She sighed and stood up.

'I will go and speak with him,' she said. 'He will not be happy. I don't think he will understand why I didn't trust him enough to tell him.'

He smiled encouragingly at her.

'I will go and see Pippa and her aunt now,' he said. 'I will be back later on and we can talk more then.'

She was about to leave the room but on impulse she turned back and bent down to kiss Philippe on the cheek.

'Whatever happens,' he said, holding on to her arm for a few seconds. 'Whatever happens from here, you must know that I have always loved you. And I always will love you.'

She smiled.

'And I will always love you.'

Upstairs, Julia hesitated at the door of their bedroom. She took a deep breath and quietly slipped inside. She closed the door gently behind her.

James was standing at the window, looking down into the street at nothing in particular. He turned as she entered the room. He was unsmiling.

'So, did you have a nice time renewing your friendship with your lover?' he said, in a deliberate attempt to provoke her.

But she ignored the jibe. She knew what she had to tell him would be painful but there was no way now to avoid it.

She did not go up to him. Instead she stood just inside the door, some distance away from him. He waited for her to begin, the silence in the room oppressive.

'There are things I ought to have told you,' she began. 'There are things about me you ought to have known before we married.'

He was grim faced.

'Go on,' he said, 'unless you want me to guess.'

She shook her head.

'No, I don't want you to guess. I want to tell you the truth about me.'

Suddenly afraid she would collapse again, she sat down in one of the two armchairs in the room but he did not move to join her.

He did not make any move towards her at all. She looked up at him, his face in the shadow against the sunlight from the window. She could not tell what he was thinking.

'I had a baby – a baby girl – some years before we got married. My mother made me keep it quiet and I wasn't allowed to tell anyone,' she said, her voice oddly composed.

'And our American friend was the father I suppose,' James interjected.

'He was,' she said simply. 'But he was posted before I found out I was pregnant and then Mother wouldn't tolerate the disgrace of me having a baby out of wedlock. She insisted the baby be given up for adoption.'

He did not move a muscle. She could sense the cold fury enveloping him.

'I assume your mother's sudden serious illness was a cover. Am I right?'

He turned towards her. He waited for her reply.

Nervously, she ran her hands over her skirt to smooth the crumpled fabric.

'You are right,' she said.

She said nothing more for she did not want to attempt to justify her own conduct. It would have been easy to blame everything on her mother. Yet she knew in her heart she had been complicit in their pact to keep her disgrace a secret.

'And that baby is where now?' James asked.

She did not answer immediately for she was struggling to find the right words. At that point, he began to replay in his mind the scene in the hotel dining room.

'Of course,' he almost shouted. 'The child – the young girl at his table – that was his daughter, your daughter. Now I understand why she seemed vaguely familiar. She looked like you.'

She had not noticed the likeness herself so she was surprised he had.

'You're right,' she said finally. 'The young girl is the baby I gave up all those years ago.'

She took a deep breath, waiting for him to say something more, but he was silent.

'If you want to know, her name is Pippa,' she said. 'Her adoptive parents were killed in a car accident earlier this year. Philippe had discovered who had adopted her and sent a letter to the family for her to have later. But she got it when her family died.'

James did not interrupt while she recounted the story.

'And the older woman?' he asked, finally.

'Her great aunt, well the aunt of her adoptive mother who was made her guardian.'

His curiosity satisfied, he looked at her as if he was seeing her for the first time. She was a stranger to him. They were strangers to each other. He felt as if their marriage was being torn to shreds before his very eyes.

'And you never thought to tell me before we got married? Never once thought I deserved to know?'

She could hear the deep anger and hurt in his voice. She paused, deciding how to answer. He was entitled to an explanation, she knew that.

'I did not think it was something that you would ever need to know about or ever find out about,' she said finally. 'I didn't want us to start married life with that between us. It would have been too great a burden.'

'You didn't think dishonesty would be a greater burden?' he retorted.

To Julia, his reply seemed disingenuous. She wanted to say: and what about your dishonesty but she did not.

Had she committed the greater sin or had he? She knew she had been dishonest about her past but she had genuinely believed the past would remain in the past. But he could not now claim to be blameless. How many times had he been unfaithful to her?

Buoyed by these thoughts, she turned the question back to him.

'I agree. Dishonesty is a great burden,' she said. 'It has been a great burden for me and I have suffered for it, even though I tried hard to hide it. There have been days when I could simply have died with the misery of having given up my child.'

It was an emotional speech. He could see she was trembling but still he did not make a move towards her. She wondered if he did not trust himself. If, with physical closeness, he might have been tempted to lash out at her.

'So where do we go from here?' he said, for the hopes he had of their marriage being revived had evaporated.

'I honestly don't know,' she said. 'I honestly don't know.'

'I think you do,' he said, 'I think you do know.'

She said nothing more, for she could think of nothing more to say.

She watched as he started to gather his clothes.

'What are you doing?'

'What does it look like?'

'Are you planning to go home?'

'Yes,' he said simply, his anger barely controlled. 'I will start back today. There is nothing to keep me here.'

Chapter 22: November 1957

The sun was low in the sky by the time Julia returned to the hotel. Desperate for activity she had earlier headed out of the hotel into the almost empty streets. Without the weekday buzz of pedestrians, a melancholy air hung over the city. She had walked aimlessly, trying to make sense of all that had happened in the past few hours

When she returned, she found the room she had shared with James empty of all his belongings. He had left nothing for her, no note, no explanation. He had simply left.

She lay down on the bed, a wave of exhaustion threatening to engulf her. But she could not lie still. Within minutes she was up. She glanced in the mirror and began to pull at her hair with a comb. She reapplied her lipstick. Once she was satisfied with her appearance, she headed back downstairs in the hope of catching Philippe on his return.

She did not have long to wait. He smiled as he spotted her across the hotel lobby and walked immediately towards her.

She noticed for the first time the hint of grey in his hair and the fine lines around his eyes. If anything his youthful good looks had given way to an air of distinction that turned heads and commanded respect.

Tentatively he put his arm around her shoulders and together they headed towards the hotel lounge. Only after they were settled and the waiter had finished serving their drinks did he begin to tell her about his afternoon visit to Pippa and Aunt Edith.

He smiled at the memory. His mood lifted Julia's spirits.

'She was so excited, we couldn't get her to sit down,' he said. 'She danced around the room.'

Julia laughed, excited by his description of their daughter's response to the news that she would, at last, meet her real mother. Absentmindedly, she sipped the gin and tonic that had been placed in front of her.

'I had a word with Aunt Edith in private first,' he said, filling in the gaps of the story. 'She was almost as excited as Pippa, but I have to say she is a sensible woman with her feet on the ground.'

Julia nodded, encouraging him to tell her every detail. Nothing was too trivial. She wanted to know everything about her daughter.

'She warned me that one question Pippa would almost certainly ask would be if we were all going to live together as a family.'

Julia frowned, worried at the prospect of them disappointing her. 'And did she ask that?'

'I have to say Aunt Edith was ahead of me there,' Philippe said, with a brief smile. 'That was one of her first questions.'

'And what did you say to her?'

There was a note of anxiety in Julia's question. Everything was moving too fast for both of them. Together for the first time since he had bidden her farewell more than fourteen years earlier, neither of them had ever considered such a question for it had not been a possibility in their lives, before today.

'I simply said we would have to wait and see, but that whatever happened, she would always be important to both of us and we would be there for her,' he said. 'And we would always love her.'

'And was she satisfied with that answer?' Julia asked.

Above all else, she wanted Pippa never again to feel that she might at any moment be let down by her parents. Philippe sat back in his chair. He noticed for the first time how it had gone dark outside.

'I think so,' he said, 'I think so. It's important to her that she can trust what I say and since I met her, I've never let her down.'

'I won't let her down either,' Julia said, 'not like I did once before.'

Suddenly, he sat forward again and reached across to hold her hand.

'You mustn't blame yourself for what happened,' he said in a reassuring voice. 'I can see you had no option but to give her up. I know your mother would not have been easy to deal with but I should have been there for you and I wasn't. If there is anyone to blame it's me.'

She smiled, grateful that he was being so concerned for her and trying to shoulder some of the blame.

'And James?' he asked, for he could not think how to frame the question but he wanted desperately to know how her husband had received the news of her illegitimate daughter.

'He's left to go home,' she said simply. 'He did not take it well.'

'Did you expect he would?'

'No, I didn't,' Julia said. 'He's always been jealous by nature. I don't think he would have married me if he had known the truth.'

'Is that why you didn't tell him? You didn't want to risk him not marrying you?' Philippe asked.

It was suddenly important for him to know just how much in love she had been with her husband but he could not ask the question outright.

'Mother pushed me to marry him and there was no one else so I went along with it,' she said, remembering their conversations and her mother's persistence in pressing her to accept his proposal.

'But I told her that I would never love James the way I had loved you,' she added.

She watched him closely to gauge his reaction. Had she gone too far? But he smiled knowingly.

'I understand completely,' he said. 'I married briefly but I'm divorced now. For the same reasons as you, it did not work out. I simply did not love her the way I had loved you.'

A new loving friendship was emerging between them as they spoke together and shared confidences about their lives.

'I don't think I told you. I have a son John who's nine,' Julia said. 'He's the spitting image of his father.'

Philippe nodded, not at all surprised by the revelation.

'And you?' Julia asked, wondering if he too had other children.

'No,' Philippe said. 'I don't have any other children, just Pippa.'

'So when can I meet my daughter?' she asked, for that was now upper most in her mind.

'Tomorrow? Is that too soon for you?' he asked. 'I don't think she's going to be able to concentrate on school until she meets you.'

He was more relaxed now. He was over the initial shock of meeting her again after so many years. His mind had begun to turn to the practical questions that faced them both.

'Aunt Edith has invited us both for lunch tomorrow if that suits you,' he said. 'She will get in touch with the school tomorrow morning and give them some excuse for Pippa to be away for a few days.'

Julia smiled, excited and anxious in equal measure at the prospect of meeting the child she had given up years before.

'That's wonderful,' she said. 'I imagine we both owe Aunt Edith a great deal.'

He nodded.

'Pippa has been well looked after and well brought up by her,' he said. 'She treated Pippa as if she were her own daughter. I think you'll see that for yourself tomorrow.'

'It's all a dream really,' she said. 'I can't wait to meet her.'

There was still so much she wanted to know, so much she wanted to ask him about the intervening years and so much she wanted to know about her daughter's life.

He smiled at her.

'You'll have to wait,' he said, 'so shall we have dinner together to help pass the time?'

Suddenly conscious of her appearance, Julia stood up.

'I must change,' she said, looking down at her crumpled skirt. 'I can't have dinner with you looking like this.'

But he laughed.

'You look beautiful to me,' he said.

But she would not be persuaded.

'Give me half an hour to change,' she said as she headed towards the hotel lift.

He smiled and relaxed, watching her as she walked away from him.

He signalled to the waiter for another drink. He had yet to tell her that he was moving permanently to live in Australia. He thought she had endured enough surprises for one day.

By midday the next day Julia and Philippe were standing nervously on the doorstep of Aunt Edith's neat suburban home. He had just raised his hand to ring the doorbell when it was opened suddenly.

Standing before them was a young girl, excited and nervous in equal parts. How many times had Pippa imagined this moment? The moment when she would meet her real mother and her real father together. And now the moment had come and she could not quite believe it was happening. She did not know how to react.

Philippe broke the spell. He moved forward to hug her. He held on to her for moment before he turned back towards Julia, his arm around Pippa's shoulder as if she needed his reassurance.

'Here is your mother, Pippa, your real mother,' he said in soft gentle voice. 'We can now tell you everything about why you were given up for adoption.'

Pippa looked at Julia standing directly in front of her, as if trying to decide if this moment was real but she did not make any move towards her. For a moment they both stood motionless until Julia reached out, her arms open wide. For the first time Pippa felt the embrace of her real mother.

Philippe could see the tears sliding down Julia's face. He understood what this moment meant to her. She had spent years never talking about her daughter, having had to deny her very existence. She had never been free to talk about her to anyone. But in the space of a day she had not only been able to talk about the child she had given up, she was able to meet her and hold her.

After a few minutes they all moved into the living room together. Aunt Edith had tactfully remained out of sight while mother and daughter met one another for the first time.

As they sat down to lunch, Julia began to hear the story of her daughter's life. She was hungry for every small detail. She lingered over the photos Aunt Edith had once shown Philippe for they faithfully recorded the stages of her daughter's life she had missed. She felt a small stab of jealously at the affection in the girl's voice for her adoptive mother Anne yet relief that she had been so loved as a child.

Sitting at the table, Julia recounted her own story. She did not dwell on her own mother's role but it was clear to her that no one, least of all Pippa, thought well of her.

Finally, as they said their good byes, Philippe and Julia were alone together once more. He held the door of the taxi for her and she got in. As he slid in alongside her, she turned to him.

'Philippe, our daughter is just so wonderful,' Julia said, her eyes glistening with tears. 'I never dreamt, I never even dared hope that I would meet her.'

He took hold of her for hand in a gesture of reassurance.

'I know how that feels,' he said. 'I never thought I would get to know her either until a few months ago. Now, I am playing an important role in her life and I can't imagine my life without her.'

But he knew Julia faced more complicated choices than he had faced.

'But what do I do now?' she asked. 'What happens now? I have a husband who probably wants a divorce. But I have a son to think about too.'

He was silent for a few moments. He did not know how to answer. Did he want to push her to resume their relationship? Had too much time elapsed? Had there been too much hurt on either side to resume as they had been? As he thought about the future he was cautious, not wanting to raise her hopes nor to create false hopes within himself. They were both older and wiser.

'I think we should take this one step at a time,' he said cautiously. 'Pippa must be our priority. Whatever happens between us, we cannot abandon her. Whatever we mean to each other in our future lives, I think time will show us the answer to that.'

She was grateful for his good sense. She did not know how her life would change in the future, she only knew it would change. But like him she was prepared to be patient and let events take their natural course. Despite the excitement of the day she resolved to think only about the next few days. After that she would return home. To what sort of a welcome she did not know. All she knew was that she was happier than she had ever been since the birth of her daughter.

Later, alone in her room, she clung to that thought as she drifted off to sleep.

At the very time Julia was meeting her daughter for the first time, James was striding across the hot tarmac outpacing the other passengers who had just alighted from the aeroplane. He quickly scanned the small waiting crowd for his sister. She caught sight of him first and waved enthusiastically. He raised his arm in greeting very briefly. It was only then Alice realised he was alone.

She greeted him with a kiss on the cheek and a brief hug, which he barely reciprocated. He knew what her first question would be so he pre-empted it.

'Before you ask, Julia is not with me,' he said. 'She's stayed behind in Sydney.'

Alice did not immediately notice the brusque way in which he had spoken.

'Is she unwell?' Alice asked.

Alice was genuinely fond of her sister-in-law and was immediately beset by concern for her welfare amid her surprise that her brother would abandon his wife in a city where she knew no one.

'No,' James said. 'She isn't unwell. It's a long story and not one I propose to tell you standing amongst a crowd of strangers in an airport lounge.'

Alice sensed his mood then. She knew better than to pepper him with further questions.

'Let's get your bag,' she said, 'and then we can get you home.'

She spoke as if he was ill for he gave all the appearance of being so, but it did not account for him returning home and Julia remaining behind. She was silent as they stood together waiting for the baggage cart to be pulled across the tarmac towards the terminal. It was a hot sticky day that was likely to give way to a storm in the early evening.

As they headed out of town, James at the wheel, he began to recount the events of the past twenty-four hours. At times Alice struggled to hear his words over the roar of the engine and the noise of the tyres on the unsealed road. But she heard enough to piece together the shocking developments in her brother's life.

Had she known anything about this, he had asked, when there was nothing more to tell.

Alice, distressed by the revelations, hardly heard his question. He asked it again, this time almost yelling at his sister.

'Did you know about the baby?' he asked. It was more of an accusation than a question. 'You were her best friend. You must have known.'

It was one of those rare occasions when Alice herself was jolted into an angry response.

'Of course I didn't know about it,' she yelled back at him. 'Do you think I wouldn't have told you if I had known. Julia and I never really discussed her relationship with the American. I knew about it but it was off limits. I didn't know the extent of it.'

She looked across at her brother and he glanced towards her.

'And William never hinted at it? He must have known about it,' he said. 'It would have all happened when Richard was overseas.'

Suddenly Alice remembered.

'Of course, that's why they came up with the story of Julia's mother needing to go to Melbourne for treatment for a serious illness. We did wonder about it as she never looked sick to us,' Alice recalled, for she and her mother had discussed it but could find no reason for the sudden absence other than the reason Julia had given them.

'Yes, it was to provide cover for Julia to have the baby and then come back and resume her life as if nothing had happened,' James said, helping his sister piece together the events of years past.

'It must have been hard for her,' Alice said, trying to imagine herself in the same predicament, having to give up Marianne and never knowing her or caring for her.

James did not share Alice's sentiments. He was angry. He felt betrayed. Above all he felt humiliated by the ease with which she had duped him.

'I can't believe she deceived me like that,' he said, possibly for the twentieth time.

But Alice wanted him to see how few options Julia had been left with.

'Her mother would have controlled everything, James,' she said. 'You mustn't blame her completely. It's her mother who would have decided everything for her.'

He laughed. It was a hollow unhappy sound.

'And they made me the patsy for their scheming and deception,' he said. 'She should have told me. I would have accepted it. I wouldn't have liked it but I would have accepted it. But she didn't trust me enough to confide in me.'

Again, Alice came to Julia's defence for she understood, better than he did, the pressure Julia would have faced.

'Her mother would have forbidden it,' she said. 'She would not have wanted Julia to risk her one opportunity of making a good marriage.'

Alice understood all too well the scheming and plotting that mothers undertook to secure suitable husbands for their daughters. She had been on the receiving end of it herself. She understood how determined Elizabeth Belleville would have been that the scandal surrounding her only daughter would never surface.

'Well, all I can say is they were very cold and calculating,' he said. 'She's been my wife for ten years, given me a son and now I find there is a big part of her life I knew nothing about. How do you think that makes me feel?'

She knew full well how it made him feel. She wanted to say his reaction was predictable but she did not. Instead she was careful how she responded. She did not want to fuel his simmering anger.

'I know you're very hurt and upset now,' she said, 'but I beg you not to say anything to young John just yet. Wait until Julia gets home and you decide between you what the future holds.'

He had given little thought to what he would tell his son. Alice's strategy had worked. He was listening to her and taking notice of her advice.

'All you need to tell him is that his mother wanted to stay on to catch up with some old school friends for a few days. Or to see her nephew Paul and take him out of school,' she said. 'He'll think nothing of it, providing your behaviour doesn't give you away.'

He nodded, acknowledging the good sense of what she said, yet he knew he would struggle to present a happy unconcerned face to his son.

'You must do it for his sake, James,' Alice said. 'Just until Julia gets home and then if needs be, he can be told what he needs to know, but don't tell him while she is not there to explain to him why he has a sister he has never met.'

Alice's words jolted James. He had not thought of it like that. He had not even considered for a moment that Julia's illegitimate daughter was his son's half sister. How would John take that news he wondered? How would he react? Would he want to meet his half sister, a girl they knew nothing about? How would he explain to his son that his mother had given birth to a baby, fathered by another man?

Before she drove away, Alice repeated her warning to wait until Julia returned home before telling John anything at all.

It will all end badly, thought James, as he wearily mounted the stairs on to the verandah to be welcomed home by the housekeeper Mrs Fry who fussed around him all the more when she discovered he had returned alone.

Alice, sworn to secrecy about Julia's shocking revelations, did not wait around. It would take all her self-control not to tell William everything but then she realised there had been things that William had hidden from her. And she was shocked to know that he had not trusted her with this deepest of secrets.

Why had William not confided in her, she wondered? He had told her about his father's bastard son. He had discussed Richard's marriage with her. But he had never ever shared Julia's secret with her, and she felt betrayed by his lack of trust in her.

Like her brother, she would have to return to Prior Park and pretend nothing was amiss. But how could she pretend that everything was as before? It seemed impossible yet she must do it for James's sake. And for John's sake.

Yes, she could do it, she thought, but only for John's sake. He must learn of the girl's existence eventually but only when his mother had the opportunity to tell him and not before.

As she turned into the driveway at Prior Park, she tried to put everything she had just heard out of her mind. She could not afford to dwell on it. If William asked if something was wrong, she knew she ran the risk of blurting everything out to him. Yet one question lingered in her mind: why hadn't William trusted her enough to tell her the truth about Julia?

It was many hours after James returned home that Mrs Fry remembered a telephone message for him that she had taken earlier in the day.

As he sat eating an early dinner, listening to his young son chatter about the day at school, and saying little in response, the housekeeper walked quietly up to the table and caught his attention.

'Someone called Violet Cunningham telephoned for you this morning,' she said. 'She did not say what she wanted, but she said it was a business matter. I told her I wasn't sure when you would be back home but that I would give you the message. She rang off then in a hurry. I think someone may have come into the room.'

In his preoccupation with his own troubles the name meant nothing to him and he shrugged his shoulders at the mention of the message. It was not of sufficient interest for him to even ponder what the message might be about.

Having delivered the message, Mrs Fry walked back to the kitchen and opened the firebox of the wood stove in her kitchen and dropped the note in. She watched the small sliver of paper curl and burn in the flame.

Later James was to remember the message and curse his stupidity. But by then it was all too late. By then it was much too late to avert disaster.

CHAPTER 23: NOVEMBER 1957

Jack Finch and Ted Lambert, the burned down butts of discarded cigarettes scattered around them, often sat together in the early evening using upended wooden crates for chairs. The single men's quarters offered spartan accommodation so they preferred to spend their evenings outside where the air at least was fresh.

Despite the hard work of yard building, this had been one of their easier jobs since the war. They rated Prior Park manager Charles Brockman as a fair man who did not drive his men unnecessarily hard. Besides they had been hired, not by Charles, but by Richard Belleville, who, they thought privately, had become unnecessarily paranoid about strangers hanging around the place.

Still he was paying their wages and good wages they were too so they kept up some pretence of being sentries for the house and grounds. They would take it in turns to walk around the house to do a cursory inspection before they turned in each night.

They expected to see nothing more than the resident possums skittling from tree to tree with unerring agility. There were rifles in the main shed but they never took them down from the rifle cupboard. They trusted their boxing prowess more than firearms. In any case, they did not expect to encounter any problems.

It was a quiet Monday night. There was no reason to expect trouble so they did not look for it.

No one noticed Alistair McGovern's car drive very slowly along the main road, its lights extinguished well before the Prior Park turnoff. No one saw him get out of the car and walk, crouching low, up the Prior Park driveway. He was careful, keeping to the side of the road among the trees and the large shrubs. There was little light except from a fading moon and from the house itself.

He walked slowly, purposefully, noiselessly. Once or twice, a dry twig cracked under foot. He thought the noise was so loud it must have been heard for miles. He was almost paralysed by the fear of discovery, but there was no response from the house. Everything remained quiet.

Half way along the driveway he paused. Just to his left he noticed a tree stump, the remnants of an old tree that had been felled before it could fall across the driveway. He decided it would be a good place to sit while he observed the house and waited for all the lights to go out.

This night was the culmination of months of careful planning. He could afford to wait. There was no rush.

He watched, his gaze never wavering, as first one then another of the lights in the house went out. He tried to check his watch but he could not see the time. He judged it to be at least eleven o'clock. He was almost ready to move but then he caught sight of movement in the shadow of the house.

On this particular night, it was Jack Finch's turn to walk around the perimeter of the house. In the darkness he missed the slightly open window of the dining room. It would not have concerned him, in any case. They had been on the job for months now without the slightest incident.

Alistair McGovern held his breath as he watched the man stride out around the house, past the garages and disappear around the back out of sight. He had not expected to see anyone so he was suddenly nervous that the patrol might be repeated at regular intervals during the night, so he resolved to wait another hour at least.

Patience, he said to himself, be patient, but he could feel his heart pumping hard in anticipation of what lay ahead.

He patted the outside of his pockets and undid the straps on his satchel. It was a nervous habit of reassurance that he repeated again and again. Yes, he had everything he needed.

He was momentarily startled by a large bird that flew overhead. It was close enough for him to see the small marsupial in its talons.

Then it was all quiet again.

He tried to count to sixty so he could judge the passing of time but he could not concentrate. He did not know if he had been there for a half an hour or an hour but he was determined to wait until he was sure everyone was in bed and asleep. It was the only way to be sure he could achieve his aim.

It was only as night finally settled over Prior Park and he had seen no sign of life for some considerable time that he judged it was time for him to move.

He crossed to the other side of the road and covered the remaining distance to the house without incident, all the time keeping close to the trees.

To get to the side of the house, which was his first objective, he knew he would have to cross open ground in front of the house. There was no protection there. If someone looked out from the house they would see him.

But everything was quiet. There was no sign of anyone stirring.

He took a deep breath. So far so good. He had reached the side of the house. He began to check for an entry point and then he noticed the slightly open window. He did not know what room it was. He did not care. But soon they would care a great deal, he thought to himself. Very soon they would regret for all time their high-handed treatment of him.

He reached up and tested the window frame. It opened further without a sound. No creaking windows in this house, he thought.

He looked around for something to stand on. He needed to be able to reach over the windowsill. Then he saw exactly what he needed. A timber saw horse had been left further along the wall towards the back of the house.

He picked it up carefully and repositioned it beneath the window. He hoisted himself up. He could now lean in to the room. He pushed the curtains to one side. He could make out almost nothing in the room beyond, except the shadowy outline of a large table.

He carefully lifted a small can out of the satchel slung around his shoulders.

It was a few moments before he could prize the lid off the can.

Then the petrol fumes hit his nostrils and he almost fell back but he recovered his balance quickly. He briefly cradled the opened can in both hands. Leaning in through the window, he carefully and deliberately poured the contents of the can onto the floor, then he began splashing it around so that the curtains too were soon covered in liquid. With the can now empty, he carefully placed it back into his satchel and reached into his pocket for matches.

A small blue flame flickered into life. He held the matchstick for a few moments then lent forward through the window, touching the match to the curtains before he let it drop. He quickly lit another and this time threw the flaming match on to the floor. In seconds the puddle of petrol was alight. He watched with satisfaction as the flames engulfed the curtains first and then began to spread across the room.

But he dare not stop to admire his handiwork. He quickly got down from the window. He knew he must work fast now if he was to fulfil his ambition.

Caution no longer mattered to him. He ran around to the back of the house. He tried the door. It was locked from the inside but there was just enough of a gap to pour fuel under the door. He had brought a second can of fuel with him just for that purpose. It had a long slim nozzle. He shook the can to make it empty faster and then he put a match to it. He could not see it but he was sure the petrol had seeped under the door and was now well and truly alight.

He knew he had only seconds left to flee but he couldn't resist the temptation to do the same at the front door. He shook the can to make sure there was still some petrol in it.

He was no longer worried about being caught. This was his night. This was his night of revenge. He would savour it for as long as he lived. He would rejoice in the sight of the Belleville's precious house engulfed in flames.

He knew they would hate him all the more but he did not care. They had denied him the one thing that really mattered to him.

Now he was about to ruin the one thing that really mattered to them, their precious Prior Park. The grand home they would not share with him would lie in ruins from his night's work. Then they would see that he was someone to be reckoned with. He could not be dismissed like a servant or bought off with offers of dirty money.

He was breathing heavily now. He could smell the fire as it began to take hold. He could hear the crackling of the flames. He stooped to pour the last of his petrol under the front door.

Just as he was about to put the lighted match to it, he felt an arm encircle his neck. He lashed out at his assailant with all the force he could muster. Charles Brockman was momentarily winded and he stumbled backwards.

Quickly Alistair lit another match and this time he succeeded. He felt a shiver of satisfaction as he watched the fuel light up and the front door begin to scorch. He could hear shouting now from within the house.

It was Jack Finch who, in one swift movement, hauled him down the steps and punched him as hard as he could. Alistair fell back under the assault but it did not matter to him now how much they hurt him. A smile of satisfaction creased his face as pandemonium broke out around him.

Charles was quickly on his feet again. He was relieved to see that Alistair McGovern had not escaped. Jack Finch held him in a headlock that threatened to choke him. Alistair turned his head ever so slightly so he could see the house and the havoc he had created but otherwise he did not struggle. He did not know just how close Finch came to breaking his neck. It was only the prospect of having to face a murder charge that caused Finch to back off.

'Tie him up, Finch,' Charles yelled, as he ran towards the back of the house. He knew it would be useless to try and get through the front door.

Ted Lambert, hearing the order as he rounded the corner of the house, headed back to the shed for rope, confident that Jack Finch would have the young man's measure. He had seen Finch beat men twice his size in bar fights. He didn't doubt his ability to keep hold of such a puny young man. He thought there was half a chance the young man would be dead by the time he returned.

Inside the house, Richard had woken first, the smell of smoke and burning stirring memories of a time when he himself had inflicted similar catastrophe.

He had opened his bedroom door to be greeted by a haze of smoke wafting up from the floor below. He knew instantly what he was likely to see but still it shocked him as he stood briefly at the top of the stairs. He could see the fire was spreading quickly. It took only moments for him to realise the danger they all faced.

He ran to William and Alice's bedroom, banging on the door, yelling at them to get up, the house was on fire.

He thanked God none of the children were in the house. Marianne was in town with her grandmother. His children were safely out of it.

'I'll get Mother,' he said to his brother whose shocked face could barely register the enormity of what he was saying.

'What about Mrs Duffy?' he called back as he turned to grab Alice by the hand.

But the housekeeper was already alongside them for she too had heard the commotion. Her room was at the back of the house but she was a light sleeper.

They were all beginning to cough as the smoke billowed around them. They could hear Charles yelling from the floor below.

'Back door,' he yelled up the stairwell through the smoke. 'Back door. You'll have to get out the back door.'

Charles had roused all his workmen but he knew there was little they could do to stop the fire spreading, except that they had managed to quell the fire in the kitchen. The flagstone floor had saved the room for the petrol had not reached the timber benches.

William tried to head down the main stairs but was beaten back by the flames and the smoke. How were they going to get out the back door if they couldn't get down the stairs?

It was then Mrs Duffy yelled to them.

'The servants stairs,' she said. 'Follow me.'

'Of course,' said William, who had not used the stairs since childhood.

The building had been built at a time of a large indoor staff. Now Mrs Duffy made do with two women from neighbouring farms for part days, and one full time housemaid, but the housemaid always had Sunday and Monday off which she spent in town with her parents. She was due to return on Tuesday morning.

She led the way past the bedrooms and ushered first Alice, then William, and finally Richard, who was half carrying his mother, down the narrow flight of stairs that came out into the kitchen.

At the bottom of the stairs, Charles hurried them towards the back door, for he was worried the building, now well alight, might collapse around them.

Alice was crying, tears streaming down her face. William had his arm around her, using his body to protect her from the embers that were flying everywhere.

No one had yet asked how the fire started. Survival was upper most in all their thoughts.

As Richard came up level with Charles, he asked quietly, 'Can we save the house?'

Charles shook his head sadly.

'It's too far gone,' he said sadly. 'We don't have enough water. We have no way of fighting it properly.'

Just then, Elizabeth Belleville slipped from her son's grasp.

'I must save a photo of Francis,' she said. She had remembered the photos in the hallway.

Before anyone could stop her, she rushed through the kitchen towards the front of the house. Richard went after her but he was a moment too late.

A large crossbeam, well alight, cracked and fell from the ceiling. Under the weight of it, the staircase began to disintegrate.

Richard watched in horror as a piece of flaming timber crashed down on his mother's shoulder and her nightgown caught fire. She fell, the flaming timber on top of her.

He quickly pulled her clear smothering the flames as best he could while trying to protect her from the shower of flames that rained down around her.

He could feel the heat of flaming shards across his back.

It was Charles who reacted decisively.

He was first to reach Richard and pull him clear of the burning debris. William was behind him and put his arms under his brother's shoulders to drag him clear. Charles, his eyes smarting from the smoke, ignored the burning embers and lifted Elizabeth Belleville clear of the fire that was now all around them. Flames licked up the walls devouring everything in their path. He heard the sharp crack of glass as it broke in the heat of the fire. Above him, nothing remained of the main staircase.

He carried Elizabeth out through the back door and into the clear night air. He laid her gently down on a rug that someone had retrieved from one of the cars. He could see immediately she was badly burned.

Richard, gasping for clean air as he tried to expel the smoke from his lungs, had mercifully avoided serious injury.

Now Charles took charge. He ordered his men to put their efforts into saving the outbuildings and the vehicles. He had long since given up the house as a lost cause.

'We need to get your mother to hospital straight away, William,' he said. 'I'll take her. Perhaps Alice can come with me.'

'No,' William said, aware that Charles was much more useful remaining behind. 'I'll take her. You stay here. What about Richard?'

He looked quickly towards his brother.

'I'm OK,' Richard said, raising his hand in a dismissive gesture. 'Don't wait around. Mother needs urgent help. I'll be fine.'

Charles moved to William's side. He put a restraining hand on William's arm.

'We'll need the police too,' he said quietly. 'Once your mother has been taken care of, contact the police and get them out here fast. We have an unwelcome guest.'

William looked at him. As soon as Charles had spoken, he knew then what had happened.

'He won't get away will he?' he asked, for he knew exactly who was responsible for the atrocity.

Charles shook his head.

'He won't,' he said quietly. 'He won't get away, I can guarantee you that much.'

Gently, they lifted the now unconscious body of William's mother into the back seat of the car which had been brought around to the back of the house. Alice got in and gently lifted Elizabeth's head on to her lap.

William jumped into the driver's seat. He remembered other times when he had been called on to make a mercy dash to the hospital. It was at these times he cursed their distance from the town.

His headlights cut through the darkness. He knew there was little chance of meeting other cars on the road at that time of night. He knew the road well but it was the kangaroos that posed the biggest danger. He drove as fast as he dared. He did not need to be told his mother was clinging to life by a thread.

For once, James felt helpless. He was desperately sorry he had not been there to help them. He had been woken in the middle of the night by a phone call from William. James knew as he picked up the telephone it was bad news but it was only as William began telling him the awful story that he remembered the message his housekeeper had given him.

He began to berate himself. He remembered months earlier having asked Violet to telephone him if a certain person returned to stay at the hotel. Beset by his own problems, he had not considered the message important. Now he understood its meaning. He could have alerted William, he could have done any number of things to prevent the catastrophe that had occurred. But he had done nothing and he was sorry for it. His own sister had been lucky to escape the inferno with her life.

Later, as night gave way to the rising sun, he had stood alongside Richard and Charles Brockman to survey the damage.

No one spoke. The morning light revealed a smouldering ruin. The house, or what remained of it, was in danger of imminent collapse. The outer walls were blackened. Nothing remained of the fine furniture that had once graced the downstairs rooms.

They watched as the local police and fire brigade began cautiously to pick their way through the wreckage looking for evidence.

Not that much more evidence would be needed with the culprit under lock and key and soon to be charged with arson. The means of his starting the fire had been carefully returned to his satchel. He did not protest when it was taken from him for examination and the empty petrol cans placed in front of him. The evidence was damning.

He had laughed as police tried to question him. He was, they told Richard and William later on, an incoherent maniac who probably belonged in a mental asylum.

With nothing more to be done for the time being at Prior Park, Richard had returned home with James. Until then he had not known his sister was still away for he had assumed that Alice had brought them both back to Mayfield Downs the day before.

Richard was grateful for a bath and a set of borrowed clothes, for everything he owned had been lost in the fire.

As they sat down to breakfast, it was James who felt compelled to confess his oversight to Richard.

'I'm sorry, I could have stopped this,' he said, shaking his head. 'I forgot I asked Violet Cunningham at the hotel to phone me if that young bastard turned up again. She did but I got the message when I got home yesterday. I had other things to think about and didn't attach any importance to it.'

Richard held up his hand as if to say 'don't blame yourself. No one could have predicted what happened'. It was only then he began to wonder why Julia had not returned home with James.

'I don't think anyone could have stopped him,' Richard said. 'He was hell bent on revenge obviously because we wouldn't accept him as a member of the family.'

Almost as an after thought, he asked about his sister.

'And Julia? She didn't come back home with you from Sydney?'

James took a deep breath. Was this the time for more revelations? He would have preferred William or Julia herself to be the one to speak to Richard.

And was now a good time, he wondered?

Here was a man whose home had just burnt down. Whose mother was in hospital critically injured. Whose own marriage was in tatters. Did he need another burden? But there was no way not to tell him. There would never be a better opportunity. Yet still he hesitated.

'There's something wrong, isn't there, between you and Julia?'

It was a statement more than a question. James's reluctance to answer had raised Richard's suspicions.

'You're right,' James said at last. 'There is something wrong between us. And it goes back many years.'

Richard said nothing. He wanted to hear what James had to say so he waited. Finally James began to speak.

'Did you know your sister had given birth to a child out of wedlock while you were overseas during the war?' James asked.

He looked directly at Richard to gauge his reaction. He could think of no way to ask the question obliquely. He knew at once that Richard was shocked by the question.

'You can't be serious,' he said, almost laughing out loud. 'You're saying my sister had a baby out of wedlock and I don't know about it!'

James nodded, his face serious and unsmiling.

'I think only your mother and William knew about it,' he said. 'And your father too of course but he died and that reduced the circle of people who knew for sure. I didn't know anything about it when I married her.'

But Richard was still disbelieving. How could such a family secret have been kept from him?

'Surely they would have told me when I got home,' he said, more to himself than to James.

He was shaking his head slowly from side to side as if the news was too shocking to be real.

'And the father of the baby? He obviously didn't do the right thing by my sister,' Richard said.

He desperately wanted someone to blame other than his sister. He assumed immediately it had to be someone other than James. If it had been James, they would have been married quickly and no one would have said anything further.

James sighed. There was no way to avoid telling Richard all the details and yet he felt he was the wrong person to be doing so.

'You remember there was an American Army doctor, the one who treated her when she and William were run off the road by the Army truck?'

He assumed that the family would have written to Richard about the incident.

'I remember hearing about that in a letter I think,' he said, trying hard to remember the details.

'They got friendly after that I think,' James said. 'Too friendly as it turned out. I don't think your mother knew about it until it was too late. And the American had been posted out by the time she discovered she was pregnant.'

It seemed strange to him to be telling her brother all this. It was as if they were gossiping about a mutual friend. He was even managing to tell the story in a detached way, as if it had almost no relevance for him.

'But why has all this come out now?' Richard asked. 'After all this time, did she finally feel she had to tell you?'

James grimaced at the memory of the moment they had walked into the hotel restaurant in Sydney.

'She saw the American in Sydney,' he said bluntly. 'She not only saw him but he was with their daughter. Right there. In the restaurant, in the hotel. He was staying there when we were there.'

Richard was about to speak but at that moment words failed him. He tried to imagine the scene but couldn't. Instead he sat in silence while James continued the story.

'It seems he had invited his daughter and her guardian to lunch,' he said. 'We walked into the restaurant and Julia saw him. She recognised him straight away. And then she fainted.'

He paused for it was a painful memory for him.

'I don't think she realised immediately who the girl was,' he said. 'It was only later when she had recovered and they spoke that the whole story came out.'

After all that had happened, now this, thought Richard. Wasn't there enough to deal with without hearing this scandal about his sister? But he felt a compelling need to know all the details despite the tactlessness of asking his sister's husband for his version of the events.

'Are you telling me that she walked into a restaurant and saw the man who was the father of her illegitimate baby having lunch with

264

the now grown up child?' he asked.

It all sounded preposterous, like the romantic fiction he'd seen in women's magazines. But here was James, sitting across the table from him, confirming this outrageous story.

His own sister, his own family had hidden a tragic secret from him but why? Because no one wanted to talk about it when Julia was trying to put it behind her? Because their mother had bullied her into giving up the child? Because they thought he couldn't be trusted?

'That's what happened,' James said.

He was finished with the story. He did not want to continue the conversation. But Richard could not resist one further question.

'And where does that leave you and Julia?' he asked.

James pushed his chair back from the table.

'I don't know,' he said. 'I honestly don't know. I don't know if I even want her back. I don't know if she wants to come back.'

But in his heart he knew. In his heart he knew she had never stopped loving the American.

CHAPTER 24: NOVEMBER-DECEMBER 1957

It was late the following afternoon. Julia was sitting beside her mother's hospital bed. She had been crying. The sound of her mother's tortured breathing was almost more than she could bear. But Elizabeth Belleville had at least survived the night although she had not regained consciousness.

Julia had been shocked by James's early morning phone call the previous day telling her the grim news of the events at Prior Park. But it was her mother's injuries that had alarmed her the most. She had hardly asked what state the house was in and James had not elaborated. He had wanted to spare her the terrible details. All her thoughts had been focused on getting back home as quickly as possible. John Bertram had hurriedly organised the charter flight which had brought her directly back to Springfield.

She looked up as William walked quietly into the room. He looked haggard, as if he had not slept at all since the fire. He and Alice had been readily accommodated at her mother's house. They had even found some of their clothes left behind on previous visits. Having lost everything, they were happy to have something of their own.

'Any change?' he whispered to his sister.

She shook her head.

'No, it's much the same as when I arrived,' she said, answering him in a whisper, as if to speak loudly would disturb the unconscious woman.

'Has the doctor been?' William asked anxiously.

'Yes, he came an hour ago,' she said. 'He said there is nothing more they can do but keep her comfortable and treat the burns.'

And the prognosis, William wanted to ask, because he liked to deal in certainties, but he did not. Instead he sat down beside his sister.

There was clearly something else on his mind.

'After the fire, after Alice and I had got Mother to hospital, and we could do nothing more, we sat together out in the corridor while they dealt with her injuries,' he began. 'Alice was upset by everything. I tried to comfort her as best I could.'

It was an unusual speech for William. Why was he telling her all this? But she let him go on.

'Then she told me why you had not come back from Sydney with James, although James had asked her not to tell me,' he said.

'But Alice and I have no secrets from one another. She needed to tell me. She needed to share what he had told her. She didn't understand why I hadn't told her about your illegitimate baby. She felt I hadn't trusted her enough to tell her, which isn't true of course. I tell her everything. I trust her completely.'

Julia took a deep breath. For a moment she closed her eyes as if she wanted to block everything out. Was this the time for such revelations, she wondered?

She had been prepared to confront her mother, to accuse her mother of treachery for intercepting Philippe's letters but how could she do that now, when in all likelihood her mother lay dying.

But her brother? What role had he played in the deception?

She had thought about it on the long flight back to Springfield. Her mother would have needed William's help to intercept all of Philippe's letters to her. She knew now her mother had lied to her and that certain knowledge of her mother's duplicity had shattered her. Yet she knew her mother well enough to know that she would defend the lies as being in her best interests.

When she did not reply, William continued.

'Is it true you met Philippe in Sydney? And met your daughter?' he asked, for he needed to hear it from her.

'Yes, it's true,' she said. 'With my own eyes I saw the man my mother swore to me had abandoned me or must be dead because there had been no letters from him. I saw the daughter she forced me to give up, to discard, to throw away. I knew then I had been lied to.'

William could not mistake the deep visceral anger in his sister's voice. She began to shake as if the emotions she had suppressed for so long could no longer be held in check.

'And you,' she almost hissed, as she turned to face her brother. 'You colluded with her. You helped her deceive me.'

William's face was sombre. He realised then the enormity of what they had done.

'We did it for you,' he stuttered. 'We did it for you. We thought it was the only sensible thing to do. No other man would have married you with another man's child in tow. And we couldn't be sure he'd come back for you after the war. We had to think of your future.'

Julia laughed, but it was not a pretty sound.

'You mean you had to avoid scandal at all costs,' she countered. 'That's what was important to you. Not me, not my child. Scandal. You hated the prospect of any scandal attaching itself to the family's name. That was more important to you.'

He could not deny it. Faced with the truth, he could only remain silent. He could not even find the words to say he was sorry.

Just then, they heard a sound coming from the bed. They had forgotten for a moment where they were.

Elizabeth Belleville held out her hand towards her daughter. It was a feeble gesture but Julia did not hesitate. What her mother had done she found unforgivable but she could not reject her now. She stood up and grasped her mother's hand. There was still some strength in it. She could tell her mother was trying to say something. She leaned in closer. She felt William by her side.

'What is it?' Julia asked. 'Can we get something for you? Is there something you want?'

Elizabeth Belleville's words were faint and they struggled to hear her.

'I'm sorry, my darling daughter,' she said. She coughed. The effort of speaking was almost too great for her. But she was determined to say her last few words.

'It was wrong what I did to you. So wrong. I'm so sorry. Please forgive me. I'm so sorry …'

Her mother's words trailed off. She closed her eyes. Her breathing slowed. Her head slipped sideways on the pillow. And then she was gone.

Julia sat back in the chair, tears flowing down her cheeks unchecked. She realised then that her mother must have overheard the conversation between herself and William.

With her last breath on this earth, Elizabeth Belleville had admitted she had been wrong. She had begged her daughter's forgiveness and, on hearing those few words, Julia's anger had evaporated. All that remained was the despair of knowing she would never speak with her mother again.

She wept silently. William, beside her, sat stony faced, fighting back his own tears.

His life, Julia's life, Richard's life … he realised none of their lives would ever be the same again.

After a few minutes he walked to the door of the room and summoned a nurse, who came in silently and drew the white bed sheet over his mother's face.

Richard and William stood together surveying the blackened remains of what had once been their grand home. Its destruction had been complete, save for the back section of the kitchen and utility rooms, which were the only parts still recognisable.

Richard began to explore the debris, hoping at least for something he could take away but there were only fragments of photo frames, dinner plates distorted beyond use and cutlery melted into strange shapes. There was nothing to salvage. Nothing of their lives at Prior Park they could retrieve.

'We can rebuild,' Richard said. 'It was insured.'

But William shook his head.

'It was insured but not enough to rebuild what we have lost,' he said.

William was thinking beyond the building itself. Much of what they had lost was what money could not replace. But neither could he begin to think about demolishing what remained of the once proud house.

'Alice and I have discussed it,' he said. 'We think we should build a smaller house in a different location.'

He wanted to say: just for us, for me and Alice and Marianne but even he was not so tactless.

Richard stepped back. He pointed to a slight rise in the landscape, a couple of hundred yards to the north east of where they stood.

'That would be a good spot,' Richard said, as if he had already thought about it.

William's eyes followed the direction he was pointing. It was exactly where he and Alice had agreed would be ideal.

'We could build an extension of this driveway without any difficulty,' Richard said, already planning it in his mind.

William nodded. Again that was exactly the plan he and Alice had discussed.

'And it should be a house just for you and Alice and your daughter,' Richard said.

He smiled at his brother. After the difficulties of the previous weeks, it was only now they were beginning to feel that life was getting back to normal again.

'What about you?' William asked, for he had not expected Richard to agree with him after so little discussion.

'I'm sure there will be enough money to buy a house for me in town,' he said.

William nodded, still surprised at his brother's decision.

'You'll be welcome to stay with us any time, and the boys too,' William said, for he was fond of his nephews.

Richard smiled and thanked him.

'So don't build too small a house then, brother,' he said jokingly. 'There'll be times when you'll need room for all of us.'

William relaxed. He'd already added another bedroom to the plan taking shape in his mind.

'We'll live differently now,' Richard said. 'The days of us all living together in one grand home are over.'

There was just a hint of wistfulness in his words. At times he had chafed against the unnecessary formality of the way their mother had insisted they live, but now he knew it would be impossible to recapture it. That era was gone, gone forever with their mother's death.

'And Catherine?' William asked tentatively.

'Ah, Catherine,' he said. 'Catherine is soon to be my ex-wife. It was unfortunate timing but I got the initial papers from her solicitor the day of Mother's funeral.'

'And did you speak to her about what happened?' William asked, for he could not recall Richard mentioning it.

'Yes, I spoke to her and she was genuinely shocked and sympathetic,' he said. 'Like me she was relieved none of the children were in the house at the time.'

'How is Anthony?' William asked.

He missed the young boy, as did Marianne, who asked about him constantly. He was sure that Richard must be missing his son terribly although he had said nothing.

'He's going well,' he said. 'He's getting ready to go to school soon and he said Uncle Edward is very good to him.'

William was perplexed. Catherine had no brothers so he could not imagine who Uncle Edward was.

'Uncle Edward?' he queried.

'Yes,' said Richard, through pursed lips. 'By Uncle Edward he means Sir Edward Cavendish who inherited Catherine's father's title. I understand he's been a regular visitor to Haldon Hall since Catherine returned to England.'

William looked at his brother and saw for the first time the hurt and disappointment he had long tried to hide.

'I take it Sir Edward is not some doddering old fool then?' William asked.

'No, far from it. He's actually a couple of years younger than Catherine, I understand,' Richard said. 'I'd say he's set about making himself indispensable to her.'

'Do you think she'll marry him when the divorce is through?' William asked.

'Probably,' Richard said. 'I'd say it's more than likely. And what

271

better way to a mother's heart than through her young child.'

He shrugged his shoulders. William could see he was resigned to the fact that his marriage was over.

'Do you still love her?' William asked.

But Richard did not reply. It was too simple a question. He could not explain how he felt, except that they were two people from different walks of life who had for a short time enjoyed life together. In the cold light of day he knew that the differences between them would in the end divide them. It had only been a question of when. He was sorry for it, but he could not change the life he wanted to live and equally he realised she was entitled to live the life she wanted.

Richard turned to walk back to his car, but he stopped.

Charles Brockman was walking towards him. The outbuildings, Charles's house, the men's quarters and the stockyards had all been saved on the night of the fire. It was only the main house that had been gutted.

He raised his hand in greeting to both William and Richard. The three men came together.

'Are you used to having a woman around the house yet, Charles?' Richard asked, for Charles had offered his spare room to the Prior Park housekeeper on the night of the fire.

He smiled.

'Well, the meals have improved,' he said, 'but she is worried about what will happen to her.'

'Tell her not to worry,' William said. 'We will go on paying her wages just as before. When the new house is built, she'll be needed.'

He did not go into details though. It was enough now to reassure her that she would not be turned out. In truth both he and Richard had given the matter very little thought but they had always expected to look after her.

'And when will that be?' Charles asked, for he was curious too as to what would go up in place of the big house.

'We'll get plans drawn up once the insurance people have processed everything,' William said.

Charles nodded, satisfied with William's answers. He nodded then towards the driveway. Another car was making its way up the road.

'Looks like your sister's about to arrive,' he said, as he walked away.

Better to leave them together by themselves, he thought. He did not want to intrude on her first visit back to her old home so he did not wait to greet her.

As the dust settled around her car, she got out and walked towards her brothers.

Together the three of them surveyed the ruin. It was the first time Julia had seen it. Although she had driven past it any number of times, she could not bring herself to turn into the driveway. Only today, seeing her brothers' cars did she feel able to look at the awful scene of the tragedy that had claimed her mother's life.

Richard put his arm around her shoulders, in a brotherly gesture of reassurance and affection. He knew now how much she had been through in the past few weeks.

'Oh my God, it's such a mess,' she cried. 'I never thought it would look like this.'

She bent down to pick up a small section of a photograph that had not been completely destroyed by the fire but then she flicked it away. It meant nothing. It was just a meaningless scrap of their lives. There was nothing she could find that was intact.

'What are you going to do with it?' She looked from one brother to the next, hoping to hear that it would be rebuilt exactly as it had been.

'We don't know yet,' William said. 'I don't think it's possible to rebuild it as it was.'

'But you must,' she said. 'We all loved it.'

'Yes, we all loved it,' Richard said, 'but that was when we were children. When our parents were alive. We're not sure we want to live like that now.'

Julia turned away from them back towards the house. Some of the highest outer walls had already been partly demolished out of fear they were unsafe.

She could hardly imagine the house, familiar as it was to her, as it had been.

'Is it money?' she asked.

'Partly,' William said, 'but not altogether. Alice and I would like a simpler smaller home.'

'And you Richard?' she asked.

'Well, it's just me at the moment, except when I have the boys,' he said. 'I'm thinking of getting a house in town. William and Alice will be happy to have me and the boys when I want to stay out here.'

She noticed he was no longer including Catherine in his plans at all.

'And you?'

The question came from Richard but William too was keen to know what was happening with his sister.

She looked down her shoes. They were covered in dirt, some of it black. She bent down to brush the dust off. It was a futile gesture but one that bought her a little time. She straightened up.

'My marriage is over,' she said simply. 'It was built on a lie. Once that lie was exposed, it crumbled.'

'And what are you going to do now? Where will you live?'

Her brothers asked the question in unison. Neither of them bothered to express surprise at her news. They both knew James well enough to realise that he would have been unlikely to forgive her. The humiliation would have been too great for him.

'Philippe is back in Sydney early next year,' she said. 'We will see what happens then. We've made no promises to one another. But I have made promises to my daughter, that I will be part of her life. And she will get to meet her brother. I can't tell you how excited she is at that prospect.'

'And are you leaving Mayfield Downs?' William asked, for she had not answered them fully.

'Yes, I'm leaving Mayfield Downs,' she said. 'I will get a house in town and John can live with me there while he goes to school and see his father on weekends. If I am away in Sydney, James's mother has agreed to have him stay with her.'

By the sound of it, she had it all worked out.

'Is James OK to buy you a house?' asked William, being ever practical about such details.

She smiled.

'You've forgotten, haven't you?' she said, with just a hint of smugness. 'I'm now probably wealthier than you are. You've forgotten I've inherited mother's trust fund.'

She could see the surprise in their faces for they had, in all the upset, completely forgotten about that aspect of their mother's life.

'I have to tell you she was much better at managing investments than our father,' she said. 'I've already had several meetings with the bank manager and with her solicitors. The trust fund is now at my disposal.'

William could not help himself. He sounded a note of caution.

'Well, you must be careful with it, conservative in your decision making,' he urged, which was everything his own father had not been.

She smiled again.

'I will be,' she said, 'because it is Pippa who stands next in line to inherit it. What greater incentive would I have than that to manage it properly.'

For the first time in her life she felt free, free to make her own decisions, free to live her life the way she wanted, free to live where she wanted.

Richard smiled at her, relieved to see her contented and happy, despite everything that had happened. He hugged her.

'If only I'd been here when it all happened with you, things would have been different. I would not have let them give your baby away.'

She could see that William was feeling uncomfortable, conscious still of the role that he had played. He had shown his sister little sympathy at the time and he knew it. With his own family now, he had mellowed. In similar circumstances he knew he would stand by Marianne no matter what. He could only excuse himself for being a callow youth who knew nothing of what was important in life.

He tried to say as much to Julia but she silenced him.

'I know,' she said. 'Let's not speak about it again. Let's all be good friends. We know what a powerful force our mother was. But now we can let that go. She is in her grave and we must remember the good things about her.'

Arm in arm they stood together for a few moments, surveying

what remained of Prior Park, each of them sad remembering the betrayals and disappointments that tarnished their collective memories but remembering too the happy times.

'I wonder what the future will hold for us all,' Richard said as he turned away.

'It's the end of an era,' William said finally as they separated.

'It's a new chapter,' Julia said. 'A brand new chapter for us all.'

They waved her off as she drove away.

NEXT

RETURN TO PRIOR PARK

BOOK 3 IN THE BELLEVILLE FAMILY SAGA

Despite William and Richard's agreement to leave Prior Park unrestored, their decision is by no means final. Can the Belleville family live without the grand home that was their great pride?

Will Julia find happiness now that she has found her daughter and reconnected with Philippe, her first and enduring love?

Will her brother Richard move on with his life? Despite Jane Warner's angry letter written in the midst of her bitter disappointment about their failed reunion, will he seek her out again?

Will Richard's soon to be ex-wife Catherine marry Sir Edward and become Lady Cavendish?

And what of the next generation.

Will brothers Paul and Anthony overcome the tyranny of distance to become close friends as they grow up or will that distance drive a wedge between them? And what of Marianne? As it stands, she will inherit her father's share in Prior Park and all the Belleville family interests but will Richard's sons accept this division of the family's assets in the future?

And what of John Fitzroy? Will he accept Pippa as his sister or will the lingering anger of his father colour his attitude to both his mother and his half sister?

CPSIA information can be obtained
at www.ICGtesting.com
Printed in the USA
LVOW12s1545100717

540824LV00004B/589/P